Bewitched, bothered, and bewildered . . .

I sold my own soul almost two years ago, and my life hasn't been the same—and trust me, that's a good thing. The soul-recruitment part of the deal is becoming old hat. After all, this is my third soul-taking. The first two were relatively easy, an assistant DA I had met at a party and the super to my old building (yes, there is justice in the world). I should be feeling an attack of conscience, some twinge of badness, but I don't.

I've closed that chapter of my life. Big things ahead. This is the end of that sort of sentimental schmaltz. Mom always said I was too pragmatic. I look Lucy in the eye. No doubts here. For just a second, I see a smudge in her mascara, and then *whoosh*—it's gone like I never saw it at all. Instinctively I reach for my mirror, check my reflection, but everything's in order. No smudges, smears, everything is beautiful.

"You don't need to doubt yourself, V. The world is your oyster, and you, my darling, are the pearl. I see great things in your future. You have to trust me on this."

Pinch me, I think I'm dreaming.

THE DIVA'S GUIDE TO SELLING YOUR SOUL

KATHLEEN O'REILLY

doWn tOwn press

New York London Toronto Sydney

An *Original* Publication of POCKET BOOKS

 DOWNTOWN PRESS, published by Pocket Books
1230 Avenue of the Americas
New York, NY 10020

Library of Congress Cataloging-in-Publication Data is available.

ISBN: 0-7434-9940-9

First Downtown Press trade paperback edition April 2005

10 9 8 7 6 5 4 3 2 1

DOWNTOWN PRESS and colophon are trademarks of Simon & Schuster, Inc.

Manufactured in the United States of America

Designed by Jaime Putorti

In memory of Aunt Mary

The Diva's Guide to Selling Your Soul

Prologue

I've always been jealous of witches. Not the incense-burning, tree-fondling kind, but the others—the ones that can cast real spells, that can turn people into livestock (I'd have turned my ex-husband into an aardvark—a faint subgenus resemblance—but that's another story).

When I was a kid, I'd watch *Bewitched* and wish for the ability to turn myself pretty and blond. As I grew older and married (my true hell on earth), I'd wish for the ability to ban housework forever. I was never meant to be a domestic servant, especially after a ten-hour day at the office. Cows should be domestic servants, not women, don't you think?

I wanted to break free. Be somebody I never was.

You know Buffy, Xena, Joan of Arc? Saving the world is for the pantywaisted. Me? I want to rule it.

Who am I?

Call me V.

One

Which publicist/designer couple have hit a speed bump in their marriage? Rumor has it that they are sharing separate quarters and that she has been seen on the arm of a well-known piano player. True love, revenge, or PR scam? Only the piano man knows for sure.

I predict big things for the Hollywood starlet opening on Forty-second Street in August. Her voice, her moves, it's the best thing she's done in ages. You heard it here first, darlings.

Fifth Avenue's most daring bag lady and her darling designers have done it again. Current buzz on the street says that the It Bag for the spring season is part of the Sonata line from V.

V. Yup, that's me. Now I own a prosperous leather shop on Fifth Avenue, and I'm not going to name names, because the purpose of anonymity is to stay anonymous. Every day celebrities waltz into the store, celebrity wannabes bumbling right after them. All to buy *my* bags. It's a hell of a rush, and I like to have fun with it every now and then. (It'll be our little secret.)

If you shop on Fifth Avenue, you'll really appreciate this one. Here's the drill:

"Are you looking for something special today?" I ask.

"I'm not sure," the customer says in that Botoxified highbrow tone that tells me she wants me to compliment her on her new $1,500 Viktor & Rolf knockoff and then find a bag to match. Do these people never learn?

"I've got just the thing," I tell her, and then, in my head, I say the magic words:

Baggara, faggara, haggara, fine, puce is what you need to shine.

Immediately her eyes zoom in on the puce monstrosity that is sitting behind the counter. We've discounted it 47 percent, solely because it's an ugly mother and no one would ever touch it.

"I love it," she gushes.

I smile and rack up the price 200 percent.

Ka-ching.

After the Page Six item, I take in orders for a thousand bags (including some in butt-ugly puce). You wonder how hype starts?

I'm telling you, it's all in who you know. You see those names that get paraded around and become forty-seven-minute celebrities? Well, if you see a certain ex-hooker at mass, I'm telling you it's a sham. As long as she's banking the advances and fighting off the West Coast producers with a diamond-studded stick, she's got connections.

That evening I take off for my usual night out. I signed over my soul to the devil almost two years ago, and I haven't regretted it yet. Having your every whim and desire—what's not to love?

Pandemonium is a trendy little joint over on 1111 Legion Street. I'm meeting Shelby and Meegan ("two *e*'s, but pronounced Megan; it's a family name"), who belongs to one of the political dynasties from Connecticut (who knew?). Shelby is svelte, tall, with a deceptively casual blond cut. Her hair was specially designed by Frederic Fekkai, and the body was designed by Oreos and Ex-Lax. A deadly combination.

Meegan is much less disciplined, a bluestocking with no sense of style at all who I had met one day while getting a facial. I promised Lucy I'd get them both in the Life Enrichment Program, and now it's up to me to show them the infinite rewards of my life. Oh, yeah, like *that's* a tough job.

To be perfectly honest, I don't care too much for Shelby. It's tougher to be apathetic about Meegan. She is genuinely nice, in a way I don't even begin to understand. We've talked a few times, and I'm feeling the disconnect. I've never spent a lot of time around nice people; that's what happens when you grow up in Hoboken.

I walk into the bar, and heads turn. Men like the lean,

Dolce & Gabbana "You can look, but you have to sell your firstborn in order to touch"–clad body, and women notice my bag. Yeah, eat your heart out, New York.

One of the Yankee ballplayers is holding court in the back, and I wink, but don't go any further. I'm a Mets fan, and it seems disloyal. Someday, when I get to be a Level 7 and earn my behavior-modification status, the Mets are going to win the pennant.

I find Meegan and Shelby near the wall in the back. I've been trying to teach them to be bolder, more aggressive, but that's easy when you have no reason to fear rejection.

"Evening, ladies," I say, picking up the martini the bartender has magically provided. It's a good life.

"V"—she didn't actually say "V," but it's really important that no one knows my real name (Life Enrichment Clause Number 473)—"you look fabulous!"

We do the air-kiss thing, and Meegan gives me an arm squeeze.

My cell phone rings, and I hold up a "just a minute" finger while I fish it out. Caller ID indicates that it's Harry, and I consider him for only a moment. Then I shake my head and put the phone back in my bag with a little moue. "Voice mail will get it. I'm with two of my favorite friends, and besides, who needs a man anyway?"

Shelby's eyes sharpen with greed. She is close; I know it. I get extra powers for each client I recruit (Life Enrichment Clause Number 10478), and I have been just itching for my next level, mind-reading, aka the Amazing V Sees All.

There's an art to the program, a stealthy give-and-take, and you never ever share the secret until the absolute moment of desperation strikes. Neither Meegan nor Shelby knows anything, although Shelby will soon. She's about to hit the wall. I can tell. With Meegan, well, let's just say she's not really the desperate type. Yet.

I push back my hair and sigh, a great, "oh, woe is me" wellspring of breath. "The shop was brutal today," I say, and then pause for effect. "There was a leak in the *Post* about the new line, and the waiting list has already started. Julia's assistant called and offered me five thou to put her at the top of the list." I roll my eyes to indicate my perpetual ennui. "Can you believe it? Like I could be bought," I scoff.

"A new line?" asks Meegan.

"Yes, Paolo has been busy. It's to die for." Paolo is my mentor, the one who recruited me. He had been the fabbest leather designer in Italy and got promoted to New York as part of the package for me. It is a big ego trip to think that my soul was worth a move to New York. I don't know what made me so special, but I give thanks every day because of it.

"I can't wait to see it," Shelby gushes.

I lean in close and smile. "I'll get you the first one."

And there it is. I can see it in her eyes. I have her, and all it cost me was a fucking leather purse. Sad. I don't like Shelby, but I think I would have wished more for her.

"You're the best," she says, joy in her voice.

"We'll do lunch tomorrow," I answer, not disputing it at all. I'll arrange for Lucy to be there. The paperwork and the legal hocus-pocus can take up to two hours, but the 1040 EZ (Lucy took great amusement in naming that one) is available for those in a hurry. Shelby looks to be in a hurry.

Meegan starts making eyes at a broker against the back wall. My gaydar is beeping overtime, but she isn't on the same wavelength. "I think he likes you," I say, just as a conversation starter. "Go talk to him."

She looks hesitant, but lonely, so she moves in his direction. I twitch my nose (purely show business, but it lends an air of mysticism), and the words just pop into my head.

Hetero, Homeo, higgledy hurl, forget your preference and go for the girl.

Immediately he turns and gives her a long once-over. His companion looks a little startled, and I giggle to myself. Just like a man. Give him a heat-seeking missile, and he'll follow it anywhere. After a short five minutes of chitchat, Meegan and her new convert are heading out the door, arm in arm. I take a long draw on my martini. Doing the magic takes a lot of energy, and I get a little sapped, but soon the alcohol is coursing through my veins, reviving the blood flow.

"She bagged him," I say with a satisfied smile.

"Lucky her," replies Shelby, bitchily.

"Ah, every dog has its day, and every woman has her lay."

"I'm being petty and small-hearted, aren't I?" she asks, completely insincere.

"That's what Prozac is for, darling," I drawl, patting her hand.

We share a moment of awkward insincerity as I contemplate my soon to be ESPness and Shelby contemplates her aloneness.

I spot him before Shelby does. An eleven-point buck in the patent-pending Armani suit. It's the shoes that do me in. Italian wing tips. I have a severe sweet tooth for Italian wing tips. Some sort of postseventies Richard Gere fetish, I suppose. He meets my eyes, and I feel nothing. However, I figure it's time for Shelby to get some sport. A kind of last hoo-haw, as it were.

I give him a wink that he won't remember—I do like playing God—and chant to myself. It occurs to me belatedly that I really shouldn't give over all my spells to the general populace, however, I will say it involves the words *wing tips, bon vivant,* and *clam dip*. 'Nuff said. (But you know, I have a tendency for prolixity, so I bet I slip up in the future. Shoot me.)

Mr. Wing Tips locks on to her, and the rest is history. They talk for a good forty-five minutes at the bar, comparing names (which neither know, but it is the ultimate game of social chicken) and complaining about the crowds at Pravda. The conversation turns racy, and I stop listening in. Eventually, they leave.

After I finish my fourth martini, Meegan returns, flying solo.

"What happened?" I ask, mildly curious.

Meegan begs a cosmopolitan from the bartender and sips. "I don't know. It was so great at first. He was Mr. Attentive, talking about how pretty I was and how refreshing it was to meet a woman who seemed so genuine, and then we're kissing, and then he gets this horrified look on his face, and can't get away fast enough. It's me, isn't it?"

My playing-God tendencies develop feelings of guilt, and I'm wondering if Lucy ever messes up. Probably not; I don't think Lucy was born in Jersey. "No, it's not you. I bet he dropped some bad acid or something." Do people do that anymore? I'm not sure, but does it really matter?

"I'm being punished," Meegan says, sounding absolutely sure of herself. And usually she's so . . . not.

Ah, I say to myself, a mystery's afoot. "Have you been bad?" I pry, because the notion that Miss Milquetoast Meegan might be laden with pepper is just—delicious.

"My mother died in a car accident."

A car accident? That is *so* not me. Some people handle death well. I, however, have a bad case of necrophobia. It's quite logical when you consider it. "Must be awful," I say, with what I hope is a sensitive smile.

Obviously I'm a better actor than I give myself credit for, because she continues: "I was in high school, and we were having a huge fight that night. I wanted to go to a weekend party at one of my friends' summer house, and she said no. I told her I wished she were dead. Then there was a big flash of light and this crash."

At this point, I nod politely and grimace. She takes a swallow and stares off into space, and I'm thinking we're done. Gee, no, I'm wrong. "I was seriously banged up, and the doctors had to remove a lot of my insides. When I woke up from surgery, they told me she was dead."

It's a heartbreaking story, but I've gone through my entire sensitive repertoire, and serious panic is starting to take hold. I take a long sip of my drink to avoid having to say anything understanding, soothing, or empathetic, only to discover that the glass is not deep enough.

"You know what I want now? More than anything else?" she says with a dead laugh. Then she's looking up at me, and I realize that she wants me to ask.

"I want a kid," she says, stealing a cocktail napkin and tearing it up.

Okay, this is better. Again with the disconnect, but I can work with this one. "Babies are nice."

" I can't have any kids of my own. Ever. It's payback, isn't it?"

And now we're talking about infertility. I look around for the nearest exit.

Meegan buries her head on the bar. "Can I have another drink?"

It's about damn time. "Bartender!" I say, and *whoosh,* a cosmopolitan appears. Slowly Meegan lifts her head, appearing eerily calm. I wait, hoping she's all talked out. However, there is a glint in her eye, and I know that glint. "That's what I want more than anything," she says. "To be pregnant. To feel a life growing inside me. And I can't. . . ."

Awkwardly I pat her head. It's the best I can do in the circumstances. She starts inspecting the men at the bar, and I know that look. Every woman knows that look when it's closing time and you're drunk.

"Maybe you should go home. Sleep it off," I say, doing my best to rescue what is left of her family values and maybe recruit her into the Life Enrichment Program.

11

"She thought I was Miss Perfect. I never wanted to be Miss Perfect."

There's a certain irony in this moment. Why is it that women are never satisfied? She doesn't want to live her perfect life in that perfect house in Connecticut, and I would have sold my soul to do just that.

"So don't be Miss Perfect," I say, because I'm not Miss Perfect, but I do understand rebellion. You can't fight it. You just have to give in when the Warrior Goddess strikes you.

Meegan is no longer listening to my advice, which is probably a good thing. She stands up, a little woozy, but she's still got that loose-cannon glint. So much for Dr. V's Philosophy of Life. I console myself with my drink.

"I think I need to go. Thank you for inviting me," she says politely, because she is Miss Perfect and will always be.

"Uh, sure. Anytime," I add.

Then I watch as she takes off through the non-smoked-filled bar, and I sit there alone, slowly getting drunk.

Crises are not for the faint of heart. I've had my share, and that's too much. Give me the even keel of a carefree existence any day. Eventually, my naturally cool demeanor returns, and I get approached by a publicist from Susan Magrino, a castoff from JP Morgan, and a lesbian from Soho. I turn them all down.

I adore Manhattan in the spring. You would too, if you had my life.

Just let me know, I'll have Lucy give you a call.

*   *   *

I meet Shelby the next day at the Gotham Bar and Grill. When Lucy's not writing the world's dishiest gossip at her Sixth Avenue office, she's there. An office-away-from-office, as it were.

I have my suspicions about the chef here, but with the whole Life Enrichment Program, there's a high level of anonymity. It lends to the air of exclusivity; that's why, for instance, I am "V," and "Shelby" is, well, "Shelby."

Anywhoo, back to the program, which is, of course, the important thing. Absolutely no riffraff allowed. You never know who's doing deals, and it's a great bit of sport to try and figure it all out. In fact, there's a special bookie down in the meatpacking district who takes bets. I put down three thousand on Alfred, but we won't know until 2033, or at least that's what the oddsmakers are saying.

I walk over to Lucy's table (I was scheduled fifteen minutes before Shelby) and seat myself. The maître d' looks offended. Save it for the pope, pal.

She is stunning, as you might guess. Black hair, dark eyes, sort of an eternal Catherine Zeta-Jones look, only a little sharper. She has two cell phones (those cool kind with digital cameras), which are perpetually ringing.

She looks up from her conversation and smiles. Lucy's actually pretty down-to-earth when you get to know her. Just don't get on her bad side. You've heard the stories; they're all true.

I order a Pellegrino and sip patiently. Eventually she kisses into the phone and hangs up.

"My God, can you believe the day I'm having? Oh, the

UN. Those poor, misguided souls. What I could do for world peace if they'd just give me a chance. And then Reverend Al is up to his usual hijinks. I have an in, though, so I'm hoping to seal that deal shortly."

I try not to look impressed, but it's hard. Some of my old gaucheness can spring up at the most inopportune times. I murmur a simpatico, "Sounds like hell." And she laughs. Lucy hears a lot of that.

"Well, so tell me about Shelby. I've got all the paperwork here." She pats the birkin, and her phone rings, a digitally modified "MacArthur Park." Lucy is a huge Donna Summer fan.

"Hello, Don." She lip-synchs his full name to me.

Because Lucy has the hottest nine column-inches in New York, everybody wants to be a part of it, and her phone is ringing all the time.

"Yes, yes. I've heard all about your troubles with rehab," she continues.

"Poor dear.

"Of course I can fix it, but it'll cost you. How much is sobriety worth?"

A very classic moue that would do Revlon proud. "Too bad. Call me tomorrow if you change your mind."

She hangs up and smiles with confidence. "We're running a little tidbit on Page Six tomorrow about rumors surrounding his 'vacation.' He's supposed to be at a spa in Arizona." Lucy laughs. "When will people learn that lies will always come out? Oh, well, maybe he'll come around before the paper goes to bed."

She dabs at her lipstick with the cloth napkin and then folds it into a perfect replica of a swan. "Now, back to Shelby. You've got her?"

I nod. "I'll let you explain the rules, but she's ready."

"You never disappoint me, V."

I smile at her, because I know. I sold my own soul almost two years ago, and my life hasn't been the same—and trust me, that's a good thing.

One average October day, just after I turned thirty-eight, I was driving down the turnpike, my average daily commute to my average daily job to my average daily life, and I screamed. No one could have heard it from the soundproofed doors in my trusty Toyota (and trust me, you don't open your windows in Newark), but I was done being Wilhelmina Lohman, bending over for every dick and dickina that came along. For me, that was it, and once I finally made up my mind, I was happier than I'd ever been before.

Part of the deal is the soul-recruitment program. Shelby is my third soul-taking, and I'm getting the hang of it. The first two were relatively easy, an assistant DA I had met at a party and the super to my old building (yes, there is justice in the world). I should be feeling an attack of conscience, some twinge of badness, but I don't. Of course, I really don't like Shelby, but still, the lack of feeling bothers me.

I've closed that chapter of my life because, well, to be honest, it pales when compared to fawning friends and high-fashion extravaganzas. And there are bigger things ahead. This is the end of that sort of sentimental schmaltz. I look Lucy in the eye. No doubts here. For just a second, I see a smudge in her mascara, and then *whoosh*—it's gone like I never saw it at all. Instinctively I reach for my mirror, check my reflection, but everything's in order. No smudges, no smears, everything is beautiful.

"You don't need to doubt yourself, V. The world is your oyster, and you, my darling, are the pearl. I see great things in your future. You have to trust me on this."

Pinch me, I'm think I'm dreaming.

And then Shelby comes through the door and spots us at the back. She looks a little stunned. Lucy does that to people. It's her aura, her image of pure, controlled power, all packaged in a neat size two. Shelby waits for the maître d' (I'm much more pushy than she is) and smiles at him politely.

I perform the introductions and listen as Lucy begins the Talk. I guess she treats everyone special, because Shelby gets a different spin than I got. Lucy tells Shelby how lucky she is to have such an orderly life, how she is saved from the rigors of the cause célèbre. I'm scanning the annals of my meager French vocabulary and think Lucy's just making that one up, but it sounds good, and Shelby is entranced.

Next comes the pitch. The surprised, "Oh, you actually *want* the fame and notoriety?" The thoughtful stare up to the ceiling. "Well, there might be a way." Shelby's intensity is palpable, a chokehold that won't let go until your soul is free.

Fascinated, I watch the whole interchange. There's profound human drama at work when someone gives up their soul. Seeing others go through the same hell and insecurities that I did makes me realize how I have grown and matured. Today, I'm above all that shit.

Shelby takes a sip of her drink every now and then, or picks at her salad, but her eyes never leave Lucy's face. Whatever you want, whatever your dreams are. Heady words. Eventually, I get seduced as well, forgetting to critique Lucy's approach. I'm sucked back into the sumptuous reverie of getting whatever you want. I'll repeat that because it's important.

Whatever you want.

Those are the dreams that fire the greed of the world.

My back starts tingling, and I look around. Eyes are watching us, some surreptitiously, some openly. Appraising and envious, all blended together in one ugly palette of emotion. It's a proud moment for someone who used to be a perpetual Z-lister, but that was a long time ago. Back before I was footloose and soul-free.

Shelby is ready to sign, the Visconti pen poised above the paper, but Lucy isn't quite done yet. She rests her chin on her hand and tilts her head in a darling Audrey Hepburn–esque manner. "I don't want you to do anything you'll regret. There's no backing out. Ever. What I try and give my clients is life without conscience. Who needs all that guilt? I mean, really."

She focuses her whole attention on Shelby, oddly intimate in the bustling setting. At this moment, I don't exist, the restaurant doesn't exist, there's only two people left in the world. Shelby and Lucy. And I'm watching the tableau, waiting with bated breath for Shelby to condemn herself to a finite, yet boundless, life.

Lucy taps her fingers on the papers. "You're sure?" she asks. Shelby nods.

Lucy continues. "We do ask for a few things in return. I'm a firm believer in rewarding positive behaviors. So, for each client you recruit for Life Enrichment, your powers will be increased to the next level. There are nine levels, and you begin an apprentice program under V's tutelage for thirty days. We do ask that you use your powers with discretion. The system works best if the world isn't aware we exist."

"What sort of powers?" Shelby asks with such repressed malice that I wonder who is going to be the recipient of the seven plagues of Shelby.

"You start with non-life-forms object creation. Basically, it's our most effective program. If Wishes Were Birkins. After you recruit another client, you move into Level 2, personal appearance modification, aka My Salad Days Are Over."

Shelby turns on me. "That's how you do it!"

I smile with teeth that are perfectly white and have never been capped. Hate me, I don't mind; I never was hate-worthy when I had a soul. "All those wasted hours at the gym. Poof! And dessert, all the dessert you want . . ."

Now she starts to fully appreciate the life before her, and her eyes start to glaze. "What's the third level?"

Lucy points to the paper in front of her. "I can't tell you the rest until you've signed. We have to have a nondisclosure agreement in place with all our clients."

While Shelby signs, Lucy brings out the Life Enrichment handbook—*I've Sold My Soul to the Devil . . . Now What?*—

and gives it to Shel. "You can take it home and pore over the details. If you have any questions, V is there to answer them for you. And remember, it's our little secret."

Lucy's phone rings, and she takes the call away from the table. I'm alone with my new convert. And after the requisite seventy-two hours (not quite standard contract law, but still a nice touch—you have three days to back out of the deal. After that, you're in forever), my power base will be upped to Level 4.

Shelby looks like a kid at Christmas. "I can just think about something, and then, voilà, there it is?"

I nod, feeling a lot like Santa. It's a good life. "Well, sorta. You have to use a spell, and then it'll appear."

She looks as if she's about to wish up an entire wardrobe from Barney's right there, and I hold up my restraining hand. "Wait. Remember. Discretion."

Her face scrunches with worry. "Oh."

Karan schmaran, heels of air, Edmundo Castillo is everywhere.

"Look under the table," I say, with all the finesse of Harry Houdini. It never gets old.

She lifts the tablecloth and pulls out the signature Bergdorf-Goodman shopping bag. Inside is a wished-up pair of Edmundo Castillo sandals. "I want to do it," she says.

Feeling benevolent, I nod and point to the Frequently Asked Questions in the back, which includes a list of the most common spells.

She closes her eyes, and I can see the magic wash over her. Clients get an almost physical glow, which comes from the four-alarm, multi-orgasmic wash of having your wish granted—immediately. She squirms in her seat and then reaches under the table. I'm curious to see what her first wish fulfillment is. Your most secret desire is a cornerstone in understanding and undermining the human psyche.

Proudly she brandishes a set of Tiffany Feathers earrings. Personally, I think they're gaudy, but I know better than to say anything. So silently I watch as she absorbs the change in her status. An instant becoming. She sits straighter, more self-assured than ever before, and there are no spells at work for that one.

We celebrate over two pieces of chocolate cake (Alfred's secret recipe) and a cappuccino. Lucy comes back in a whiff of custom-designed perfume, something mysterious and musky, as old as the world, then she waves good-bye and departs for places unknown. All eyes follow in her wake. I feel a surge of admiration for this fascinating female who lifts us above a cheap imitation of life. Shelby and I toast her new soul loss, and she smiles in an almost drunken fog.

Today I can rule the world. Well, okay, I'm only an almost Level 4. But someday . . .

After all, what good is a soul? Can you borrow against it? Dress it up and parade it down Park Avenue? I feel the eyes gravitate in our direction once more, and I brush back my hair, a modest gesture to acknowledge the silent tributes that are flowing our way.

Just remember, *you can have it, too.*

Two

Today's politicians have fallen a long way from merely chopping down the cherry tree. A statesman from Albany was found in, um, a rather indelicate situation with the coat-check girl at a renowned restaurant on Fifty-sixth Street. Both parties insist she was removing something from his fly. And I wonder what that was? Page Six snoops indicate business at the restaurant is now booming.

In more uplifting news, the rumor that Don B is back into rehab is absolutely false. Sources at the Kabala spa in Arizona confirm his presence at the yoga paradise. I'm sure there are those who are prepared to believe the worst, but they'd be wrong.

*And lastly, a perky morning talk-show
hostess is flirting with taking the dragon-
lady title from the infamous Miss Oh So Lo.
First the water wasn't sparkling, then the
music was all wrong, and now she wants
the show's stylist fired for insubordination.
Appearances can be deceiving, can't they?
And here I thought she was such a doll.*

Sunday afternoon is the day I play chess with my ex-husband's great-aunt in the southern part of Central Park. Yeah, right there above the rink with all the kiddies. It's embarrassing, but Blanche says that Columbus Park is full of punks and Washington Square has "too many damned hippies."

Every time we come to play, Crazy Yuri from one of those Stan countries shakes her down. "You must pay. Five dollars. This is my park. These are my tables." He has those Brezhnev eyebrows that never reflected well on the Soviet Union. If I had those eyebrows, I would have declared the cold war over, too. Just so I could go to the States and get a decent brow wax.

Secretly I think that Blanche has a crush on Uri, even if he is a "leftist Commie." She gets all dolled up, wearing forty million bangles up and down her arms, and they jingle when she moves. As if that's not enough, she has this huge four-carat faux rock on her right hand that is truly bigger than her fingers. When you're seventy-three, crushes are cute.

She doesn't get out much anymore, and I like spending time with her. Sometimes I can even forget that she's related to the mealymouthed Marv who ran off with a cunt. There's no accounting for genes, that's for sure.

Yuri comes over and shakes us down. I hem and haw, but give him the fiver (he prides himself on his Art of the Deal negotiation skills). Blanche laughs, her arms ringing like bells.

"You like opera?" he asks her.

Opera? I'm thinking to myself. Now that's a wasted artistic endeavor.

Blanche beams up at him. *"La Bohème."*

Nervously he smoothes his eyebrow with his forefinger. "We should see it. Together."

I start humming the *Love Boat* theme, but Blanche chooses to ignore me. She dips her head in a coy gesture. "That would be nice."

"I will call," he states and then stomps off with that anti-capitalistic stomp that only true Communists have mastered.

"Does he have your phone number?" I ask, ever practical.

"No," she answers, ever the optimist.

I shut up, and we begin to play.

Now, I'm not a great chess player, but I can hold my own against Blanche. Chess is a cerebral game, and she considers herself one of the first great intelligentsia of Queens. Tell me, who can argue with that?

"V, you gonna move, or have you turned into one of those statues?" she says, the bracelets clanking as she pushes up her glasses and gives me the big-eyed Mr. Magoo stare.

"I need to think," I say, but secretly I'm coveting this little felt chapeau that some NYU coed is sporting across the way.

My marvelous long and flowing hair is the exact shade of mahogany brown that I adore, and pink is one of my best colors. Pre–Life Enrichment, I had a dish-mop head highlighted with streaks of gray. The memory makes me shudder, and I run my hands through my silky ponytail (très chic) just to convince me that the nightmare is over.

When I turn back to the board, I notice the gaping hole that Blanche has left for me to jump into. Others might have qualms about trouncing a senior citizen at chess. I, however, am qualmless as well as soulless, and immediately move my queen to D6, while her king waits blissfully for death—just like the horny cheerleader in one of those slasher movies. I'm telling you, it's a guilt-free life. You should try it.

Eventually I win, and I pocket the five-spot that Blanche owes me. Starting tomorrow, I get my Level 4 ESP powers. I bet it's morally wrong to gamble when you have mind-reading abilities. So sue me.

We play two games before the clouds roll in and a light rain threatens to fall. I notice Blanche shivering and realize it's time to pack it in. Weather powers are beyond the realm of the nine. If you hear someone claim they can harness the wind, I'll be the first to tell you, they're lying their ass off. In lieu of pocketing another fiver, I hang my king out to dry.

"It's getting late," I say, waiting for her to put me in check.

"Got a hot date?" she asks, moving her queen into exactly the wrong position.

"Of course," I lie, this time setting up my pawn. "Your

nephew is a schmuck, Blanche. He should have appreciated what he had."

She sees the opening and zooms in to commandeer my pawn. "Don't I know it. That Kimberly is going to bankrupt him. Just wants his money."

I smile, my happiness complete. "Probably."

Blanche mistakes my vindictiveness for worry. Too naive, that's her problem. "It's a shame he left you. Stupidest thing he's ever done. Look at you now, and look at him." She raises her eyebrows over the thick lenses for emphasis. "I bet if he saw you now, he'd fall for you all over again."

Oh, let me think. Derek, Marv. Harry, Marv. Charlie, Marv. Oops. Marv, you lose. "I'm sure he would, but I'm not letting him within nuclear fallout range. The man is trouble, Blanche, and my troubles are over."

She leans forward, bracelets jangling, which means this is important. "But if he did get in a jam, you'd help him, wouldn't you?"

"No." When we were married, I would have given him anything. Today, the aardvark spell would be my only present to him.

"Come on, V. He's family."

"He's a dick."

Her mouth purses together in disapproval. Well, I'm sorry, I'm going to call a spade a spade and a dick a dick. Even if he is family. To Blanche. My only best friend.

Shit.

"I bet he'd shoot himself before he asked me for any help,"

I say, which is a complete lie because backbone and Marv don't belong in the same sentence, but I'm trying to appease Blanche here.

"Promise me, V. Promise an old woman. He's driving a new car. Flashy thing, too. I worry he's up to no good."

Marv? No good? *You think?*

The bracelets jangle again, and there's worry magnified behind the Coke-bottle lenses. Oh, God, she's going to make me do this. I hold up my hands in surrender. "Blanche, all right, already. I promise. Let's talk about something else."

Conversation is averted because some mangy dog comes running through our table, his leash dragging behind him. I jump to my feet, dreading what dog hair will do to dupioni silk.

Immediately I'm trampled by what feels like an entire army and thrown to the ground. I jump to my feet—again—and flash the official Hoboken hand-jerk at the tiny figure chasing after the dog. The dog, who now has my Chanel silk scarf trailing behind him, runs even faster.

"V, she's just a little girl," Blanche yells after me, as if that should make a difference.

I start after the pair, anger giving me speed I'd never dreamed I had. You try running in Manolo Blahnik slides. It truly is a fucking miracle, but I don't realize it now. The dog is heading toward the reservoir, toying with my scarf, having a good old time, and I'm just flat-out pissed because that scarf had sentimental value. Jimmy Fallon had given me that scarf, and okay, he's a little passé now, but well, he's still Jimmy Fallon.

My eyes widen in disbelief as the dog takes a flying leap into the water and the girl dives after him, my beautiful scarf floating like a bit of Chanel flotsam on the surface. I, being intelligent on a good day, skid to a somewhat graceful halt. My Jesse Owens career is over.

Unfortunately, then the real nightmare starts, and yes, the scarf is heartbreaking, but that's not what I'm talking about. The girl is floundering around, and I'm thinking, what sort of idiot kid jumps into a lake if she can't swim? I glance around and notice a few old geezers shuffling just over the horizon, but no young and vibrant parental unit leaping to the rescue.

It's all up to me. Don't you hate it when that happens?

The little girl bobs up and down like a bottle, the damned dog barking around her, and I'm thinking, Why couldn't this dog be Lassie? Go get her, girl!

I'd just jump in myself, but God, Lucy would have my hide (it's one of the basic ten commandments—do not interfere with the will of the devil). And I know exactly what lake water will do to dupioni.

The little girl is holding her own, and I hold my breath. My toe creeps forward, just enough to wet the leather of the slides. No, V, no. You can't!

I look back toward the hill, willing someone, *anyone,* to appear, but the hill is empty.

But out of nowhere there's an old homeless guy standing right next to me, a seedy Charlton Heston in rags and reeking of eau de vodka. He smiles, one of those blank smiles that shoots right through you. I'm thinking that he's expecting me to jump in. I'm thinking, No way, buckeroo, the vodka has pickled your brain. He smiles again, raises his arms, and then FUCK! I'm thigh deep in water. Silk is floating around me like a shroud and I'm really, really hating this. The bastard pushed me!

The little girl starts to scream. Couldn't she be a little more appreciative? "You need to be quiet so that I can think," I yell at her, scouring my brain for spells that might get me out of this mess. Unfortunately, spells are implicitly designed to satisfy wants and desires, not for something as multipurpose as parting water.

I watch the girl go under, and for one time-stopping moment I feel shame. Have I gone so far to the dark side that I'm going to let a kid drown?

Stuff like that sends you to hell.

Of course, I'm going to hell anyway . . .

Oh, fuck.

I start wading through the water, all the while thinking that I can tell Lucy that I was pushed. There's nothing like the truth to get your ass out of a sling.

The water gets deeper, and I swim over to where she's floundering, and then just as I reach out to grab her—Holy Waterworks, Aquaman appears! I tread water, feeling one shoe slip off into the dark depths below, and watch as the sleek dark head starts towing her in.

"Hey!" I call out, really pissed now. I secretly like the idea of being the hero, and if I'm going to get in trouble, I want to get in trouble for something worthwhile.

"Can you get the dog?" he yells.

Oh, yeah. That's me. Dog-saver extraordinaire. I almost tell him no, but then Fido swims up to me and starts licking my face. I hate dogs, especially ones with bits of pink Chanel clinging to their teeth.

I grab the stupid leash and tow him to land, praying he doesn't have rabies. Slowly I drag myself out of the water and stand on the shore, me dripping and Fido leaping for joy.

By now a crowd has gathered, and there's applause and cheers. Aquaman is a hero. No one cares that I saved the dog. I don't even care that I saved the dog. I look down at the ruined silk that is clinging to my body—and not in an attractive way.

Blanche rushes over to me, bless her heart, and oohs and aahhs. The mother of the brat finally appears, and as I wipe the bits of slime and water from my face, I watch in disbelief as Brat-Mother fawns over Aquaman. Go down and kiss his feet, why don't you?

As if he could read my mind, he looks up and smiles at me. And suddenly I'm thinking, Aquaman is a little studly. Then Aquaman is walking over, and I'm trying to think of my über-model appearance spell, but my mind is blank.

Shit, shit, shit. Unfortunately, that is not only a convenient curse word, but also a description of my physical situation. There's the nightmare of the crowd, which by now has grown to monumental proportions, and I'm grateful when Aquaman gives me his jacket.

"You're a brave lady," he says.

I blush. Oh, God, I blush. What the hell is wrong with me?

"It was nothing," I answer back, thinking to myself, NO, YOU MORON, IT WAS SOMETHING TREMENDOUS AND THE WORLD SHOULD KNOW ABOUT IT. My pragmatic self tells my megalomaniacal self to shut up.

Because my day is not bad enough, a reporter noses in, scrawling notes in his little stenopad. I have to say, this dweeb is no Clark Kent, more like Ted Koppel on a bad hair day.

"Ted the Nose Knows from the *Post*," he says, dragging me deeper into the hell-pit of this moment. The *Post*. *Lucy's paper*.

"I'm sorry, I think we should wait for *Newsday*. They pay," I answer churlishly, clinging to that last little bit of self-preservation that will not die. There's a punishment for doing good works. Life Enrichment Clause Numero Uno.

Aquaman smiles. "You're a hero. They just want the world to know about it."

And I'm thinking, Okay, strictly on the surface, this is going to look like a good deed. The punishment for goodness is at Lucy's discretion. But this wasn't truly a good deed. I mean, I was pushed. All I saved was a dog.

"Actually, I can't claim any credit at all. This drunk homeless guy pushed me in," I say, looking around for the drunk homeless guy.

Everyone looks for the drunk homeless guy, except for Aquaman. "I saw you. I saw you jump in. There wasn't anybody around you for miles. You took off after the girl, flying, I've never seen anyone run so fast, and then you did this great dive into the water."

My eyes narrow, and I glare. What a pile of shit. I'm immediately suspicious. Maybe this guy is a client, too, and doesn't want to incur Lucy's wrath. Pretty damn smart. Okay, the guy has brains as well as looks, but I'm still not going to let him railroad me into being the hero here.

"I don't know what happened, but hey, you got the little br—girl. I just saved Fido." Immediately that earns me a lick on my privates. I slap the dog in earnest. No animals in my sex life, no sirreeee.

Aquaman turns to the reporter. "I'd like you to leave me out of the story. I'm just a John Doe, you know? This lady here. She's the one you want to interview."

Blanche pipes in to help. "She's my great-niece by marriage. V *bleep, bleep*. That's spelled *bleep, bleep, bleep, bleep, bleep, bleep* [you didn't think I'd forget, did you?]."

I'm seeing my grave get deeper and deeper, and now I'm sure Aquaman is a client. That would explain the studliness.

The reporter drags the kid in front of me, and the little girl, sensing the daggers I'm throwing in her direction, starts to cry. Her mommy shushes her, but she just bawls louder. This is not a Kodak moment, and I'm hoping Ted the Nose Knows will be smart enough to figure it out. But no, Ted is a doofus. He snaps the picture: me in drippy, ugly dupioni silk, a bawling child, and Fido giving me another personal kiss.

God.

The brouhaha loses some of its haha, and eventually the trivialities of the world return and the crowd dwindles away. Blanche is a media hog, which I never realized up until now.

I'm going to remember that in the future. Aquaman, who has remained stubbornly silent on the subject of identifying himself, begins to walk away.

I, determined to know his name, for my sake as well as needing a fall guy for Lucy, rush after him. With one shoe off and one shoe on, it is an awkward rush at best. "I've got your jacket," I say in some stupid, breathy, Kewpie-doll voice.

"You'll need it," he says, giving me a once-over that causes me to shiver.

"Then I should return it to you, after I get it cleaned, of course. Who are you?" I ask, frantically wishing I was up to the level of behavior alteration (Level 7) and could just hocus-pocus it out of him.

"Nathaniel Stevens."

I file it away in my memory bank and hold out a hand. Where is my self-confidence, my poise, my magic? My energy is sapped like I've done a veritable grab-bag of spells. Alas, all I am now is a pre-soul-loss schmielazoid. "Call me V," I say. "Do you have a card?"

He laughs. Why is that funny? Everyone has a card. "I'm in the military. We don't have cards."

"That's nice," I say, wondering why a client would be in the military. I mean, you could get killed. The old necrophobia grabs me by the throat, and I take a step back. He couldn't be a client, unless he's a masochist, too. Now there's a thought.

He reaches over like he's going to touch me, but instead takes a pen from the jacket pocket. Disappointed, V? *Moi?*

Then he writes a phone number down. "Call me when you want to give it back."

I realize I'm wearing one of those bomber jackets. I thought the guy had just bought it at Bloomingdale's—now I realize it's a real bomber jacket. "You're a pilot?" I ask, trying to sound intelligent. Definitely not a client. He was just born naturally studly. The cad.

"No, I'm in the army," he says. "I got it at Bloomingdale's."

I nod. "Okay, I'll call you."

He stuffs his hands in his pockets, drawing attention to a first-class pleasure package. I don't stare. "Sure," he says. "And, V . . ."

I look up. "Yeah?"

"You did good today."

The feeling of impending doom returns. That's exactly what I was afraid of.

That night, there is a showing of the fall collection of Marc Jacobs at the Boranski gallery in Chelsea. I have heard no word from Lucy, so I can only pray that the afternoon park-rescue will fail to make the morning paper. If the Olsen twins go to dinner, the rescue will get shelved into the circular file and I'll be trumped by a pair of over-the-hill actresses who're under twenty. I can hope.

Tonight will be the first test of my new Level 4 powers. Mind-reading. It'd be nicer to test out these powers in say, Atlantic City, where I could actually profit from my abilities, but for tonight, Chelsea will have to do.

When the car arrives, I have my first trial run. "Driver, I think I want to go to New Jersey this evening. Perhaps Newark."

His answer comes through crystal clear.

Jersey? What the fuck does she want in Jersey? The tip better be worth it. It's a hollow-sounding echo, like it's coming in from far away. Very Hollywood. I bet Lucy invented this.

"No, never mind," I say, just to take the pressure off. "Take me down to West Twenty-second Street. The Boranski gallery."

Praise God. The Lincoln Tunnel is hell on Fridays. Now I can get home for Survivor. *Wonder if Cheryl would come over. I could get laid.*

I tune him out after that and lean back to relax. Mind-reading snippets from a livery driver is not my idea of fun.

Finally, we arrive. I have to say that art galleries are a world apart from me. And that was true even before I lost my soul. I don't understand contemporary art, but I pretend to, which is what I suspect 90 percent of art patrons in the city do as well. The gallery is one of those renovated warehouses with thirty-foot walls of sheet metal, which must cost a fortune to heat. I've learned to wear fur to gallery showings—not only as a fashion accessory, but because I get cold.

Tonight's event is a fine combination of art and fashion, highlighting the fall collection of Marc Jacobs. Everyone has shown up wearing Marc Jacobs glasses as well, and I'm not sure if that is a joke or not.

I am met by my date, the illustrious Harry Harrison, heir to the Harrison Bread fortune and professional trust-fund playboy with a unique chest-beating elitist attitude that's very

Cro-Magnon in a contemporary sort of way. The New York gossip columns eat him up. I, of course, only date him. When he's lucky. Ah, it's a wonderful life.

When I think back to my soulful days, I was such a loser. Guys like Harry Harrison wouldn't give me change for a meter, much less a date. Run-of-the-mill Marv was the best I could do, and after ten torturous years of Weight Watchers and the gym, he runs off with Kimberly the Cunt, who I used to think was a friend. Makes my blood boil over in a fit of rage. I try not to dwell on the past, but sometimes a piece of it just comes up and slaps me right off my ass.

Like now, for instance.

I spy Kimberly in a marvelous Dior creation, and I'm wondering, How did Marv swing that? Or, even better, Maybe he left her, and she's found new and improved greenback pastures in which to flash her 36D udders.

There's that rage thing again. I really should see a therapist. When I achieve Level 8, I can actually abracadabra a person. It's transitory—you only get to keep your neo-friends for a maximum of twenty-four hours, and then they disappear (it's Da Rules), but I figure a good twenty-four hours with a shrink would do wonders for me.

But then Harry comes up to me, and Kimberly the Cunt is forgotten.

I hear his deep thoughts echoing inside my head. *Tonight I'm going to get laid. First step, compliment the dress.*

"V, you look absolutely stunning this evening. What is that? Halston?" he says.

He's only a man, I remind myself. He can't help himself. Then I twirl prettily, letting him admire my sleek lines, nattily attired in sequins and black. "You noticed!" I give him a kiss because I like kissing Harry. He's a great photo-ops kisser. He manages to snag you just when a member of the paparazzi is skulking by, and then he dips you into this delicious, romance-novel clinch. I, liking the spotlight fine, do not object. We kiss for the cameras, and as soon as they pass, he immediately raises me up and wipes lipstick from his mouth.

Yeah, Harry, love you, too. I pounce upon the first glass of Moët that passes in my direction and take a long gulp.

Across the room, Kimberly has spied me, and I'm wondering if she will approach. I polish my appearance with a truly magical glow.

Sunlight from the south of France, candlelight from a twilight dance, moonglow sparkle in my hair, kiss my eyes with starlight's stares.

(That was a freebie because I'm feeling generous, and because every lady should know how to look her best. This is especially handy in those "morning-after" moments—the ones that nobody wants to talk about. You can thank me later.)

Kimberly is feeling brave and approaches. I smile graciously and wait for her to speak.

"V! Imagine seeing you here! How long has it been? Too long."

Yeah, that's what happens when you boff your friend's husband. Time flies. My smile gets harder. Of course, the last time she saw me, in my soulful days, I was a pitiful sight. I was at the end of my rope, with a diet that never worked, thighs that were never smaller than Kansas, and a husband who never believed in monogamy.

When Paolo singled me out at a little no-name boutique in Newark, I thought I'd died and gone to Condé Nast heaven. I, who followed the bag industry like a fiend, knew who he was, an import direct from Italy. My God, everyone who had an innate sense of style knew who he was. It was Fashion Week, and he was in town for the shows. We started discussing types of leather and bindings, and not in that tacky S&M way. No, he was treating me like an equal, and to be frank, with my self-esteem issues at that particular time, I was like a flower blooming in the Tuscan sun. I had never thought I could compete in the cutthroat arena of high fashion; my skills are more in the business/financial end of things, but Paolo seemed confident. Two weeks later, I met Lucy and I knew. Finally, someone who could appreciate me for what I wanted to be. After I signed on, I waved bye-bye to Marv. And all his bimbos. Like Kimberly.

"We'll do lunch," I tell her, in a voice that implies hell will freeze first.

I test out my new mind-reading powers, expecting to hear, *She's turned into such a bitch*, but instead I get, *My God, that bag! A Sonata. They look even better in person.*

Whoa, I could get used to this.

Kimberly doesn't let me see her bag envy, but that's okay, because I know, and she doesn't know I know. We used to go bag-shopping together (Canal Street, and not the good parts), and I know just what she likes. She wisps her scarf around her shoulders in a Nora Desmond move. "I'll come by your shop. I've been dying to see your Sonata line."

"How is Marv?" I ask, then nearly bite my tongue off. I should never have asked, but ten-year-old habits die hard.

Her eyes focus on the cement floors of the gallery, and she sniffs. "He left me for his secretary."

Blanche hasn't said a word about this, but she and Marv don't talk every day, and Marv is enough of a weasel to keep quiet.

I watch Kimberly with something suspiciously akin to pathos zipping into my heart, and I'm tempted to tell her about the aardvark spell. It would cost her her soul, but trust me, sometimes revenge is worth it.

Instead, I say, "I'm sorry." Two words that I never thought I'd utter to Kimberly. Okay, so maybe I was a little harsh on her and she's not really a cunt, but she did boff my husband. In my bed. I feel the panic stirring up inside me and struggle to breathe.

But then I flash her a smile. It's the peace of practicing self-actualizing Tibetan meditation (not really). Mainly it's because I'm me, and she's not. Doesn't that sound marvelous? I've been waiting forty-two years to be able to say that. I don't think she realizes how bad I hurt back then. I had really high expectations, even for Marv. God, I was such a sap. The bag business helps these days, but memories like that don't go away. Ever.

"You're looking really good, V. Maybe a little nip here, a little tuck there, huh?"

My eyes narrow to slits. "If you're trying to suck up, Kimbers, implying plastic surgery is not the best way to go about it."

She has the grace to look ashamed. "Sorry. But I love the pocketbooks, V." She cast jealous eyes over my purse.

I would kill for one of those. Maybe she'd let me borrow it. Just for one night.

For a moment I consider leaving Kimberly alone and letting her go on with her little bourgeoisie existence; however, mere bag envy from an old friend who stole my husband is not enough. By nature, I'm a flaunter.

"Why don't you stop by next Wednesday? We'll go to Elaine's for dinner," I say magnanimously. Her eyes light up with a joyous excitement that I used to be intimately familiar with. I now realize that she's not wearing Dior, but a Victor Costa design at one-tenth the price. If I were truly an evil person, I would invite Kimberly out for a little soul-taking. The low-hanging fruit is always the easiest to pick, and Level 5 is mind alteration, including but not limited to selective amnesia and memory implants. (Excellent for when the doormen don't recognize you and the velvet rope is the only thing between you and three column-inches in *Boldface Names*.)

However, I am not truly evil, just selfish and somewhat myopic, so I demur and leave her alone. It's the flash of excitement in her eyes that gets to me. I remember the days when it would take nothing more than a night out to make my entire year. Now every night out is a night out.

We plan a little more, and then Harry approaches with that "Ready to leave, babe" swagger. I don't need to read his mind to see the lust in his heart. Trust me, the man has a perpetual hard-on, both mentally and physically.

Kimberly eyes him with prurient interest, and I'm thinking, Don't waste your juices; Harry's first love affair is with himself.

But I leave that night on Harry's arm, and we take a limo back to his penthouse. One thing—and I do unfortunately mean ONLY ONE THING—leads to another, and we have a rollicking romp with a faux-induced orgasm that could shatter glass. I dress and listen as Harry talks about himself. By 4:00 A.M., I call a cab and drag myself out the door, feeling unsatisfied and alone. And I notice the morning's headlines staring up at me.

BAG LADY'S DARING DUNK SAVES TOT

My cell phone rings. Caller ID says that it's Lucy.

Hell.

Three

Well, we've certainly all had bad-hair days, but the photo shot of the glorious V at rescue central has to take the cake. And speaking of V, sources say that Paolo is threatening to leave the top firm and spin off his own designs. Where would V be without Paolo? Dunked in a lake without a paddle.

A supermodel that will remain nameless (but I will mention that she is the "top" NY model) was pulled over for speeding by one of the state patrols. Seems when he tried to write her a ticket, she launched into a French tirade and slammed back into her Ferrari and zoomed off. He caught up with her three miles later and threw

her into jail. If only she had spoken Roman-
ian instead.

New York Dog is a wonderful addition
to the New York literary landscape. I was
approached to do a cover and write their
Doggy Style column, but instead suggested
a dear friend, who is just now being pen-
ciled in on everyone's guest list. Pick up the
June issue and meet Shelby and her
adorable dog, Mooshoo.

Lucy's little hell on earth is on the thirty-fourth floor of Central Park West. As I take the private elevator up, I contemplate my future while an orchestrated version of Prince plays in the background.

Okay, I know that I'm in trouble, but, how bad can it be? It's not like she's going to rip my powers from me—is she? *Is she?*

No. I shake my head, telling myself I'm being silly. As long as there are souls to be recruited, I think Lucy needs me. By the time I arrive at her door, I'm feeling cocky and secure. Yeah, baby.

She opens the door before I knock, sort of the mental version of Caller ID, and it throws me for a moment, but I recover admirably. She's wearing a gorgeous black peignoir that flows when she walks. I follow her inside.

I've never seen the penthouse before, and now I stand in awe. The antiques are tasteful and plentiful, and I notice a cute little tapestry that features Eve's fall from grace. You know, I bet Lucy needlepointed it herself. It has that personal touch.

The Manhattan skyline is lit up in the darkness, the Empire State Building outlined in red tonight. It could be a tribute for the Heart Association, or it could be a testament to Lucy's influence, I don't know.

Under my feet, the building sways as the wind whips outside. Inside feels safe, secure, and—yes, I'm shocked—cozy.

In one corner there's an entertainment center disguised as a Louis the XIV armoire, and it looks like the real deal. Vases of flowers are tucked everywhere. It's really quite nice.

As my eyes skim around the room, I notice the sumptuous pièce de résistance. On the side wall is a dark wooden bar with inlaid leaves hand-carved in the wood, and Holy Antonio, adorning the bar, is a shirtless bartender. Oh, those pecs, those abs—which will soon grace my best fantasies. Level 9, baby, Level 9, and then I can have a bartender all of my very own.

I drag my gaze away and try to regain some of my poise and sophistication. It's impossible. I'm still entranced by the lodgings of the devil, and so I continue to gawk.

Really, the place is great. You should see it! Très chic, and not anything like the fire and brimstone that legend speaks of. A cheery blaze burning in the hand-carved marble fireplace brings me back to my current troubles. I take a step over to see if I hear any screams coming from the flames. None. Secretly I breathe a sigh of relief.

Lucy laughs. "That's so cliché, V. Drag yourself off to the new millennium."

Mind-reading. Damn. Forgot about that one. Instantly, I think to myself, Doesn't Lucy look lovely this evening? Is that a new haircut?

I think she knows what I'm doing, but she doesn't call me on it. I smile. "You rang?" I say.

Her smile doesn't weaken at all, which really worries me. "Did you think I wouldn't read my own paper?"

I wave a "pish-posh" hand. "Oh, you know how those reporters are. Always making something of nothing."

"Lying to the devil is not a good idea."

Fuck. "Okay, but I was pushed, and I didn't even save the kid. It was a dog, for God's sake. Only a stupid dog. And he took my scarf. My Jimmy Fallon scarf. You would do the same if you were in my shoes."

She walks over to the window, her black skirts swirling around her. For a moment she stares out into the night, and then she turns to face me. "Rules are rules, V. I haven't asked you to kill anyone, not even lie, cheat, or steal. No, all I ask for is apathy. In this day and age, that's all I need. A do-nothing attitude can do wonders for my Life Enrichment Program. And unfortunately, you did something."

"I was pushed," I repeat stubbornly. "And I didn't even save her."

"You tried. You could have just let her drown."

A creepy little voice buried deep in my mind said, "No, you couldn't," but I ignore the voice. I need to play this right, or there'll be hell to pay.

I stand firm. "There's no point in arguing over this. You

called. I'm here. It won't happen again. I swear on my mother's grave."

"Your mother's not dead."

"No, but someday she will be. She smokes a gazillion packs a day. And there'll be a grave." I shrug, just as any selfish, evil, mother-killing client would.

Lucy stares at me; a long, hard stare that makes me more than a little nervous, but I'm wearing an armor of Halston and I can persevere.

Then she walks over to the bartender and picks up a glass of tonic water. Mr. Fantasy Man watches her adoringly.

She lifts a hand, and the fireplace starts to scream, this high, piercing scream that slides down my spine like ice.

I've always considered myself a brave, though sometimes foolhardy woman, but now I am scared shitless.

Lucy starts to laugh, and thank God, the screaming stops. I stop shaking, too.

She takes a long sip of her tonic, and I concentrate on the ice cubes floating in her glass. That little bit of normalcy calms me—somewhat.

"Why are you fighting me, V?"

"What are you talking about?"

"Don't you know what's inside you? Who you're destined to be? I remember the day I first met you. I'd never liked one of my clients before. Oh, some were better than others, but I liked your style. You didn't pretend to be anything else but who you are."

"Thank you." *I think.*

"You always made it so easy for me. I know what you think before you do. I know what you'll do before you act. You're just like me." Then she sighs and shakes her head.

Now here I have to say that I think Lucy is cooler than anybody else in New York. She has the world in the palm of her hand, and I feel intensely flattered about the things she just said . . . and yet . . . I'm not really comfortable with the whole "just like me" part. I haven't really thought much about Lucy as a person vis-à-vis Lucy as the devil. For instance, I don't think I would ever make a fireplace scream—it's just not in me, and to be perfectly honest, I don't want it to be in me, either. I choose to keep these opinions to myself for the moment, and Lucy continues: "I hope you had a chance to check out your mind-reading powers, because they're gone now. As are your transitory emotion powers, which should tell you just how greatly you've disappointed me. I think you'll do nicely at Level 2, and I wouldn't plan on wearing a bathing suit anytime soon," she says.

The Halston tightens noose like around my thighs, and I get that itchy feeling in my legs. "You wouldn't," I say, but it's too late.

"I did. It's only half an inch. I'm not that cruel, V darling." Regally she seats herself on a straight-backed armchair and crosses her legs in a graceful manner with thighs that do not smash together. "And as soon as you give me another soul, you can have your thighs of steel back as they were."

The old feelings of inadequacy do it for me. It's 5:00 A.M., I'm tired, and now I have fat thighs. It's not my finest moment. I nod tightly. "We're done?"

"Yes, we're done." A little washrag terrier comes bounding into the room and bounds into her lap. She strokes the little guy, who laps her adoringly, and I'm wondering if the little dog was once a human. Lucy looks up, mind-reading in her eyes.

Damn.

She smiles and pats the dog. "V . . . don't let it happen again."

"No, Lucy," I say, not wanting to live the rest of my life as a Pekingese. "It won't." Then I turn to go. But all the way down in the elevator, as I listen to the Muzak version of "King of Pain," I'm wondering if I was actually telling the truth.

It scares me some to realize that I might have just lied to the devil.

I have dreams that night, really scary dreams, I'm trapped in Lucy's fireplace, and there's no getting out because my thighs have ballooned to a size gazillion. All the while, Mr. Fantasy is laughing in a Vincent Price manner and pointing at my legs. For the first time I wonder if I made the right choice about giving up my soul. For some time I toss and turn, but then the sun comes up, just as it always does, and I get out of my bed and stare into my infinite closet. I remember what I had before—namely a one-bedroom apartment in Newark, a dead-end job as an accountant, and Marv—and it just doesn't compare.

I soak in the tub a little longer than normal, dress slowly, and then go into the shop. It's Monday, which is usually a slow day, but I need to occupy my brain.

The first thing I notice as I walk in the door is that the collection of homeless guys is larger than normal. Now, this is New York, and there are supposed to be no homeless guys on the street, only in shelters. We pay high taxes (even the soulless render taxes to Bloomberg, like he doesn't have enough millions) to make sure that the homeless guys stay in shelters. The world should be a neat and tidy place, and it irks me (and my fat thighs) that this morning—of all mornings—it isn't.

Gradually my confidence returns, my savoir flair emerges in the most Clintonesque manner, and I'm selling bags like there's no tomorrow.

The store always helps to toughen my hide. Just as I'm getting back into true form, Paolo appears, dressed in a Liberace red cape, which causes me to laugh. I know what you're thinking, a designer, a cape—V, he's gay! Well, my friends, no, he is not. Paolo is a closet heterosexual. He can tell you the best clubs to pick up men, the perfect way to tie a half-Windsor, the best restaurants to be seen in—because, of course, a designer has to be gay to be any good.

I've tried to convince him to come out, but he doesn't listen. One of these days, he's going to be caught picking up a hooker or tipping a topless dancer across the Canadian border. I've told him, but he's got to "be his own man." Ha!

I bring up the article in the *Post,* but he denies he's leaving me. We argue over the future of his designs at my store, complete with arm-swishing and finger-snapping gestures (on his part, not mine), and I'm still not convinced, but I let him off the hook. For now.

Right after lunch (Craft, divine as usual) Shelby charges into the shop and motions me over like we're in some *Spy vs. Spy* thriller. I roll my eyes, but I'm her mentor—lucky me—and according to the laws of the Netherworld, I have a job to do.

I look over her new shoes and jewelry—Shelby's been busy—and smile. It's what New York is wearing this spring—greed.

"Did you see the *Post* today? This is so cool."

I'm assuming that she's not speaking of the hatchet job that Lucy did on the store. "Doggy style, Shel? I don't know."

"My phone's been ringing off the hook. Openings. The *Daily Show*. Can you believe it?"

I glance at the cell to see if I've missed any messages. None. I flash her a look of stylized ennui. "Of course. That's why you joined the program. Lifestyles of the Rich and Famous. That's us."

"I'm thinking about a new doggy perfume. What do you think?"

At first I think she's joking, but sadly, she's not. "That's nice, but I think you should get a dog first."

"I hate dogs. They smell. Thus, the perfume."

Why do I try? "Why are you here, Shel?"

"I've been trying to conjure up a new Jaguar, but I'm having problems with the spell."

Mentally I crack my knuckles. There wasn't a spell I couldn't cast, a Jag I couldn't conjure, a man I couldn't do. "First, let's go over the four steps. Do you have a quiet place?"

"My apartment."

"City noise at a minimum?"

She raises an eyebrow. "I'm on the thirty-fourth floor."

Like I couldn't guess. "Good. Step two. No observers."

"I was alone."

I frown. This is tough, but I'm on the case. I remember my first time, nose to the book, memorizing, getting each little iteration just right. Your first spells are a special time, just like your senior prom should've been—if, unlike me, you actually went. (Don't tell. I snuck out of the house, and to this day, my mother doesn't know that I was wandering the streets of Hoboken alone.)

I'm racking my brain. "What about step three?"

Shelby crinkles her nose. "That's the one I'm not sure of."

Aha! Step three messed me up, too. "TV off."

"Check."

"Microwave not running."

"Check."

"Stereo?"

She shakes her head.

I put on my Sherlock Holmes face and quirk a brow. "Cell phone turned off?"

"Off?"

"Off. It's the interference. It's like takeoff and landing at the airport."

"I didn't know."

I sigh. Oh, to be so young and naive. "Shelby, you must not make assumptions."

She laughs, sort of embarrassed. "You won't believe what I did."

Remembering the trials and errors I went through, I was willing to imagine.

She starts to whisper. "I was out on my roof, dancing in a circle."

I remember my first time. "Well, at least you had your clothes on."

"V!" she says with a laugh, and then she whispers, "I tried it nude, too. My doorman thinks I'm a pagan."

I laugh as well. Here I am, bonding with a woman I don't even like. There's an awkward silence, and I don't need to be Level 4 to know what she's thinking: *I don't even like this woman.*

I smile. "As your powers mature, the interference goes away. Soon you'll be chatting and shazaaming, all at the same time."

"I'm waiting to get to Level 3. I have two friends lined up already. They're dying to meet Lucy. They can't *believe* I really know her."

She looks really excited about this. I don't do my friends. Of course, I don't have many, so that makes the pickings slim, which is probably why I don't do them. But still. "Level 3 is great fun," I say, avoiding the fact that Lucy has knocked me down to Level 2. "It lends new meaning to the term 'players on the stage of life.'"

Her face turns sly, and her eyes move off into never-never land. "I have plans of my own."

"Do you have an ex-husband?" I immediately ask, because I understand that need to imprecate your ex. It comes with the divorce settlement.

"No. Just plans," she says, still a long way off.

I think about donning my mentor hat and giving her a lecture on how not to piss off Lucy, but I think better of it. Shelby is a big girl. I shrug my shoulders. "Whatever."

We talk about nothing much—spells, men, she asks about the sex. Everybody wants to know about the sex. I confess, the orgasms are truly great at Level 3. Technically Level 7 is the money shot, though. *Actual behavior modification.* Shelby is quick, and she sees the upside to this level right away.

After a bit more meaningless chitchat, her eyes start to shift nervously. I'm ready for anything, as long as it's not about death.

"Do you? Do you ever"—she looks around—"regret it?"

I think. I think very hard. I actually have trouble wrapping my tongue around the word *regret*. I don't think about turning back the clock, only barreling forward. When you're damned, regret will only get you depressed, because when you're in, you're *in*.

I shake my head. "No. That involves knowing pleasure in your soulful life."

Was it the smartest thing I ever did? HELLO? A woman selling her soul for an eternally (well, not quite) perfect body and great shoes? I mean, what kind of idiot would regret that? (Don't say it, don't even think it.)

Outside, thunder starts booming, and I'm wondering if Lucy's powers are omnipotent. A homeless man steps into the shop, and instantly one of my salesclerks, Fifi or Phoebe, or something, shoos him away. He meets my eyes, and I recognize Charlton Heston from the park.

Maybe he's one of Lucy's spies. I didn't know if she had

spies, but I couldn't think of another reason he'd be watching me.

As he crosses the threshold out into the pouring rain, a true customer steps in, pulling off her dripping sunglasses. She looks around, and immediately her eyes pick me out from the rest.

"V?" she says.

I nod regally, deciding to grant her an audience, simply because she has marvelous taste. Then her gaze moves to the right. "Oh! Shelby!" she cries, and then strides forward, waving the glasses. "You look exactly like I pictured. The newspapers don't do you justice."

Who is this? We all know that Shel's nothing special.

Shelby gets a shy smile, which is an interesting look for her. "Have we met?"

I send Phoebe a casual nod, which means, Be prepared to call the cops, this woman is a fruitcake. As I watch, said fruitcake wipes away a tear. "No, we haven't met." Then she closes her eyes and sniffs, regaining control. "Forgive me. I'm just so honored to be in your presence."

What a load of crap. Is Shel really going to fall for this one? I look over at Shel, expecting her to give said fruitcake the boot.

Instead, she looks touched. *Puh-lease.* "Are you here to shop?" Shelby asks her, and I must say, it's about time that someone remembered where they were.

Of course she's here to shop. This is the only place to find a genuine Sonata bag. And because she's a friend of Shelby's, maybe she won't go home with a puce one.

The fruitcake, who, okay, has nice taste in purses after all, shakes Shelby's hand, more of a gracious touching of fingers than anything else. "Amy *bleep*. Women's Projects for Manhattan. Showing Women a New Way of Life. I'm not here to shop. I have a cause. A cause more noble than mere scraps of leather."

Phoebe sniffs, but I'm immune to the arrow.

The fruitcake is a do-gooder. As someone who has fat thighs from her recent dip into do-goodness, this does not impress me. Phoebe sends me an anxious glance, silently asking what to do. I'm thinking we need to show Amy A New Way of Leaving. Of course Shel the schnook is still listening, and then she asks the exact worst question to ask: "What do you want?"

And it's like opening day at Ellis Island, Amy rushing in before the doors are shut. "You're just the person we need. We have a charity bazaar scheduled for the end of June, and I'm collecting prizes to be auctioned off. The benefit's for improvements to a women's homeless shelter in Lower Manhattan. You should see these women. Grasping and crawling their way through life, most with a newborn baby with a rare heart condition to care for. And even worse, some can't even remember their own names. Amnesia. It strikes more than you know. It's all so heart-wrenching, and it's time for us to take a stand. We're thirty percent of the way to our goal, and I think this silent auction/spaghetti potluck will put us right over the top."

Potluck? Poor Shel. She looks completely flummoxed. Being new to all this fame and fortune, she just doesn't know that you have to be careful. I grab Amy by the arm. "Well, Amy, it's been a real pleasure to meet you, but I think . . ."

"Wait," Shelby says. Horrified, I stop.

She can't. She won't.

"I'll help."

She does.

Amy starts to glow, and I start to sweat. I pull Shelby aside for a little heart-to-heart, even though, technically, both of ours have been MIA for a long, long time.

"You can't do this," I tell her, my thighs swelling with fear alone.

"Why not? The girl needs me."

"Yeah, Shelby, the entire state of Mogadishu needs you, too, but are you dropping everything to go off and save the world? I don't think so."

"I can't tell her no," says this new and improved Shelby, and frankly, I want the old model back.

"Lucy will kill you," I say. "Trust me. Her punishments are creative and designed to inflict maximum pain and collagen, and it ain't settling on your lips, sweetie."

That seems to resonate with Shelby, so I keep going. "You want to be a Level 3? You'll never see this side of Level 1, unless you cut out this charity crap."

"You really think so? But what if I did help out? I mean, think about this, a roomful of the unrecruited, subject to the awesomeness that is my new life. They would be crying to get in. Think of how many souls I could put on my roster in just one night. I think Lucy would love the idea. She's looking for creativity. She's looking for new things to try all the time."

I've heard these words before.

Did Shelby get the same postrecruitment talk that I did? Heaven forbid. But there is a certain elegance to the plan. I mull for a little longer. It could work. And in a true moment of self-actualization, I realize that it would work even better for *me*. This could be my way of proving my own potential within the organization. How many souls could I add to the V-roster? Mentally I pat my fat thighs. How incredibly serendipitous.

"Shelby," I say, "you gotta stand firm. You're a new person, you're moving in new circles, and you can't be mingling with the hoi polloi."

"Bad idea?"

I shake my head. "The worst. Go home and practice your spells. Cook up some new shoes, maybe some little doggy outfits. Although you need to get a dog."

Then I push Shelby out the door, into the rain. Bless her heart, I hope she can find a cab. After she's safely out into the crowd, I rub my hands together and turn to deal with Amy.

"Amy," I say. "You don't want to work with Shelby. She's a diva, and she'll be asking for all sorts of special favors for her and her entourage."

"She has an entourage?"

I nod. "About a dozen. And six bodyguards. They like to drink. Heavily. There are rumors of drugs, but they've never been proven."

Amy is a bright girl and immediately gets the picture. Her little face falls, but I don't want her to stay disappointed for too long. "May I offer some advice?"

She nods. "Please, do."

"You need a big celebrity. Somebody bigger than Shelby. Somebody with that New York cachet that knows how to get people to open their wallets. And keep a smile on their faces the whole time. It's a talent that not many people have."

"Do you know anybody like that?"

I scuff my foot (Gucci) against the floor. "You know, I'm a very busy woman. But I see something in you. Something that reminds me of me." I realize how that sounds and backtrack. "That was a long time ago, though. But the more important thing is that you need help."

Her face takes on a look of hope. It's so cute and sweet. "I'd love to," I say, not wanting her to worry for one extra minute.

Her smile blooms even bigger. I have made her day, and possibly contributed several millions to the Lost Women of Queens or the Bronx or wherever the hell they're from.

And then I feel it. My heart is pounding inside my chest, and something warm and slightly icky washes over me. Like a mud wrap at the Four Seasons. (If you've ever had one, you understand what I'm saying here.)

I think I feel good about this.

I shouldn't feel good. Well, not *this* good.

I remind myself why I'm doing the deed: dozens and dozens of souls for the picking. But it doesn't help. I still feel a tinge of goodness about the whole charity-women-in-need-starving-babies thing. I tell myself it's because of the look of total adoration on Amy's face, but just between you and me, I don't think that's it.

Shit.

Nervously I look around the shop, trying to find someone else to blame, but everyone is too busy buying leather goods that celebrate their inner diva. Gradually a nightmare of Empire State Building proportions looms inside. My conscience. My God, what if it's alive?

Tell me why this had to happen today. You know, a bad person without a soul, that's not a loss. You're damned anyway. But if you're good . . . Oh, God, what if somewhere inside me there existed something that was good?

I'm a little disturbed, because I truly believed I was rotten to the core. I want to be bad. Life is easier that way.

Yeah, life is definitely easier. All I have to do is take a few souls along the way. What's the real harm in that? I tell my conscious to take a hike.

Outside the thunder booms again, louder, and *moi*, who is absolutely never scared of storms, jump a good six inches. Scares the bejeezus right out of me, because I know exactly what is going on.

The devil is alive and well and lurking on Fifth Avenue.

Fuck.

Four

Monday was a busy day. The phones were ringing off the wall regarding rumors of a sex-for-stocks investigation involving some of the top names in NYC. Check the headlines tomorrow and see who's at Ben Benson's dining with their lawyers.

Yesterday at Michael's I ran into an old friend who is still broadcasting after all these years. We had drinks and laughed and she gave me the dishiest sort of dirt. Oh, I shouldn't tell . . . I shouldn't tell . . . I shouldn't . . . Okay, twist my arm, but don't tell. Do you remember the box-office darling who got ten million for her last picture? The four Oscars? She's gone slumming, because she could certainly do

> *better, but reliable sources have reported*
> *her staying overnight most nights at her*
> *ex-husband's ex-wife's West Village loft.*
> *Which brings adultery to an even newer*
> *level of confusion. Is it really cheating if you*
> *sleep with your ex's ex?*
>
> *And lastly, because this just came over*
> *the wire: Harry Harrison is out on a new*
> *lady's arm this week. She's a darling and a*
> *wit, and already her looks are blooming. I*
> *think she's in love. The name of the new*
> *greyhound from the A-list? Shelby. I'm*
> *thinking wedding bells by August.*

It's Tuesday morning, and I'm still a Level 2. Whew. That was a huge bullet-dodge. I see the paper, which makes me suspect that I'm not Lucy's favorite soul right now, but I can live with that. Harry is SO not worthy. Although I miss my transitory emotion induction powers. When you aim to rule the world, Level 3 is the equivalent of shock and awe. With a few magic words, I can make you feel both. After a nonentity life, being an entity is quite addictive, but I must content myself with body beautification (and fat thighs!). See, if I'm not careful, I'm going to royally screw up this addictive life that I've created for myself.

I do my morning soak in the tub (using lavender for its extra calming abilities), and contemplate these small bouts of goodness that have been peppering my hereinbefore heinous existence.

I've never been known as a good person, never been defined by my generosity or my unselfishness. I told my fourth-grade teacher that my mother beat me, and it took about six months before Mom and Youth and Family Services finally forgave me. At fourteen I wrecked Dad's car. I told him that it had been an emergency, and I had to borrow it in order to rush Mary Salarno to the hospital, but he didn't buy it and I was grounded for three weeks. At Rutgers, I skated through by bribing the TAs with pot and selectively dating the class brains. I'm sure you're wondering, Is that how you met Marv? Oh, yeah, and I've got a Brooklyn Bridge to sell you, know what I mean? My moral precepts went downhill fast after Marv. I would say more, but it involves the IRS, so let's just leave it at that. No, never in my wildest dreams did I imagine that I would grace the pearly gates. Some people were destined for heaven, just not me. So when Paolo started hitting on me, I found the perfect answer. If I'm going to hell, I'm certainly going to live the high life while I'm still breathing.

Why not? Why not? WHY THE HELL NOT?

I sink low into the water, feeling the warm bubbles soak over my skin, and I know I've made the right decision. It's not like God has been knocking himself out to get to me, you know? I swear off my better half, and in the future, I'll content myself with apathy. Well, after this charity benefit is over, anyway. But the benefit's a veritable swag-bag of souls, right? Right. So I know Luce will be okay with this, which begs the question of why I wasn't planning to tell her, but I'm not going to go there.

Ten minutes later, I'm dressed (Valentino pants that are supposed to be cut loose in the butt and thighs; today they are embarrassingly tight), and my doorman knocks. He's got Nathaniel's jacket back from the cleaners, and it looks brand-new. I give Ed a big tip for his trouble and listen as he talks about the upcoming doormen's strike. Times are tough for the soulful in New York City, and if the doormen go on strike, then the soul-free will be opening doors all by themselves. Sometimes shit rolls uphill, too.

I transition my thoughts to Nathaniel, which is an easy thing to do. I finally have my reason to call him, so I take out my cell and dial.

I've been looking forward to this moment for several days, and I try to talk myself into poise and confidence, but the longer I wait for him to answer, the more I fail and feel like a girly-girl once more.

He answers on the fourth ring, which startles me—by this time I've decided he must be a call screener—but I recover and tell him that I have his jacket. He asks me to breakfast tomorrow, which I think is strange because I usually don't get up before nine. Apparently he's only staying in the city for a couple of months until he is restationed overseas, and while he's here, he runs every morning. I shudder at that; however, it nicely proves my latest theory that he can't be a client. Clients do not run; they stroll leisurely. And they stroll only when necessary and no limos are available.

I don't let myself talk too long, or linger on the conversation. Nathaniel is not part of my world now (okay, he's a hunkarooni, but other than that). I like my new world, but these thoughts, thoughts of Nathaniel walking out of the pond at Central Park, preferably nude, keep invading my head, and I am too weak to resist. So I lie down on the bed for an extra ten minutes, just me and my Nathaniel thoughts. It's a private time, with no spells necessary. I won't say more.

The store is busy that day, and outside the street crews work on repairing the potholes from the Blizzard of 1985. Moon craters don't grow this big. Maybe I should talk to Bloomberg about signing over. We'd have those pesky potholes fixed in a wonderfully timely fashion, and no unnecessary noise. Hmmm . . . I'll think about that.

I've promised Lucy that I'll call Meegan that morning as well, but I put it off. I'm just too busy. You'd think with my fat thighs and measly Level 2-ness, I'd be just jumping at the chance, but I simply don't feel like chance-jumping this morning. Maybe I should have another cup of coffee, I don't know.

I wallow in my ambivalence until Kimberly shows up after lunch (Petrossian: caviar, of course).

She's still not warming the cockles of my heart, but I notice that I've dropped the automatic "cunt" modifier, so that is something.

"V, I need your help," she says, as if I would actually *want* to help her.

"What can I do?" I ask, with a heavy sigh.

"It's the SEC. They're investigating Marv."

I start to laugh. Oh, even in my wildest dreams I could not have done something so ingenious. Marv *never* plays the market.

He has a broker that he entrusts with all his sacred (i.e., involving money) decisions, and his broker is just not that good—or he didn't used to be. "Oh, Kim, you must be popping the bubbly."

She looks at me, confused. "No, I'm being charged in the investigation as well."

I suppose that could put a cork in anyone's bubbly. "Club Fed really isn't as bad as they say it is," I respond, a small attempt at consolation.

She looks around for a chair, but I have none in my store—that would detract from its minimalist beauty and style. Finally she leans against the wall. "I can't go to jail—I didn't do anything. It was Marv. He hooked up with his secretary-cum-stripper, who was feeding him tips, and she got indicted by a grand jury."

Juries? Strippers? This is serious. I snap my fingers for Phoebe and arrange for a glass of brandy. Could this small blip inside me be pity? I analyze my behavior and decide that such generosity and concern for Kimbers is not a good thing. The thought depresses me.

However, I need to segue right back from my favorite subject, me, to my not-so-favorite subject, Kimbers. I have Phoebe bring me a glass, and I stand next to Kimberly and sip the brandy, too. Empathy drinking. It's a great bonding moment. "Blanche didn't tell me any of this."

"Blanche doesn't know."

I'm wondering how this is going to go over with her. Although Marv was never Blanche's favorite, still—he's blood.

And then, like the next day after bad sushi, I get a pain in my stomach and remember exactly what I told her. That I'd help him if he ever needed it.

Fuck.

But does this situation really constitute a need for help? In the truest definition of the word? I think not. There's got to be a better way.

For instance, if Marv and Kimberly died in a fatal bus accident, all their problems would disappear.

And then Blanche would be heartbroken.

Or, for instance, if Marv pleaded guilty to all counts and was sentenced to life without parole at Sing Sing, preferably with a he-devil named Loretta as his cell-mate.

And then Blanche would be heartbroken.

Or alternatively, if Kimberly, in a fit of passionate rage, fatally stabbed Marv with an ink pen, his problems would be solved, and Kimberly would experience the wonders of prison sex.

And then Blanche would be heartbroken.

Thoughts of fun and revenge drift away, and I take a deep sip of brandy in order to calm my now-queasy stomach. But would it be so bad if Marv and Kimbers realized the absolute coolness that is the new V? That might be kinda nice. They could start up a V fan club, even sell bags in the store, at minimum wage, of course. Yeah, I could do it. I sigh to myself, resigned to doing good and planning accordingly.

Kimbers mistakes my sigh for denial. "V, you've got to help me. There's nowhere else to go. We used to be friends, remember that?"

"Friends? This from a woman that had intimate relations with my husband? I think you're overstating the case, Kim."

"Marv was a mistake."

I raise my brow at her. Marv was always a mistake. For any woman that met him. "You made your flea-bitten bed. Now why don't you get out of my store?"

"I'm sorry, V. I was being stupid."

"Yeah, you were."

"Remember that time that we went shopping at Tiffany's, and I told the salesgirl you were a countess from Tunisia?"

"The past is dead, Kimbers. It won't work."

"Or how about that time we met up for tea at the Plaza, and I had a huge hole in my thigh-highs and the waitress wouldn't even serve us? You laughed at me for two months, V. We had good times."

"Why'd you do it to me, Kim?"

She looks me square in the eye. "I was lonely. That's all."

Damn, she's pretty good at this. Not as good as I am, of course, but given a little time . . . In fact, if I reeled in Kimbers, I'd be a Level 3 and could do a lot of damage to the prosecution with transitory emotion induction.

Hmmm . . . You wonder how Lucy gets all the power? It's from paradoxical decisions such as this. Even while I'm considering the slim possibility that my soul might actually have been worth saving, I'm thinking about pulling my husband's ex-mistress over to the dark side with me.

"I really don't think there's anything I can do," I tell her, not really meaning that, but needing to twist the knife just a little bit longer.

She sniffs, real tears welling up in her eyes, a very genuine touch. "You could talk to Marv for me. His testimony should clear me, but I think he's going to lie and say that I knew about the tips and might have even given some to my hairstylist."

Oh, that's a good one. I bet Kimberly would do well in the Life Enrichment Program, and Lucy would get her off. Lucy is an expert at making nasty legal troubles go away. Remember that DA I told you about? My soul-taking number one? Well, see, there was this little matter of a bribery scandal going on that he was at the heart of it, and poof, now he's running for governor of Connecticut.

So if Kimberly got off, the pièce de résistance is that Marv would be left to rot in prison . . .

And Blanche would be heartbroken.

So once again, thoughts of diabolical revenge are stripped away. I'll talk to Marv, rescue his little aardvarkian butt, but check with me again tomorrow, because I turned a perfectly darling pair of pants into fat pants today, and I'm not happy. Hooking up with strippers. What was he thinking? I ignore my own rhetorical question because I know exactly what he was thinking.

"Come on, Kim. Tell the truth here. You were in on this, weren't you? Do I have Sucker tattooed on my forehead?"

"Yeah, I was in on it. He said it'd be easy money."

"Easy money? I can't believe you fell for that line," I say, remembering how he talked me into altering our 1995–2001 tax returns. Easy money is what he said then, too. "What do you expect me to do?"

"I want him to forget I was involved. Just lie. He lies about everything else. Do you know how much I made off those stocks? Thirty-eight dollars and forty-seven cents. And I'm supposed to go to jail for that?"

I wave a calming hand. "Cool your jets. Okay, I'll see what I can do. Is he in custody?" I ask, hoping that he is.

"No, he's out on bail."

I nod and finish her brandy. "I'll go talk to him tomorrow night. You owe me, Kim. For this, you owe me big."

"I know. I won't forget this, V."

I send her out the door and chalk up a win in the "Good" column in my brain. That should bother me more than it does, but I shrug my metaphorical shoulders. Helping an ex-cunt escape jail time because she shared my deplorable taste in men is not feeding the hungry masses. I feel secure in my inner badness. As for rescuing Marv, trust me when I say that if wasn't for Blanche, he'd be practicing daily shower aerobics at Sing Sing.

I turn around and search out the clientele in the store. The dumpy broad overloaded with diamonds is who I set my sights for. I fix my most potent smile on my face and head over. She'll buy two bags and a pair of Jackie O sunglasses before I'm done with her. My smile gets a little broader. I really do love my job.

That afternoon a messenger arrives with an engraved invitation to a Friday-night fund-raiser in Williamsburg for the Starving Artists Newly Immigrated from Some Third World Country Because of Religious Persecutions. And Yes, That's Just What We Need in America, More Starving Artists Who Don't Even Speak English.

I RSVP because it's the pre-opening night of a new grunge club, and I want to see what it looks like. My cell phone rings, and it's Lucy. I consider call-screening the devil, but decide that's a bad idea and answer.

"Yeah."

"I'm having drinks at the Hudson Hotel at five-ish. I want you there. It's been six months since your last performance appraisal, and I think it's time for a chat."

My stomach drops, and I swear I feel an extra inch on my thighs. I find my special place and relax before I break out in wheezes. "I'll be there," I say. A good-employee answer if I ever heard one.

We hang up, and I anguish over what to wear. Finally I settle on a red Oscar de la Renta suit with a fox-fur collar. Genuine fox, not that faux fox. It just screams, "I'm a bad person," which is the look I'm going for.

The Library Bar is a great place for quiet conversations where you want to be seen and not heard. I don't go there often. I like being heard. I think it's because of my Jersey roots. Maybe I just like being noticed. Anywhoo, I arrive before Lucy and find a wing chair near the back, but far away from the fireplace. Just in case Lucy is mad.

For a while I ponder the gargantuan cows that adorn the walls. I really just don't get the art thing. Not at all. Then Lucy arrives with a dramatic entrance, pausing in the doorway, a red pashmina casually draped about her shoulders. I really have to say that I like her style.

The waiter takes our drink order (two vodka martinis—

mine with an olive), and then Lucy pulls out a pack of papers. So far everything is all smiles and good fun. I'm okay with this.

"I brought your marketing plan that you presented to me almost two years ago. You do remember this, don't you, V?"

I remember frantically scrambling to put a document together late one night. Going through my address book and scamming the society pages of *New Jersey Today* for likely soul mates. "What do you need?"

"Well, according to our timelines, you should have delivered your fourth soul more than three months ago. I have such big plans for you, V. You should see what your future entails, but you're falling down on the job, darling. And with your shop and your new connections, I assumed that souls would be raining like manna from heaven." She takes a sip of her martini and stares up at the bookcase-lined walls that tower to the ceiling. "The boutique was a marvelous idea; if Mohammed won't come to the mountain, the mountain opens up shop on Fifth Avenue."

There was a certain elegance to her scheme. "And the bags are nice, too."

Lucy blinks, and I'm noticed again. "Yes, darling, the bags are nice, too. But how are we doing on Meegan? I admit, I wasn't enthused at first, but I overlooked the benefits that she brings to my table. Her father's Rolodex alone could get me four more seats in the Senate. Politicians really don't need my help to get into hot water, so I usually ignore them. But you, my dear, you were certainly on your toes. In fact, it was a stroke of pure genius. Bravo."

Me and my fat thighs puff even larger under the praise.

Yeah, I knew Meegs was a good idea when she told me her whole fucking pedigree, but I had no idea that Lucy would see the brilliance as well. I smile at her. "I thought so."

"So when is she signing up?"

Now there's the main problem with brilliant ideas. You're actually expected to deliver on them. "There may be a few difficulties with Meegan."

Lucy leans her chin on her hand. "Such as. Let's brainstorm together."

"Well, I think my biggest worry is that she's such a good kid. Maybe I was aiming too high when I tossed her name into the hat. Maybe I should go for somebody a little less challenging. You know, work my way up the soul-free ladder." It wasn't exactly true. I was good. Hell, I was great. I could have got Meegan if I wanted to, but Lucy isn't exactly my favorite person right now, and I—

Oh, God. She glares at me like she can read my mind, because, *yes—she can.* I keep forgetting that little piece.

"You shouldn't forget that, V," she says. "Let's talk some more about Meegan. What does she want?"

I turn on my charm, ready to explain to Lucy the impossibility of the situation. "She wants a baby."

Lucy's smile gets broader. "Ah, family. I understand."

"You do?"

"Of course. To have someone who's always there as a confidant. Someone to share your dreams with."

"A family? Share your dreams with?" I start to laugh. "You never knew your parents, did you?"

Her eyes sorta soften, and I'm thinking I might be getting my thighs back.

She wrinkles her nose at me. "Not yet. Let's go back to the baby."

I take a sip of alcohol, because I guess I'm just not getting through. "You don't get it, Lucy. There is no baby on the horizon. She's infertile. I can't fix that for her. Not even if I were a Level 9. With steely thighs."

"Haven't you heard of miracles? I can give her a child. At the club opening." Her whole face lights up, very Broadway. "That's what we'll do!"

"Do what?"

She shoots me one of those "moron" looks. "V, you're thinking too small. Didn't you see *The Omen*? I can do anything." Then, as eerie music starts playing in my head, she shuffles her papers, just as calm as can be. "So who else should we put on your list?"

Stop the presses here; I'm still focused on the child of the devil. "You know, I could be wrong about Meegan. She was talking about the kid thing, but everybody wants a kid when they don't have it. It sounds like such a good idea, but is it really?"

Lucy's gaze zooms in extra-close, and I shift a little nervously. "I've always wanted a daughter," she tells me.

"Yeah, I've always wanted a mother, too. Look what that got me."

Lucy looks down at her paper. "I need names, V."

My mind goes blank. I just don't have anybody else to offer

up right now. Truth is, I'm not so quick to act. I think I'm starting to actually *like* people since I've been branded a hero and lauded with accolades by the entire tri-state region (not really, but I have a vivid imagination), which puts a big damper on the whole soul-taking experience. "How about Marv *bleep*?" I ask, because he's the sole exception, pardon the pun.

"Would you like me to add him to your opportunities profile?" Lucy asks as she picks up her pen.

I think carefully, mulling over the tableaux. If Lucy took Marv's soul then he'd be out of trouble, Kimberly would be out of trouble (maybe), and my ex would be on an express train to purgatory. The whole "express train" thing had a nice ring to it.

But then would I ever have the personal satisfaction of turning him into an aardvark? Do I actually want him to have powers to achieve short-term happiness, wealth, and movie-star good looks? I chew on my lip, but I already know the answer. No way in hell.

"Let me get back to you on Marv."

She nods. "Meegan's coming with you to the fund-raiser?"

"She hasn't returned my call," I say, just as my cell phone rings. Caller ID reads MEEGAN'S MOBILE. Lucy holds up the "you should answer that" hand, like I'm her minion or something.

I stall for three rings, but I do answer. "Hello."

"V, Meegan here. You've got tickets to Club Skank?"

I nod my head encouragingly to Lucy. "Yes," I tell Meegan.

"What time should I be ready?"

"The auction starts at nine," I say, thinking I don't want to do this and wondering if I could wish up a cold or some stomach bug for myself.

"Don't even think about it," Lucy whispers.

I bat my eyelashes at her. "No, I won't."

"What did you say, V?" Meegan asks.

"No, I don't know what you should wear," I say, speaking louder into the phone, and around me heads turn.

"But I didn't even ask yet! You are such a card."

Yeah, that's me. A real card. "I'll pick you up in the limo. Friday. Eight-thirty. Ciao."

We hang up, and I smile at Lucy. "Satisfied?"

"Of course. And you can have one of your levels back. Transitory emotion induction. Congratulations, you're officially a Level 3. Again."

Which is all well and good, but a stellar negotiator knows when to keep at the bargaining table. I can live without the Level 4 mind-reading powers for now, but there are more pressing issues. "Eh-hem."

"You can have your thighs back as well. I'm not the total demon you think I am."

Instantly my legs shrink, and I press my palms against the toned flesh, welcoming my babies back home.

After that, I get out of there mucho fasto. Out on the streets of New York where a person can really breathe. I barge through the smokers that are puffing and thronging on the sidewalks, and make my way to the corner of Ninth Avenue, where I attempt to find a cab.

Normally this is not a problem for a Level 3. But the thunder claps, and I'm competing with a gazillion other meteorologically challenged Gothamites. There are no unoccupied cabs to be found. Resigned to the banalities of exercise, I begin my walk home. The clouds move in even lower, and now it starts to rain. Since rain sucks, I think about the conversation with Lucy again.

The child of the devil? On an evening like this, when I'm stuck in the rain, getting soaked, and I can't even manage to get a cab (and I have powers!), it's easy to visualize all sorts of bad things happening. I saw *Rosemary's Baby*. I know this is not good. I shiver to myself, wondering if there's anything I can do, or to be frank, if there's anything I want to do. I mean, look at me, I'm back to being a Level 3.

Maybe Lucy's just playing some sick joke on me. Not that I buy into that one; she's not really the cutup type, but maybe I'm worrying for nothing, or at least prematurely. From what Lucy says, it looks like I've got a couple of days before anything will happen. So I back-burner that nightmare and give in to the more pressing horror: walking home in the rain.

But you know what? With each passing cab, my step gets a little springier, because hallelujah, now I have my thighs back.

Five

Ah, springtime in the Hamptons! And what would springtime be without the East Enders creating new bars to drive through? Last night's opening of Selkie's saw a notorious party girl dancing on the tables and tossing her shirt into the yawning crowd. Find a new act, darling, that dog's getting too old to hunt.

I told you, I told you, I told you. Did I not mention a certain hot Scottish actor who is impregnating his way to an Oscar? We're up to four wee Scottish buns that we know of, and the latest womb belongs to a top screenwriter for Warner Brothers. Selective insemination or just luck of the sperm?

I had a marvelous conversation with our

fine New York statesman, asking whether a
run for the White House was in her future.
After dodging the issue in a true Washington fashion, she finally (after two drinks) in-
dicated she was giving it some thought. It's
been too long since a New Yorker was in
the White House. Don't you think we could
show those Texans a thing or two about
how to run the country?

When the morning comes, I do the usual getting-ready routine
before my breakfast meeting with Nathaniel, although I must
do it FOUR FUCKING HOURS earlier. All of you who are
soulful are probably thinking, "Well, V, the rest of the world
has to get up earlier." Yes, I'm aware of that; that is why I sold
my soul. So I would not be like the rest of the world. So please
don't let me hear you complaining again.

But today is breakfast with Nathaniel, which has a certain
je ne sais quoi–ness about it, and a certain look is required. I
end up with a white linen D&G pantsuit that is cut tastefully
low. Not slutty, yet subtly provocative. I take a cab to Andrew's
Coffee Shop and snarl at the cabdriver. He doesn't understand
English, so my snarling is wasted. Sigh.

When I get to the café, he is already there. Let me repeat
this last bit, because it's important.

He's Already There. Waiting for Me.

I yank on my reality reins and calm myself. He's only a
man. A mere mortal. He is not worthy.

This would be a much more effective credo if he were not so absolutely gorgeous, even without Italian wing tips, which gives you an idea of my fascination with his physical presence. There's an appreciative glint in his eyes, which is the normal way that men approach me these days. However, I sense there's an answering glint in my own eyes as well.

In deference to my "I must be cooler than all below me" image, I smile, 220 watts of pure V voltage, blasting right in his direction, and the appreciative glint turns to something much more—primitive. Yeah, I still got it. Then he stands and helps me into my seat, good-mannered boy that he is. That earns him points.

The waitress appears and takes our order (I haven't had scrambled eggs in years), and I remember the purpose of our meeting.

"Here's your jacket," I say, completely boring, nonwitty, and so very Jersey.

"It seemed the least I could do. You looked cold, a very nice cold, but cold nonetheless."

"I was. That day is something I'm really hoping not to re-peat," I say, rubbing a fond hand over my newly reclaimed per-fect thighs.

He asks what I do for a living. (Obviously he doesn't read the *Post*.) I tell him I run a purse shop. He looks curious, but not overly in awe. Men do not understand the Power of the Bag.

"So you're one of those fancy designer types?"

"More of a merchant than designer. I like to think of myself as the brains behind the bags."

"That explains the look."

"What look?"

"The high-dollar outfit with accessories to match."

I smile. "Thank you."

He laughs at me, but in a nice way. I am charmed.

"So what's an army guy doing in New York?"

"I have a reunion at West Point in a few weeks. Fifteen years since I graduated. It matched up with my leave."

"A military academy. Sounds very nice," I lie. "So, you married?" I blurt out, before promptly sticking a forkful of eggs into my mouth in order to not embarrass myself even further. What happened to my poise? My "look, but don't touch" coolness? I know exactly what happened to it. I cue my Wicked Witch of the West voice. *It's . . . melting . . .*

"I was married once. She didn't like being a military wife, and I was drinking too much."

Ah, a drunk. That would explain much, but I like it; it makes him tormented and flawed, much like me. "Alcohol can cure a lot of ailments."

"I quit."

Strike the flaw. I'm still holding out hope for tormented, though. "What have you been doing while you're here?" I ask, my conversational skills drifting further into Garden State geekdom.

"I've been walking a lot. I ran in the Race for the Cure a few weeks ago. Did some shopping." He laughs and points to the jacket. "I didn't think it would be this cold in April."

"The weather has been horrible this year. I don't know why.

I remember the summer of 1983—" I snap my mouth shut in horror. *No, no, no.* I will not discuss the weather.

"You were saying—the summer of 1983?" he prompts gently.

"It was shit. It was all shit," I snap.

He gets this empathetic look in his eyes (they're dark, by the way), and leans his elbows on the table. "You should try summers in Afghanistan. A hundred and eighteen degrees during the day, with winds that just slam the sand in your face."

I want to scream. Now not only are we discussing the weather, we're discussing the weather in a country that I don't even know about.

"Have you been all over the world?" I ask, struggling to be polite.

I've only seen New Jersey, New York, and Pennsylvania, and I don't want to know of a world outside mine anymore. I want to be cocooned in my new life, sort of a reverse metamorphosis. As a larva, I saw much too much of the real world. Now that I have my glorious butterfly wings, I think I'll stay in the silken cocoon that binds all twelve miles of Manhattan. It makes me happy.

"Not to any fun places," he answers with a laugh. "Afghanistan, Fauslhamabaad, the usual tropical paradises."

"Oh. I've seen pictures on the news," I say, even though I've only Tivoed the news, and never watched it since my Life Enrichment days first began.

He tells me stories that Katie and Matt would never report. Raids and shootings. Death. I hate death. These dark, dreary things make me aware of how lucky I am. Of course, I've always thought I was lucky to be chosen by Lucy, but it's a co-nundrum to think that I might actually have been lucky be-fore—in my soulful days. I didn't have great shoes or a perfect bod, but I wasn't starving in a bombed-out hut in some desert in one of those eighteen-syllable countries with no vowels.

I spy my strappy Jimmy Choo sandals and shake my head. No, I wasn't lucky before. In a world of haves and have-nots, Gotham exists only for the haves.

"Tell me about your family," I ask, hoping to move the talk into nondeath water, which is where I currently want to be.

"I'm the black sheep."

Okay, this is good stuff. We're back in business. "What did you do to get excommunicated?"

"I joined the army."

Not exactly murder or mayhem. In fact, it's not even close to selling out your friends for a designer label or perkier breasts. "Your parents still alive?"

"Mother is."

"So she doesn't want you killed, huh? That's understand-able," I say, although I suspect my own maternal Machiavelli would lose no sleep if I were to bite the big one.

"Nah, she just doesn't believe in war."

"Oh. And you do?"

"It's got its place in the world."

"Bad things for a good cause?"

"No, mainly just justice."

Philosophically we are polar opposites, which I suppose ac-counts for the intense attraction on my part. Or it might be the way he makes me ogle him. Or maybe it's because I think he's a good person. Just like I think I'm not.

"Are you going away soon?" I ask, not just being polite anymore. Nathaniel is elusive, and appealing. Like the toy I never had at Christmas. I can see him on my arm, in my bed.

"I've got a couple of months before I'm reassigned."

"Good," I say, although I'm thinking we're going to have to work on those conversational skills. Now this is the moment where he should ask me out. I wait, silently, for the words.

There are no words. There's a gleam in his eyes that means he's definitely jonesing for me, so why isn't he taking the next step? Now I wonder what Nathaniel is like when he's head over heels, when his eyes light up with joy at the sight of me.

I should help him along. Only just a bit. Other than a blatant attempt at manipulation with my morning-after spell (which really doesn't count because it's a basic survival spell), I have not used my powers. I haven't needed them.

But opportunities like this are why I need Level 3. And so I tinker. Because I can.

Merry Cupid, love's supply, take your arrow, let it fly. The man I touch, let him see, the fabulous, decadent, marvelous V.

I have a heart-stopping moment when I nearly miss Nathaniel and zap the old man at the next table instead, but I recover. And lightly, oh, so lightly, tap Nathaniel on the hand.

He blinks, and his dark eyes turn deeper, and richer, and I fall right into them.

Then he lightly clasps my fingers, and I feel ten gazillion shivers running wild through my blood. Oh, my. I could really,

really get used to this. It makes me remember why I sold my soul.

A half-smile starts at the corner of his mouth, and he looks a little embarrassed. "I'm sorry. You make me stare."

"That's okay," I murmur.

"You kicked me in the gut from the first time I saw you dive into the lake. I'd never seen a woman do something like that."

Guilt flashes neon bright, and momentarily removes nine of the ten gazillion shivers. "We don't need to talk about that."

He strokes my cheek, my mouth. "You don't need to be modest."

And yes, for once in my life, I want to be modest. "You were impressed?" I ask, mainly because I'm not naturally modest.

"Oh, yeah. You didn't even want anyone to know who you were." He moves in closer, and I can smell his soap, his toothpaste, his man-scent.

"I like my privacy," I lie.

"Come take a walk with me. Or a movie. Or maybe we can just find a bench somewhere and talk."

I am charmed, and appalled. It sounds so mundane. So common. So *tempting*. "I have to go to work," I say, lest I be tempted anymore.

He doesn't reply, just kisses me. And of course, it's a magical kiss. The kiss of true love always is. I'm forty years old, divorced, and a size 14 when dressing while not under the influence. Statistically, it's more likely that Nathaniel will be killed in battle than that I will ever know true love. Do I let that stop me?

No. I jump right in, and I kiss him back for all I'm worth, because this is my one moment, and I'm taking it.

Before he opens his eyes, I undo my own spell. Regrettably, magic only goes so far, and you have to use it sparingly or it stops being magical.

When he opens his eyes, the intensity is gone. I'm no longer his one true love, simply a woman he's being polite to because he doesn't know anyone else in the city. He scoots away and laughs awkwardly. "Sorry. I wasn't going to do that."

I feel a bit of shame, but I have a feeling that I'm not going to see Nathaniel again, so my shame is overshadowed by a memory that I can hold to myself forever.

What could have been. I avoid his glance and pretend it never happened, which tells you how good a liar I really am. I've never been a "could have been" person before. Maybe I've never had a "could have been" that was worth it. Don't know.

On our way out, I spy the waitress in the corner watching me with something akin to awe. I know that look in her eyes. I smile at her, because I've been there, too, sister.

I spend the afternoon lounging in my apartment watching CNN and talking on the phone to Meegan, trying to convince her to stay home on Friday. She is unconvinced. I attempt to bribe her with the idea of a girl's night out, just me and her hitting the clubs, but apparently the thought of Jamie MacGregor, in all his Highland hotness, is more appealing than *moi*. Go figure.

After several (one) hours of analysis, I have determined two reasons that I want to keep Meegan in the baby-free zone. First of all, I don't like Lucy's attitude. She takes everyone for granted. I don't even know that she truly can predict what happens. I've heard of the chaos theory. I think it describes my life. She thinks it's just Lucy this, Lucy that, like she's ruling the world, and I know that's not the case. I'm going to hell all on my own, thank you very much. Yeah, she's got cool stuff, but in the end, it's me who decides. Nobody else.

Reason number two is much more altruistic, which is a new word in my vocabulary. A baby is Meegan's heart's desire, but Lucy's baby has all sorts of ancillary consequences, not all of which I know, but I suspect none are good. Sometimes heart's desires get us into all sorts of deep shit, and Meegan's not a person who's equipped to handle deep shit. Now that I'm back to Level 3, there's all sorts of spells I can cook up to keep her safe. I'll take her, and show Lucy that sometimes things don't turn out exactly like we planned.

My moment of thoughtfulness is over, and I turn back to CNN, which is certainly a yawner. So far I have learned that Mr. Greenspan is very important, the Democrats are scratching their Republican asses, and Fauslhamabaad is still one very fucked-up country. I understand how Marie Antoinette felt; but I choose to order Chinese instead of cake.

Have I told you about my apartment? I should, because it's perfect. Thirty-seventh floor, Trump Grand Palais. Two bedrooms, a view of the park. It's not as cozy as Lucy's place, but it has that Trump cachet. I'm happy.

And then my mother calls. Immediately I am sucked into a

whirling vortex of maternal diarrhea. If you've been there, you know what I mean, and it's not pretty.

"I'm going to shoot your father. I think you're the trustee of his estate, so don't kick your mother out of her only home," she says, in that raspy voice that no daughter could ever love.

"Good afternoon, little short person," I say, because my mother is four feet ten, and shrinking.

She never lets my insults get to her, and she ignores me. "I'm serious this time. He won't throw anything away. Our neighbors have started complaining. The community won't permit rubbish, and Dorothy Powell thinks that his lawn-mower repair business is rubbish."

"They won't throw you out, Mother. You own the house. They can't do that," I say, even though I have absolutely no knowledge to back me up here. But really! My mother thinks the condominium community is more powerful than God.

I suppose it comes from some prefeminist desire for domination and a craving for interminable ass-kissing. I don't know. I don't understand. All I can say is, thank God I didn't inherit too many of her genes.

"I can't sleep anymore, and I've given up my third cup of coffee."

"Still smoking?" I ask.

"My generation considers it very sophisticated," she says with a cough.

I know smoking causes cancer, reduces life expectancy, and limits my time on earth. As such it is a Bad Thing. However, this is my mother's life, so I shrug and study my toes. *Maybe a rose-petal scrub would do the trick.* "Don't shoot Daddy," I say, as I pencil in a trip to Brigitte Mansfield on my calendar.

"I might do it. I just might do it. I need a break. He just wants to go on those god-awful tour buses everywhere—"

"That's because it's not safe for him to drive, Mother."

"I don't care. Hanging out with all those old people."

"You're an old person."

"Age is a state of mind."

"There you go, Mother. Already you sound calmer."

"I'm coming to visit."

Immediately I hang up.

Immediately she calls back. "Did you hang up on me?"

"Sorry, Mother, but no," I lie. *And a massage, too. I could really use a massage.*

"I mean it. This time I'm getting on a plane."

"You hate to fly."

"I'll take some Xanax."

"You hate the city. You told me that Florida is where you've found your place."

"I miss the old house. I could go see Estelle Moyers. Bet we could paint the town red."

"I thought she died."

"No, no, I think that was Stella Myerson."

"Well, if you're determined to visit, I can arrange for a hotel suite at the Waldorf."

"Don't go to all that trouble. I'll just stay with you. After you walked out on Marv, I bet you get lonely."

"Marv left me, Mother."

"A girl needs her mother."

And where were you when I was getting a divorce? I want to ask. Hell, where was she when I was getting married? Instead I bite my tongue in a vicious manner and say, "I don't have room for you here, Mother."

"Nonsense. I sleep fine on a couch. My back don't let me sleep well anyway. I never should have listened to your father. What was he thinking, asking me to lift that motor? No sense, I tell you."

"Mother, you can't stay with me," I answer. And then, because I'm absolutely determined to have the last word, I hang up.

I don't want to see my mother. We don't have anything in common, and she *expects* things of me, as if I'm still five years old. V, is your room clean? V, look both ways before crossing the street. V, make sure he wears a condom. V, where are my grandchildren?

AAGGGHHHHHHHH. For once I'm glad I've lost my ESP powers, so that I can't hear her buzzing around in my head. Of course, I still hear her buzzing around in my head, even without the ESP powers.

I'm *definitely* going to get a massage.

I promised Kimberly I would visit Marv, and I have stalled as long as possible. I haven't seen him since the day we signed the papers about, oh, two years, three months, and twenty-one days ago.

Marv now lives in a one-bedroom prewar apartment on the Upper East Side, and don't kid yourself that this is one of those prewar charmers. Oh, no, it's a dump. And best of all, there is no doorman.

I ring the bell and announce myself.

"V?"

"Yes, it's V. Let me up."

He buzzes me in, and then I'm on my way to see my ex-husband. Oh, God. The Joy. Hold me back. However, I remember my promise and choose not to run away.

When he answers the door, I immediately notice that his hairline is receding. "What are you doing here?" he asks, looking sorta happy.

I barrel in and find a chair. "Do you get HBO? Have you seen those guys on OZ? You'll die, Marv, or turn into some cross-dresser with Spike tattooed on your privates."

"You heard," he says, disappointing me because there is no fear in his eyes, only sadness.

"Of course I heard. What the hell do you think I came here for? You're going to give Blanche a heart attack. You're not taking my best friend from me. And look what you've done to poor Kimberly." Take note the new Kimberly modifier is "poor" as opposed to "cunt." It's not that we've bonded, but Marv has dumped her. I empathize.

Slightly.

"I don't need this from you," he says, a surly contrast to Kimberly's begging. This is no fun.

"I was going to help," I say, popping up from the chair and heading for the door. "I'll go."

"You came to help?" he says, still not begging.

I wave. "Toodles."

Immediately he's there, barring my way. "You can't go. Please. Come on, you've got connections. I know you've got connections."

I hide my smile because today I have all the power. "I don't have no stinkin' connections," I say, because I want to hold his balls in my hand and squeeze. You think that's depraved, don't you? You've never found your husband with his head buried in someone else's pâté de foie gras. It's not pretty.

He leads me back to the chair and then sits on the arm. His hand starts sliding over my shoulder. This is Marv's version of foreplay, so you see why I have issues. "V, V, V," he says, in a deep, silky voice that makes me remember why I married him. "You're looking good these days. I always knew you'd make it big."

It all starts coming back to me, and I feel slightly less vindictive, but only slightly. Until he hit his midlife crisis, we had some good times. Momentarily I weaken. "I can pull some strings."

He brushes the hair back from my face, and I realize he's going to kiss me.

And then he's kissing me, and I'm trying to figure out if I like this or not. It's not the Kiss of True Love, but then it's not magically induced either.

"I didn't come over here for that," I tell him, because I recognize that glint in his eye. "Tell me who's in charge of your investigation."

"It's Calvin Bassano," he says, his lips against my neck.

"I'll talk to him," I say, and then Marv shuts me up.

And while he's kissing me, I'm remembering all the late

nights that he lied to me, all the sit-ups I did for him. All the days I raced home to have the perfect dinner made. And I'm getting madder and madder. And he's kissing me like crazy and divesting me of garments that cost more than his annual salary.

Eventually I'm down to a pair of La Perla stockings and my Roger Vivier heels, and absolutely nothing else, and let me tell you that I never—I repeat, never—looked this good married.

I lie back against the chair doing my best *Playboy* imitation, and I can just see the combustion piling his pistons.

No, V, no, you say! You can't let the evil man have his way with you!

Hehehe. Oh, ye of little faith.

I smile and glance at my watch. "Look at the time! My God, I'm late." I gather up my clothes, and put them back on, feelings his balls clench tighter and tighter, and then I walk out the door with a fabulous wave. "Ta-ta, Marvin."

"V! Wait! You look amazing, so . . . different."

I start to hum to myself. *Whatever Lola Wants.*

A deal with the devil: One soul. Body perfection: Two souls. Seeing your ex's face wilt with pain because he can't have you anymore: Priceless. Because there are some things that money can't buy.

Anyone of you that have ever been divorced, give me a call and we'll chat.

Marv follows me out into the hallway. "V, you know, I don't think I've ever wanted you so much, and you seem to be much more *uninhibited* than you ever were."

"Yes?" I ask, because I sense he's going to beg, and that is a favorite fantasy of mine. Right up there with V Takes Over the World.

He gets this really earnest look in his eyes, and I can see the aardvarkian resemblance. "You're so cool, and I've been such a schmuck. I really want to ask you something . . ."

"Go ahead," I say, with a royal tone that suggest he get down on his knees, like a good fief.

Marv, being permanently obtuse, grabs my hand. "What do you think about doing a video? You, me, Kimberly. I'd make a mint."

So much for begging. This is Marv, and he is a shit, and he will never let me forget that he is a shit.

Immediately I drop his hand.

"You know, Marvin, one of these days you're going to wake up and look in the mirror, and you're an aardvark. And you're going to wonder, How did I become an aardvark? And then you're going to say, You know, V told me I was going to be an aardvark, and you'll come to me on your little aardvark knees, begging, and I'll laugh at you, Marv. *I will laugh*. You just don't get it, do you? The world does not revolve around Marv. For ten years, it was Marv, Marv, Marv, Marv, *Marv*. Well it's my turn now. Today, tomorrow, and everyday. From now on— it's all about V."

I push him back into his measly one-bedroom nothing-land and slam the door in his face.

Marv opens it. "Is that a no?"

That's it. Tomorrow I'm learning the aardvark spell.

Six

The Best of the Best will be out in full tonight for the art exhibition, I Support Ethiopia. Proceeds will be going to help those needy Ethiopians and keep the Republicans out of Albany. A win-win all around. Be there, and be the first to see Jamie MacGregor since he's arrived in New York. I know I can't wait.

Today it's all about politics. In the spirit of peaceful activism, Graydon Carter will be organizing a smoke-in at the Condé Nast Building in protest against the New York smoking ban. Outside, the American Lung Association will be picketing. Beyond the picket line, Philip Morris will be protesting *the American Lung Association. You gotta love this country, hmm?*

Last little item, a delightful Euro-dish. At Soho House (because the best British things belong in New York), there was a bit of a to-do about the wife of a newly knighted import caught in a to-don't with a world-famous soccer sensation. Lots of sugar, but no spice at all.

The next morning, I get a surprise visitor to the store. Nathaniel. When Phoebe, loyal employee that she is, spots the studly man with a telltale U.S. Army T-shirt and perfectly packed jeans coming through the door, she's ready to leap into action. I, however, do not lose my cool.

"Phoebe, why don't you take a break. Go get yourself a cup of coffee. You're looking a little sapped."

Nathaniel looks pleased at my actions. I plaster a cool look on my face. One of the lessons that I have learned about men is that they can always disappoint you, and therefore you must never make hopeful assumptions. Of course, now it's just the two of us. Alone.

"So this is your store, huh?" he says, walking around and inspecting each design carefully.

It's a noncommittal comment, and I've already decided that he's going to have to take the next step this time. "We don't cater to window shoppers. If you're only looking, you can leave now."

He turns to me, thumbs hooked in his pocket, and surveys

the perfection that is my body. My ego swells, as do other parts that shall remain nameless. "I've always stayed away from women like you."

"Women like me? That doesn't sound good. Who is a woman like me?"

He moves a little closer, failing the "staying away" test even more. I can see temptation in his eyes. As a soulless person, I am on a first-name basis with temptation, and I move even closer. "Confident, spoiled, the sexiest woman I've ever seen."

"If I was so spoiled, then wouldn't that mean that I'd always get my way?"

"Don't you?" he says, and the distance between us grows smaller.

"I'm not getting it now," I answer, and then back up a step, just because I don't want him thinking that I'm too fast.

"What are you after?"

"If I told you, I bet I'd scare you," I say, backing up until the wall hits me in the ass.

His smile says he's got me right where he wants me. "Nothing scares me. Absolutely nothing."

"I should. I'm a wicked, wicked woman."

"I know," he says, placing a kiss just at the corner of my mouth.

Such land mines of tenderness decimate my arguments. "So why are you here?

"Go out with me," he says, and there's a little too much confidence in that face for me to say yes. At least, not immediately. I'm not stupid.

"After you said I was spoiled? I don't think so."

His body moves in close, until I'm trapped (*trapped* being a metaphorical term, of course) right smack against him. "Sometimes you gotta take a chance. I bet you like to take chances."

The man really has no idea, but his parts are pressing against my parts, and I'm growing more enthused about the idea of taking chances. I can feel that he is growing more enthused as well. "Maybe."

"We'll do dinner. Italian. I miss good Italian."

"You throw in dancing afterward, and it's a deal."

Regrettably he unsticks himself from me, and I'm left solo, pressed against the wall. "Done. I'll pick you up on Sunday night."

After he leaves, it hits me: I have a date. It's not a date designed to get me in the papers. It's not a date that will sell 3,000 more bags. It's simply a date with a man I want to be with. How whacked is that?

I do a little happy dance. Nothing overt, although a passing window shopper looks at me strangely. I shoot her the finger, which seems to make her feel better. New Yorkers don't know how to handle happiness. Neither do I.

On Friday, Meegan and I ride in a limo down to Club Spank—whoa, bad slip there—Club Skank. I think tonight is a mistake, but Meegan is determined. I consider a spell to keep her home, but ever since I got my thighs back, I've seen the wisdom in not denying Lucy anything. At least not to her face, you know?

There are purple lights dancing on the town car's ceiling as we cruise through the streets of Williamsburg. In the old days, it was the Village that was all grunge, but now you have to go to Brooklyn—excuse me, fucking Brooklyn—in order to find true skankiness. Eventually, you will have to go to Jersey, and my life will have come full circle.

I sigh.

Meegan interprets my moment of self-pity as an invitation to chat. Another conversational disconnect. You wonder why I have these problems with her?

"I can't wait to see Jamie MacGregor. Oh, God, can he *be* even hotter in person?"

I don't tell her that I used to have those same feelings about NSYNC. (They're in the dictionary. Look under "Geeky Teenage Crush.")

"I'm sure he is," I murmur, all the while taking a long sip of vodka and rolling my eyes. Jamie is a pussy compared to Nathaniel, but Meegan is young and has much to learn about men.

"If I get a chance, I'm going to do it. Of course, he'd have to notice me first," Meegan says, pushing her hair out of her eyes. Normally she's doing a nice straight, boarding-school coiffure. Today she got a blowout, giving her a Newark big-hair look that is belied by the innocence in her eyes. I'm not so far gone that I don't recognize it.

"Driver, turn us around," I say, but Meegan's having none of it.

"Club Skank. And if you don't go with me, I'm heading out solo."

There would have been a time when I would have applauded Megs's newfound, Madonnaesque personality. She's turning fun. However, when the devil is thinking about using said Madonna for baby-making of the 666 kind, now is not it. "Meegan, you're not going to be playing Lolita to his John Wayne Bobbitt, am I making myself clear?"

"I'm over twenty-one," she says, looking me square in the eyes. She's gone high-octane with the mascara this evening and I can see she's going to give me trouble.

Time for a little harsh truth; I've gotta crush her in order to protect her. "You don't have the right credentials, Megs; namely a Hollywood pedigree. Jamie will notice the wallpaper before you."

"I know," she says, and now she looks like she wants to continue in the self-analyzing loser mode, but through divine intervention, my cell phone rings. I check Caller ID. Oh, cool! This one I'll take.

"Rolf, darling," I coo and revel in the deep baritone of his voice (it's faux deep, but I'm okay with that, it still gives me shivers). I'm almost positive that Rolf is not a client. There's always been those rumors about his sexuality; not good for box-office hunk. The whole thing just smacks of devilish intent.

He wants to know if I'm going to the benefit, a benefit I don't want to go to, but I'm not willing to put my ass on the line, either. "Save me a seat at the bar," I say and then click off with an air-kiss into the phone.

Meegan is impressed, which is, of course, the whole point.

"Rolf?" she asks.

"He's a friend."

She sighs.

I'm happy.

We make it to Williamsburg, all the Yiddish graffiti proclaiming "Hipsters Go Home." The Williamsburg Jews are having it out with the miso-establishment vegans, but the yarmulke set should be heeding the writing on the *pupik*. Do they honestly believe that Brooklyn would be a safe haven? Heh.

Club Skank, if you're really curious, is dark. Lots of black, tattoos, bare skin, and silver. Catwoman meets Jerry Springer. And amidst this cesspool of style, we have the ear-exploding whimsy of Eve. Three females with bare navels, beer bellies, and all the musical talent of the Bangles—before they made it big.

Meegan is close by my side, breathing something akin to hero worship. Yeah, I'm touched. Of course, with all the flash here, it's not surprising. This is the Manhattan Party Crowd. Tara (still drunk), Derek (still a Yankee), Lenny (still with bad hair), Ethan (still dirty), Nicole (still gorgeous, definitely a client, no way is that complexion for real), and Paris (still anorexic and annoying).

Tonight's gala event is the auction of two dozen foundation garments (bras—like we don't know the difference), artistically enhanced by various New York celebs. Studs, feathers, leather, and diamonds. Each work of discerning refinement is tastefully presented on its own rotating pedestal. You wonder why I have problems with art?

All the big names have personalized their support for the cause—Candace, Monica, Lil' Kim, Boy George, Chelsea, and

Lauren (did you know she was still alive? I was really surprised).

Even Martha Stewart has shipped in some art, showing some real talent by using a combination of Burberry plaid and leather trim in her design. Très cute, and really classy next to the Lil' Kim bling-bling abomination. (The glare alone would blind you.)

It is hard to resist bidding six figures for such a good cause, but I am strong and migrate to the back rooms, where the noise is coming from. Meegan follows in my shadow.

In the bowels of the bar (and you think that's just a literary term, don't you? But this place *smells like shit*), I spy Jamie MacGregor. He's a handsome devil. Snapping brown eyes and this "I will take you to bed and you must pleasure me while I think of other women" grin that all women seem to fall for. I myself was married to Marv; my doormat days are over.

"I think he's looking at me," whispers Meegan. "I could bear his children."

At that moment, a lightbulb flashes in my head, and I remember the baby gossip about Jamie. I connect the dots, and a pentagram appears, wrapped in swaddling clothes.

I look at Meegan, who is now rubbing her belly.

Aw, shit.

"I heard he carries every sexually transmitted disease ever given to womankind," I blurt out, just in case some miracle happens and he does notice Megs. "Just think of where that Scottish hymenator has been. Ewwww."

Meegan smiles, not getting the visual. Perhaps if I mention the possibility of a genetic birth defect (i.e., horns), it'll help.

Although maybe I'm unable to intervene. Maybe the fates have already spoken, and civilization is damned. Considering the current state of art, it's not a big leap. I should just go home. I look around for my bag.

No, V. No!

Ha. Had you going for a minute, didn't I? I'm such a kidder.

Of course I'll keep an eye on Meegan. I toss my hair and smile at her in a superficial manner. "I think Jamie's looking my way. I didn't mention the torrid affair we had last winter in South Beach, did I?"

It's a lie. He's so not my type, and I hate the state of Florida (my parents live there, do I have to elaborate?), but I know the best way to keep Jamie MacPreginator from fertilizing Megs, and that is by casting myself as the Bitch-Friend from Hell.

She doesn't look deterred.

Not a problem. When in doubt, use a little magic.

Ugly, schmugly, Depardieu, see the men and say adieu.

The anti-Cupid hits his mark. The dumbstruck bemusement on her face disappears, and Jamie is forgotten. I crack my metaphoric knuckles, completely impressed with myself. When you have powers, nothing is impossible. Unfortunately, Jamie has noticed me, and is instantly captured by my innate sexuality

There is a rising level of tension in the room. He meets my eyes, nostrils flaring (it's more attractive than it sounds) and walks toward us.

I frown, not wanting to encourage him. When I turn my

head, Meegan is wandering off toward the bar. I grab her hand and pull her back in visual range. I have a job to do tonight.

Jamie smiles at me, and somewhere a Clay Aiken song is playing.

Oh, yeah, right. Actually, the music is something by Outkast, and at that moment Lucy comes through the door, her devilish eyes directly on me. Now tell me, how does the woman sense every single fucking time I'm in the midst of doing good? My God, it's worse than my mother (actually, it's not. My mother is ten times the demon that Lucy is, but I'm prone to exaggerate).

Anywhoo, Lucy spots me, and I raise my arms in a "who, me?" gesture. She smiles, and I'm sensing a crisis averted as she is thronged by her throngs of admirers. She really does have this great presence. It's just no wonder . . .

Suddenly, there's a typhoon blowing in my ear, and a strange Scottish hand is awanderin' up my waist.

Jamie wraps his fingers in mine, a boyish gesture, and I understand why girls ♥ him. "Fook me. You're V, aren't you? It's such a fooking head-trip to see you in person."

I let him fawn for a bit. Then I see Lucy watching carefully, and I sigh, remembering Meegan.

Diversion is the theme tonight.

"I affect a lot of men that way," I answer back, noticing that Meegan is looking restless, like the magic is wearing thin. I consider another spell—something stronger, perhaps a coma—and then Lucy meets my eyes.

She looks very nice this evening, wearing a black leather miniskirt that shows off her legs. When I'm her age, I hope I have legs that look like that. I let my mind suck up to her a bit longer, until she turns away, convinced that I'm still her faithful partner in crime.

Jamie, however, is one lusty rogue and rubs on me like Paris on anything. "I have to fooking have you," he says, this ego-stroking urgency in his voice. My ego swells with a thematic crescendo.

I sneak a look at Megs, keeping my thoughts under Lucy's mental radar. I think the coast is clear. Meegan is setting herself up against the back wall, drowning her boredom in a cosmopolitan, which is just so last year. I can see the headlines in the paper. "V Saves the World: Spawn of Satan Plot Aborted." Gracefully I yawn. Yup, just another day in the life.

Jamie's hot beer breath is misting my neck, and his Wee Scottish Weenie pokes against my butt. I'm not turned on, not aroused, not even interested.

"You know, Jamie, I think you're really cute, but I'm looking for someone a little more"—an eight-by-ten of Nathaniel flashes in my brain—"military."

He stares at me, but I don't think the rejection is cutting through the stone. "You're so fookin' luscious. I'm just going to—"

Out of the corner of my eye, I see Meegan walking through the back exit of the club. Oh, not good, not good, not good. I brush off Jamie and follow her.

"The fookin' alley? Oh, you're a wicked, wicked lass," he says.

I push open the door and look both ways, but Meegan has disappeared.

"I don't have time for this now," I say, but Jamie is one stubborn Scottie, and he grabs me with those strong, Hollywood-toned arms and presses me against his abs of steel.

"Dinna kin your bit of ass—"

I know you're concerned, you're thinking that he's gonna jump me. Right here in the fookin' alley. Tell me, why does everyone underestimate me?

I shoot Jamie a come-hither look, just to make his year, and then whisper a one-two combination guaranteed to ring his bell.

Ohken, fawken, Scottish sod, libations send him back to Nod.

Immediately Jamie conks off against the brick wall. If I were a nice person, I would prop him up so he wouldn't fall over. I'm not a nice person, and he falls—*crash*—right on the pavement. I adjust my Dior blouse (Christian has never been so shamed) and take off to find Meegan.

Unfortunately, when I go back inside, Meegan's nowhere to be found. Lucy's alone at the bar, giving me the evil eye. However, I can plead stupidity and ignorance. I do that well (and as a bonus, it's currently fashionable).

"Did Meegan go home?" I ask innocently.

"No."

I sip at my martini, surreptitiously checking out the bar for some sign of the currently MIA Megs. Lucy looks up at me (she really is very short, and I'm a stilter), and her dark eyes read my entire life. I can see it flash before her eyes. Very *Twilight Zone*. Not recommended.

I lift my glass to my lips, and then I see the imagery inside it. It's Megs (I think), and she's getting laid in the bottom of my martini glass.

Instantly I put it down. After I blink, Meegan is still there, and there's a guy with her. A total dweeb. Okay, my anti-Cupid spell had problems. That's the headache with doing magic on people; it's a little unpredictable.

Lucy just laughs.

This is not good. I look in her eyes to see if this is just another facet in Lucy's devilish sense of humor. Unfortunately, she looks serious. Definitely serious.

Fuck.

You know, I truly believed that I could handle everything. Me, the mighty Level 3. I was wrong, and worse, I think Lucy knew exactly what I was doing the whole time. I like to think of myself as unpredictable and elusive, as changeable as the wind. Instead I'm a lab rat running for the cheese. It's bad for my image. And speaking of image, Lucy's wearing a new one this evening. Evil. Tell me, why would I underestimate the devil? I want to like her; she's very cool. But Lucy is like having a pet cobra, and when you're a lab rat, as I suspect I have been, a cobra is a very deadly creature. Hypnotic, but deadly nonetheless.

For a moment, Lucy lets me ponder my failures in peace. Then she raises her glass. A little devil toast. "She's an opportunity for you now. Just another soul. You should be proud of what you've done," she tells me, rubbing some iodine in the wound.

"I don't think she's cut out for the program, Luce," I say, because I'm feeling those hot spots of conscience. I failed Megs tonight. I should have just forced her to stay home and faced the consequences with Lucy myself.

"Don't beat yourself up. Wait till she sees her baby. She's going to love her new life."

And we're back to the baby again. The nightmare spawn. "Can I ask you a personal question?" I say.

"Sure."

"This baby. Now, it's a stretch that you're giving her a kid just out of the goodness of your heart, because, well, you're the devil, albeit a kinder, gentler devil, but still . . . So, what exactly is your plan?"

"It's more than just a plan, V. I want a daughter. This is my way to have her."

I slam my drink, but even alcohol doesn't help me now. "I don't think hijacking Meegan's womb is going to give you the results that you're looking for."

"You'll see. Everything's all laid out in front of me. I know what you're going to do. I know what Meegan's going to do. It's all predestined."

Please note that I'm smarter than to buy into all that predestined shit. If I were preordained, I'd still be in Newark, but I'm not. I'm sitting here (with the devil, mind you), with the best eyeballs in New York City fixated on me, all dying to be in my place. I glance over at Lucy and realize my position is a little more precarious. I'm not stupid, and I choose not to argue her point.

Unfortunately she reads me thoughts. "You can't interfere, V. People will do what people will do. I know the future. All of it. Including yours."

"Silly me," I answer, which is much more polite than the "fuck you" that I'm thinking, mainly because I'm pissed at my own gullibility.

"V, V, V. What am I going to do with you?" she says, but her eyes are nice.

Why couldn't she have red eyes or something creepy like that? However, I've learned my lesson, and nice eyes or not, I know I'm gonna pay for this one. I hold on to my thighs for dear life. "You're going to zap me again, aren't you? Go ahead. I can take it," I say, praying she's not going to take away my powers, because now I really need them to help Megs, and also to continue living in the manner to which I am accustomed.

Lucy just smiles, still with the nice eyes. "No, I'm not going to zap your thighs. Just wait."

A surprise. I hate surprises. I always have. I always will.

She laughs her little devil-may-care laugh and prisses off on a really great pair of Manolos.

Damn.

My mother is waiting for me in my apartment when I get home. My hell is now complete.

"How did you get up here?" I ask.

"I lit into your doorman when security didn't want to let me up, and when that didn't work, I faked a heart attack. After that, he said he knew we were related."

Already my blood pressure starts to rise, and I can feel a pounding in my head. My mother is the most self-centered person on the planet. "What are you doing here?" I ask, but I know. *This is Lucy's surprise.*

Why couldn't it be something simple, like the plagues or floods or the end of the world? Oh, yeah, the world might really end (I've seen the devil-kid movies), but I can't worry about that right now, because, yes, my mother is here.

"I'm moving in." It gets worse.

"You're not."

"I am."

I go to my bedroom and change into my pajamas. When I come back, she's still there.

"You can leave in the morning. I'm too tired to have this conversation with you."

"If you wouldn't stay out until four A.M., you wouldn't be so tired. Pretty soon the only bags you'll be wearing are the ones under your eyes."

I swish my hand through the air.

Mom shuts up.

Whoa. I did that. *The magic works on Mom.*

Instantly I'm dishing out spells.

Mommie Dearest, Mommie Mine, freeze thy tongue till end of time.

Mother just blinks. "I need my suitcases brought up. The doorman wasn't happy. You should find yourself a better building."

It wasn't quite what I was going for. "This is Trump Grand Palais. There is no better building," I snap and then try again.

Double, double, toil, and truark. Find thyself on path to Newark. If thy path should start to stray, get thyself to JFK.

"You're leaving in the morning, right?" I ask. (Please, please, PLEASE!). "I'll get a limo to take you to the airport."

"I'm not flying," she snaps.

"You can take the train," I snap back, thinking of other spells, more powerful spells. I try them all. My mother is immune. Exhausted and defeated, I fall back on the couch.

"The train takes too long, and I could buy a new car for the cost of the ticket."

Weakly I raise my head. I have danced with the devil, but my mother is going to land me in Bellevue. "I know you're dying to leave."

"You need me."

"I don't need you."

"You think I can't read the papers? Look at this."

Tell me why I'm cursed with the only human being that won't respond to my spells? This is more than just Lucy spanking me for being good. No, God is having a huge joke at my expense. Well, God, I'm onto you, and it's—not—funny.

Then I look at the paper.

Seven

Where to begin? I told everyone not to miss the I Support Ethopia Benefit. And look what happens? It's the sort of day a gossip columnist, excuse me, human events reporter, lives for.

Can you spell D-I-V-O-R-C-E? The broken marriage news of the day is that a certain Pop-Tartlet (and no, not THAT one) is splitting from her "You've made my career, now get out" husband. She's booted him from their Tribeca loft, and the TV cameras have been kicked out as well. Who predicted this one first? Well, actually everyone. Apparently, MTV is salivating to buy the rights to the divorce as well.

What newly widowed singer has already

signed away the memoirs of her late husband's indiscretions? I heard the book pro-
posal was finished before the eulogy. A
"nice" deal. How sad when your life doesn't
even rate six figures.

And who's the newest alley cat at Club
Skank? The last thing this Sonata girl needs
now is a bun in the birkin. Tsk, tsk, tsk. Get
a room!

"Are you proud of yourself? You've taken the *bleep* name and
dragged it through the mud."

I ignore her to gather my thoughts.

Okay, thoughts are gathered.

Lucy is pissed. Megs is possibly going to birth the child of
Satan, which, according to Ira Levin, foretells the end of the
world. My mother is visiting for an indefinite period, and the
end of the world can only be a good thing. To top it all off,
I've started having these night sweats of conscience inside me,
and I think it's getting worse.

(No, it's *not menopause*, don't be snippy. Clients don't have
menopause. Cool, eh?)

My mother, all three feet eight of her (okay, I'm exaggerat-
ing, she's actually four-ten), stares me down. As I register the
waves of hostility emanating from her, I sense something
buried deep underneath the waves, and no, it's not love. Man,
are you on the wrong planet.

"Can you lay off the lectures, Mom? I've had a bad day." I

rub my head and try to ease that throbbing pain inside it. Oh, yeah, can't. It's my mother.

"I think you need a stronger influence up here. I've let you run wild for too long."

"I'm forty years old."

"So, we start a little late . . ."

Where is all this concern coming from? Certainly not from maternal instincts. And then I see the way her beady eyes are looking at my stuff. The pristine white rugs, the plasma TV, the authentic leopard-print sofa. "You're jealous, Mom. Why don't you admit it? I've got everything you always wanted, and it's eating you up inside like a cancer." (I just threw that in, because Mom really hates the C word.)

"You really think that because you're living this Park Avenue lifestyle, everyone must be jealous?"

"Yes," I answer truthfully, not knowing whether that was a rhetorical question or not. "For as long as I can remember, me and the whole eastern seaboard have heard your whine. A town house in the city, a summer house in the Hamptons. Sundays in the Park."

"I must have overlooked the poke in the alley," she says, her mouth pruning in disapproval.

Far in the distance, rumbling cuts from the ceiling above. Either God is laughing at me, or my upstairs neighbor has taken up the drums.

I ignore God, standing firm in my own righteousness. I was trying to do the right thing. Mother, the little drama queen, misses my firm stand, forges onward, hand over her heart: "You have shamed me, shamed my family."

The Italian blood begins to boil in my veins. It takes a lot to boil me, but two seconds with Mom, and now I'm ready to maim. "Get out. Get out now. I don't know what the punishment in the state of New York is for matricide, but I swear it'll be worth it."

Bing-bing-bing. We have a winner. Her hand falters a bit, and she lowers the shield of moral rectitude. "Your father left me for another woman. I don't have anywhere else to go."

I sit there, frozen, wondering if she's making a piss-poor joke, because everyone else seems to be doing it.

But it doesn't seem to be a joke. She sits down and calmly lights a cigarette on my leopard-skin couch. And did she ask if she could smoke in my apartment? Oh, no. Queen Prima Donna will do whatever she wants. If I were a sensitive daughter, I'd feel sympathy, pain, or sadness. However, the only thing I feel is anger. She's sitting there, quietly taking a long drag, and I can feel the smoke pouring out of my ears.

This is it. No more.

"Well, you finally did it, didn't you? You finally chased him off."

"He left because he's a bitter old man who thinks he'll be happier without me. Taking up with some floozy. What was he thinking?"

"Big surprise, huh? You made him that way, Mother. You made us all that way."

"While I was out dancing under the moon with the joy of my life? I was miserable, too."

I'm so tired of all the whining, the "poor me" vitriol that

I've been drowned in all my life. "Why don't you go away, Mom? Get a hotel. I don't want to see you, okay? Dad's a decent man. He was about the only thing decent in my life, and now you've taken that away, too."

Her dark eyes flicker, and I recognize that flat look of feigned apathy from the mirror. "I don't have any money."

Are you surprised? I'm not surprised. Once again V is being played, but this time by my mother. It's one step below being played by the devil. It took me forty years, but I finally have something in my life to be proud of, and of course, she wants it. I'm tired, and my feet hurt. It's been a long night, and my ocean of sympathy has long since dried up. "Gee, Mom. Go find a job. I hear Dairy Queen is hiring."

"I don't want to be a burden," she says while tapping her cigarette ashes on my Alberto Rosselli table. I remain silent, and she senses my conflicted self. The bigger part of me that wants nothing to do with her, and the tiny part of me that spent my formative years searching for a relationship with her—in vain. Sadly, I can see my future written in the Marlboro-gray ash. I'm a schmuck. Tell me, why don't I have a sister or a brother? Somebody else to shoulder parental responsibility? However, I'm not a complete schmuck. "Three conditions. One, you're looking for a job, and two, you work hard to patch things up with Dad. Three, this is temporary. Four weeks and you're out of here, unless the world ends first. *Capisce?*"

"*Capisce,*" she says, as cool as a cucumber. Maybe we're not related. Maybe I was adopted, because I don't sense any shared DNA at all.

* * *

On Saturday, I wake up and Mom is gone. At first I imagine that it was all a horrible nightmare, but then I see the note. "Gone to walk in the park and buy myself a decent breakfast. What do you eat here?"

In my soulful days, I would have screamed, raged, or arranged a mugging for my mother, but now I must maintain a cool demeanor in order to resolve Megs's issue. You didn't think I'd just roll over and play dead, did you? Nah. I've got my powers. I can do lots. However, what if Meegan's truly pregnant? Of course, Lucy could be pulling a fast one on me, and Meg's not pregnant, just ends up with some STD, and then parts start falling off, and she's willing to sell her soul in order to get well. But Lucy wants a daughter. And I know what that means. It's one thing to say you're going to hell, it's another thing to perpetuate the demise of all civilization as we know it. People would really hate me for this one.

To bolster my energy level, I zap myself a Starbucks grande venti tall mocha with extra whipped cream and pick up my cell phone to call Dad. Just to figure out what's going on.

"Dad?"

"Speak up, I can't hear you."

I raise my voice. "Dad. It's V."

"Me? Yes, it's me. Is this a crank call?"

Damned phone. I move to the window, where my reception is better. "Dad. It's me. Mom's here. You've got to take her back."

It's too late. My father has hung up on me.

If your cell works in Manhattan, please tell me now. I've sold my soul, and I *still* can't get decent coverage. But enough bitching about the Dead Zone, I'll call him later. I have to go visit Meegan and see what's up. I'm holding out for the hope that Lucy's wrong. I go to my closet and swish up a head-turning little snakeskin sheath (Versace). Sarah Jessica had wanted it first, but she wasn't willing to sell her soul. Her loss.

The schlep to Brooklyn is killer; it takes me thirty minutes to get to Meegan's. I should get her to move to the West Side, but right now she's situated in a quaint (i.e., small) little brownstone in Dumbo.

"How're you feeling today?" I say, settling myself on her couch (vintage IKEA, this from someone with money. *Ack!*).

"I'm okay," she says, still standing, arms tightly crossed across her chest. I spy the *Post* in the corner, and she's taken a marker and put little devil horns and black teeth on the picture of me with Jamie.

Okay, obviously I'm not her favorite person. "Still hung up on him?"

"I was feeling a little weird early on last night, but yes, I recovered nicely, V. Thank you for your concern."

"I'm sorry. I thought I was doing you a favor."

"You didn't," she says, still pissed.

"I'm not the enemy here," I say, because after all, it's not *me* who has the Daughter of Satan in utero.

"You knew I wanted him. You knew he was the only reason I was going to the club that night. *The only reason.* I told you that."

"Who are we talking about, Jamie?" I say, repugnance in my voice, my gaze, my very bearing. "And we certainly didn't wait too long to go legs-out with someone else, now, did we?"

"How did you know about that?"

I could admit that I saw an image of her copulating inside a martini glass, but I'm wondering if she'd really believe it. "Is it true?" I ask, keeping my fingers crossed that it's not.

"It's not your business, and I don't think I want you for a friend anymore. Can you go now?"

"What if you've got some communicable disease? Did you think of that?" I ask, blithely ignoring the invitation to leave.

"Do I need to call security?"

(I have to know, does everybody else get treated so shitty when they're doing good? It's no wonder the world is going to hell in a Kelly bag, just no wonder at all.) In the face of such snotty treatment, I'm tempted to leave, but I demur and use my powers instead.

Caesar, Brutus, mend your fences, find yourself the best of frences.

Instantly she beams, recognizing me for the savior that I am. I sniff modestly. That's more like it.

Then she starts to pace, her little brow marred with wrinkles. "I don't know."

"Who is this guy, anyway?

"I don't know his name. I met him at the bar. He was the barback," she says, ending in a little voice.

Oh, Megs. I feel a twinge of pity, but the seriousness of the situation means I must shove it away. "You didn't have to do that. You should have come and grabbed me and talked. I would have talked you out of it. We could have gone and shared some cosmopolitans, you know?"

"Cosmopolitans would have been nice," she says with a weak smile.

"That's my girl. Now let's talk contraception. Are you taking anything?"

"No. I can't have kids, V. Remember?"

"Megs, I know you believe this is impossible, but I think you're pregnant," I say, deciding that truth, or at least part of it, is the best solution.

"I'm infertile. It's impossible."

And that's the real kicker. I don't want to tell her what I know; I can't. Meegan isn't me. She isn't equipped to deal with the badness that is second nature to the damned. "What if the hospital screwed up, Meegan? Did you ever think of that? What if they lied to you all those years ago?"

"Why would they do that?"

"I don't know, but I think we should consider the possibility. I don't think you can gamble with your future. We can run off to Duane Reade. They have those I-can't-remember-what-happened-last-night-and-I'm-damned-sure-not-gonna-take-any-chances pills." I wrinkle my nose. "You know, just in case."

Megs looks at me in horror. "If I'm meant to conceive, this is a miracle, V. I'm not going to interfere with God's will."

Now she gets religion. Where was religion when she was on the rocks with Mr. Harvey Wallbanger? I try another angle.

"Can we talk about Meegan's will for a minute? Single momhood. You don't need that hassle."

"A child is not an inconvenience."

"Don't kid yourself. This one would be a doozie."

When she looks up at me, there's hope in her eyes. "You really think I could be pregnant?"

Hope. Trust me when I say that hope is a dangerous thing. I didn't want to give her hope; I wanted to give her fear. I manage a smile. "In this day and age of medical incompetence, anything's possible. We'll wait awhile, and then you do a test. If that comes back positive, you go see a doctor. Immediately."

She launches into my arms and gives me a hug. "V, I never thought it was possible. But now . . . Oh, God, what if? You know, I actually feel pregnant."

I endure her hug for a short moment and then put her to one side. I'll let her have her moment of happiness, because I suspect that a moment is all she's going to have.

That night I go partying at Revelations. You say, "V, what about the end of all civilization as we know it?" I say, "My mother is at my apartment. Already it has her smell. You worry about your own problems, I'm getting drunk."

Revelations has a nifty VIP entrance in the back for the hoity-toity crowd who want to make an unobtrusive entrance. I *always* use a limo at the front.

It's an average night; the usual faces are here. No big whoop. A few young models, the old *Sex and the City* gang, sans Kim, and even the Samurai of Swat, who is downing Cristal while sporting a Nike hat. I look up and see Jamie in the VIP lounge.

He stares longingly at me. I smile cheerfully and wave in that "I swear I didn't leak anything to Gawker" manner.

This is my world, my domain, the reason that I sold my soul. And since there's no going back, I better be fucking happy about it. All the guys are hitting on me, buzzing around me like flies. Happiness returns, and I've got my bearings once again.

The crowd gets worse as the evening progresses. The bar is a round circle of red light, with a caged dancer on top, flames licking at the base. It's a puritanical look, but in these post–9/11 days, it works really well.

All around me, there are Sonata bags, most in the darling kelly green that I adore, but I notice three in butt-ugly puce. In my soulful days, I would have carried a puce purse. Whoa. Tiny loser moment. I take a deep breath and smile. Then I buy each of the three ladies a drink and tell them about the new scarlet evening clutches that will debut in the spring (they look so much nicer). Hopefully they'll take the hint.

Later in the evening, I see Shelby balancing herself between Harry and Damien Wasabi, last year's New York wannabe, and another size-plus brunette who is unfamiliar to me.

"V!" Shelby launches herself at me, a vision in white fur (I would bet two levels it's Michael Kors, and many baby seals died for her to look so good, even in April. *Not jealous. Not jealous. Not jealous*). "I need to talk to you," she says and whisks me away.

I am easily whisked (four martinis).

"I'm loving this stuff! Look!" She twirls around, her white fur billowing and catches the poor guy next to her off-guard. He stumbles. She ignores him. "And check this out!" She pulls a matching muff from the pocket of her coat.

The muff starts to bark. It's a little white dog. "Meet Mooshoo."

"You got a dog?"

"It's a rental. It's part of my new business empire," she says, and I smile tightly at the Chia pet until she stuffs him back in her pocket.

"You must be swimming in souls. Recruitment going well?" I ask.

She nods toward the unfamiliar brunette. "Regina Bassano. She's my ticket to Level 2. Body beautification, here I come."

"Bassano? Daughter of Calvin? SEC prosecutor?" *Surely it's a coincidence.*

"You know Calvin? Isn't he a laugh?"

Instantly I'm wondering if old Cal is a client as well. It would explain much. "Is Calvin on your marketing plan?"

Shelby nods. "At this rate, I'll make Level 9 before the end of the year. Lucy told me that she's planning a celebratory jaunt to Saint Lucia for those of us who achieve the Golden Circle in less than twelve months. You should come. Bikinis. Piña coladas and a personal cabana boy to polish your nails and feed you grapes. It sounds like paradise."

Paradise lost, more like it, if Lucy is planning this gathering. I watch Regina out of the corner of my eye. She's flirting with Damien, who wants nothing to do with her. She's ripe for the plucking, and unfortunately Shelby knows it.

I shake my head, clearing off the fog of alcohol. The martinis are going to my brain, and I think about interfering, which is kinda sad. I'm not nice, and no matter how much I try to be, it just doesn't work.

No, for tonight, Regina's on her own. "You'll have a great time," I say, still watching Regina. I stare at her, seeing the awkwardness, the insecurity. She must have been about twenty-four, but she could have passed for twelve. I was like that when I was twenty-four. Hell, I was like that when I was thirty-eight.

You know, the strong ones like Shelby, they don't make me sweat at all, but the weak ones, Meegan, Regina, *those* make me nervous. And there is Blanche to think about. I could use Regina to bail Marv's ass out of his sling. The way I look at it, if I *were* to salvage Regina, it's not really something noble or anything. I'm just helping out a loser woman.

"Shelby, I need to ask you a huge favor. I need Regina."

She shoots me a you-bitch look. I am immune. "I'm not going to let you poach in my territory. You've got to find your own flock of souls. I talked to Amy. She told me about your stab-me-in-the-back. I thought you were my best friend, V."

Yeah, that's me. I damned you for all eternity, but I'm your best friend. "I had no choice, Shelby. You don't want to stray too far off the Life Enrichment path at the moment. You're too green. You don't need all those powers."

"Yes, I do."

"Now you just sound desperate."

"Do you want to hear about desperation? I can't get in to see Dr. Karp until 2010. I sent a pair of Manolos to his receptionist, and she laughed in my face. *Laughed.* If I don't get to Level 2 soon, I'll be ruined. Look!" She slaps a hand under her chin.

I sympathize, but stand firm. "You're doing this all wrong. You're working with Tribeca Pre–De Niro. Raise your standards, Shel, you can do better than that." I flash a scoffing look at Regina. "She's no challenge at all."

Unfortunately, Shelby sees my high-standards talk for the filibuster that it is. "A soul is a soul is a soul. I don't care if I get my looks from Mother Teresa or from a serial killer. I just want my firm jawline back, like it was a mere TWO YEARS AGO!"

There's no arguing with a desperate woman. I sigh. In my drunken stupor, I succumb to the inevitable. "I'll get you some other souls. Swear."

Her look sharpens. "How many?"

"One," I answer, shocked, *shocked,* by her greed.

"I want five."

"Fuck you, Shel."

She looks contrite—and rightly so. I can't believe the fur-covered balls on this woman. "Four," she murmurs.

"I'll do two, but that's my final answer. You're getting transitory emotion induction as a bonus, so don't look a gift soul in the mouth."

"Deal, but I want the souls delivered by the end of the month, or I'm taking Regina back."

I try to avoid staring at her chin, and eventually close my eyes at the horror. The clock is ticking.

"Deal."

Regina is charmed to meet me—of course she has heard of the Sonata line and is dying to have one. Magically, the latest bag appears from underneath my seat, and I place it in her hands. (How to Win Friends and Influence People 101.)

After plying her with three Pink Ladies (ugh!), I broach the imminent investigation.

"I understand your father's has been working some overtime lately with that insider trading case. Sex for stocks. It's been all over the news."

She gulps down her fourth drink and seems perfectly sober. "It's been really hard on Daddy. I've hardly seen him since the investigation started."

"It must be difficult, prosecuting a case on such flimsy evidence."

"The brokerage statements were more than enough."

Statements? Oh, man. Marv left a paper trail? It's enough to make me divorce him all over again.

"Regina, I need your help."

"Really?"

"I'm organizing a charity auction at the end of June—it's for a woman's homeless shelter in Lower Manhattan."

"That's so nice of you," she gushes.

I nod modestly. "A person really needs to give back to their community, don't you think? Would you be willing to help out? I have a personal assistant who is organizing the whole thing, and I know she'd love some extra hands. Maybe I could meet with you and your father and get some Wall Street types to help support the cause."

She bounces on her bar stool, and I look around, hoping no one has noticed. "Daddy would love to. Ever since I met Shelby, I've been telling him that he's so out of touch and boring."

Calvin is one smart dweeb. "I can't wait to meet him."

"Let's get together" she says.

"Dinner. Nobu. Two weeks from Friday," I say, stalling for some time.

She points a finger at me. "We'll be there."

I cringe. "Can't wait."

Eight

Apparently, one Scottish actor has been struck with a v., v., case of love—unrequited, if last evening was any indication. The original bag lady seemed oblivious to the huge brown puppy-dog eyes he was casting in her direction. So what does a Scotsman wear under his kilt? According to knowledgeable sources, it's a tim'rous beastie....

What wealthy publishing tycoon was recently hit up for a donation to the homeless? The size of his contribution made the earnest altruist gasp and his too-too comfortable daughter sweat million-dollar bullets as she watched her inheritance shrink by a good ten figures. And no, ha, ha, we're not kidding.

In yesterday's lowlife column in the Europe Observer was a full-fledged castigation of America's obsession with celebrity. And of course, the very next paragraph contains the lowdown on his too-too dinner at the Pump Room. Hypocrisy, thy name has seven syllables.

The next morning I wake up late, hoping to avoid my mother. Sadly, she's in the kitchen flinging coffee grounds everywhere and in general making a mess all over my Italian granite countertops, which she will definitely not clean up.

"You have to clean that up," I tell her, even though I have maid service. Far be it from me to take advantage of my hired help.

"I will," she says, promptly brushing the coffee grinds onto the floor. I swallow all the scatological terms that leap to my tongue.

"Found any great leads in the classifieds yet?"

In retaliation she lights up a cigarette. Oh, she knows just which buttons to push. "Have you talked to your father yet? Is that floozy still shacking up at our home?"

Ready to nip this stall tactic in the bud, I pick up my cell and walk over to the window. Last night I put Dad on speed-dial.

"Dad? It's V. Listen—"

"This is Ben and Laurie, we can't come to the phone right now..."

I click off and turn to Mom. "Who's Laurie?"

She tries to look nonchalant and fails. "The floozy."

We maintain an antagonistic silence until finally she can't take it anymore. "So, what fun things have you planned for me today?"

"I have a private fitting scheduled for this afternoon. I won't be here. And tonight I have a date."

"Couldn't we do something together? A little quality mother-daughter time?"

"If you'd like, we can go to Per Se for brunch," I say, like I'm a frequent patron of that highbrow establishment (which I am). It is a bitch-slap, cleverly cloaked in olive-branch silk.

Her eyes narrow, and I wonder if she'll cut off her daughter to spite her face.

"I'd love to," she answers stiffly.

"Do you have something to wear?" I ask, taking in her red-striped duster.

"No," she says, not disappointing me at all.

"What are you? A fourteen?" (I get my hips from her.)

"Twelve."

"Let me see what I have in my closet."

I come back with a YSL pantsuit, a frilly Narcisco Rodriguez dress, and a classic Donna Karan sheath circa J. C. Penney.

My mother, the Florida fashion maven, goes for the Donna Karan. I am shamed.

We break bread, but not bones, over brunch at Per Se. There's much tension and cattiness, and the general aura of two women who share the same blood but would gladly spill it if sharp objects were accidentally placed in their hands.

A hush falls over the room, and a pack of men in black suits, sunglasses, and little hideaway earpieces appear. These are not D&G models, it is the Secret Service. The eaglet has landed.

Mother's eyebrows have disappeared, and she is all aquiver with anticipation. As the first daughter scans the room, searching for her lunch date, she just happens to glance in my direction.

Now, when life hands you the first daughter, you do not squander the opportunity.

Squealing, trilling, child of POTUS, no bag of mine will miss your notice.

"V! Oh. My. God. I love your stuff!"

I look at my mother and blush with delight. "I didn't realize you were a fan."

"Of course! First with the Tempo design, then the Largo. When Sonata hit *Vogue*, I wasn't surprised at all."

I sneak a glance to make sure Mom is taking this all in. Her mouth is open, but there is no drool. I lay it on even thicker. "If you'll give me a shipping address, I'll make sure you get the first one for the fall season."

The first daughter begins to squeal, turning more heads. This will be in the morning papers. Note to self: get extra staff to support 30 percent increase in sales tomorrow. Still squealing (she's not by nature a squealer, it's just the spell), she turns to Secret Service Man #1 and gives him a look. Without saying a word, he hands me a card.

WHITE HOUSE. 1600 PENNSYLVANIA AVENUE.

WASHINGTON, D.C.

All casual, I put it on the table and watch Mother's gaze zero in on it. Eventually the first daughter (code name Twinkle) moves on to find her date, and my mother is alone, with only me and my hubris.

"Care to go shopping?" I check my watch. "I have thirty minutes before I need to meet up with Amy at the store. Big charity plans. Auction. Fashion. Stars." It's a lie. Amy is Tuesday, but Mom's eyes are bigger than a Harry Winston solitaire, and I'm on a roll.

Actually I'm going to play chess with Blanche. I'm thinking about asking her advice on a few things. Like for instance, what do the ancient prophecies say will happen when the child of Satan appears on earth. Blanche's old. I bet she would know.

Mom gathers up her purse (Old Navy!). "Shopping is good," she says with a smile.

"First thing we need to do is get you another bag."

She pulls it close to her side. "I like this purse."

"Are you going to argue with the president's daughter?"

She looks suitably shamed, and I take her arm. We haven't been this close in ages. I love it when I'm right.

I pull a Kobe and dump Mother and my charge card at Sak's. I'm off to meet Blanche, and the tension dissolves from my shoulders as the miles between myself and the demon who spawned me grow longer. This is why I adore Blanche. She is the mother I should have had.

The park is crowded, mothers with babies, tulips in bloom everywhere, the spring lambs grazing in the field (I just made that up).

However, Yuri is not here to shake us down when we find our table, and Blanche seems a little worried, her bracelets jangling more than usual.

"You don't think he's dead, do you?" she asks while I'm setting up the game board.

Now, Yuri isn't in the first bloom of youth, but I think he's got a lot of good years left in him. I usually weigh in on the optimistic side of longevity. "He's fine."

Blanche looks at me, considers my answer, and finally nods. "He's dead. I feel it"—she strikes a fist to her chest—"here."

I have to say, I'm tired of dealing with all this stress. Megs's maybe-baby. Mom's visit. Marv's problems with the SEC. Helping Amy out. It weighs heavy on a person. And now here's Blanche, my friend, who thinks she's lost her one true love.

"There's no reason to think he's dead, Blanche. You're just making something out of nothing." I'd like to think we're all making something out of nothing.

"You truly believe that?" she asks, giving me her big-eyed stare.

I wave my hand. "Of course," I lie. "Can we get back to the game?"

Blanche feels better, but I've got the willies. I mean, for two years, I've had my own paradise on earth. But recently, it's just one disaster after another.

To take my mind off things, I put my queen in serious jeopardy three times. Blanche misses them all, which worries me even further. She's a vindictive opportunist, which is why I love her so much.

"It's your move," I say, after sitting quietly for about ten minutes, which is about the extent of what I can tolerate without either screaming or needing to hit the toilets, neither of which is a good idea in Central Park.

"No, V, I just went."

I blink and look at the board, double-checking the layout. Everything is exactly the same.

"No, I moved my pawn to D4. It's your turn."

She stares at the board, shaking her head. "I could have sworn that I moved."

"Nope."

She picks up her queen, ready to take my queen, and then she puts it back down. "I've been forgetting things lately."

"Well, yeah, like how to play chess, for instance."

She picks up the queen, I hold my breath. She puts it back down, I exhale. "I'm not sure if I turned my coffeepot off."

I roll my eyes and pretend this is not a big deal. "Blanche, this is normal. Everyone forgets that. That's why they invented automatic shutoff."

She picks up her queen. I have learned my lesson and no longer hold my breath, merely contenting myself with watching the bangles around her wrist move back and forth. "I lost my hat last week on the bus."

"You actually rode the bus?" I ask, thinking that Blanche *has* really lost it.

"I've been doing it for several years now. You're a snob, V."

There are worse things to be called. For instance, the Devil's Own Handmaiden. "Blanche, do you think I'm really a snob?"

"You're a snob, V. Get over it."

"Does being a snob make me a bad person? I mean, what if I did something even worse? What if, for instance, I sold my soul to the devil?"

Oh, God. I did it. I hold my breath. I actually told someone. I look around, checking for the flames of hell, something to indicate that I just did a Very Bad Thing in Lucy's Book of Bad Things That Should Not Be Done. There are no flames, only a curious sensation inside me. A moment of freedom. It feels kinda nice.

Blanche looks up, her queen still in hand. "No man is worth the loss of your self-respect, V. Don't turn yourself into a slut."

And back to reality. "What the hell you talking about, Blanche?" I can't believe this. I'm trying to make a confession here, and she turns into Carrie fucking Bradshaw. "I said I sold my soul, not my body."

"Your soul? Am I supposed to understand what we're talking about? What soul?"

"You know, the one inside me."

"What did you do, V? Really."

"I told you, I sold my soul to the devil."

"Yes, we've already covered that. Now then, exactly how did you sell your soul? What did you really do?"

"I signed some papers. . . . She made a lot of promises. It all sounded really good." As the words come tumbling out of my mouth, I realize how naive I was to believe Lucy. But you should meet her, she's very earnest. I suppose that's how she got so big.

"Is she some shylock named Gotti? Your business in trouble?"

You know, it's very difficult talking to Blanche. I don't confide to many people, though, so maybe it's just me. "My business is fine. Lucy took care of all that."

Blanche gets really still and stares at the board. After a few minutes she looks back up at me. "This Lucy. She your business partner, or . . . something more? You know, this day and age, it's anything goes, but I'd still expect to meet her. I don't like the idea of you getting involved with somebody I don't approve of. Not counting Marv, you're really all the family I have."

"She's just the devil, Blanche. She's not a lesbian."

Blanche nods, and sucks her lip until it disappears. "Good. When you insert homosexuality into female friendships, it goes all wonky."

"Can we talk about my soul here?"

"V, I know you're in trouble, and I know that it's serious, and when you're ready to tell me the whole story, I'm here for you."

And that's it, the conversation is kaput. I don't know what I'm doing telling her my darkest secret anyway, because it's not like Blanche is going to be able to help me.

"You know, I've been helping Marv."

She moves her knight and spears me with a look. "That's what he said. Thank you for helping him."

"You're welcome, Blanche."

Then she lifts her queen and takes mine without any regrets.

"Blanche, you're heartless."

She smiles as she takes my ten dollars, and I notice the bracelets aren't shaking quite so much anymore. "I know."

Sunday night is my date, and I know you're thinking, well, V, I already know that, but I feel like I should remind you again, so you can experience my moment. Lately I haven't had so many, so I must relive it many times.

Nathaniel picks me up at my apartment, and we take the subway (ugh!) to the restaurant. I survive the vibratious ride only by checking out my date. He has an aura of potent sexuality that rises above his fashion sense. I have to say, I like the way he watches me. His eyes cover me all the time, and I think at any moment he's going to jump me, but in a good way. Most New York men (unless they're very drunk) think they must conceal their passion or they will be branded uncool. There are unspoken rules of cool in this city, and sometimes the rules really suck.

I survive the subway, and we arrive at a cute little Italian place on the Lower East Side, which you'll never read about in any papers, except the freebies they try and throw at you on the subway.

Over dinner we talk more about things that I have skimmed from CNN. Nathaniel is very into the world and has an opinion on everything. Eventually the talk turns to my favorite subject: me.

"Have you lived in New York all your life?" he asks.

Now this one is a tricky question. I never admit to actually domiciling in Jersey, except to those who already know. It adds a facet to my personality that I would rather deny. "Not all my life," I answer. "Where'd you grow up?"

"Trenton."

I eye him with new respect. He has transcended his Jerseyness and shaped his life into something more meaningful, which I believe is a genetic anomaly. I lean in low over the table and check for prying eyes before admitting my second-most-secret secret. "I'm from Jersey as well. Hoboken."

He pulls me closer to whisper in my ear: "I know."

I pull back, shocked. "That's impossible."

"It's your accent."

Immediately I close my mouth. My mouth always gets me in trouble. However, I can't keep it shut for long either. "But just my accent, right? I mean, nothing else gave me away. Did it?"

"Saving the girl was a big clue. Most rich bitches from the city wouldn't mess up their clothes."

See, statements like this indicate his distaste for the icons of

New York style and fashion, of which I am one, and I wonder what he's doing with me. Can sexual chemistry of Jurassic proportions overshadow giant cultural inequalities? I would like to explore this conundrum further, preferably in a physical manner. "You're making too much out of nothing," I say and switch the conversation to something else besides me, which shows just how much I am actually bothered.

I am selfish. I am wicked. Most important, I am going to hell, and there's not a damned thing I can do about it. Nathaniel knows I'm wicked, he knows I am selfish, but when you delve past the lust in his eyes, there is something else there when he looks at me. That something else is a little scary because it gives me hope, and that's just fucking moronic. So later that evening, I decide to show Nathaniel a little piece of my reality.

The club is known as Plaid. There is a line to get in, but I glide through. The DJ is some rapper wearing lots of gold (I know, you say, "V, be more specific," but I truly can't. I look silly dancing to it, and I'm not into the whole "ho, bitch, death" way of life).

Nathaniel does not even attempt to dance, but instead sits and watches the crowds with anthropological eyes. There is a Sally Johns clone in the corner, left over from Studio 54. Whoops, that really is Sally Johns. You could bounce a quarter off those cheekbones. What the older women are doing these days to look good. I shake my head. It's pitiful, truly pitiful.

On the far side of the floor is a British actress who I think

Lucy wants in the program. She's making out with another actress who I'm guessing is already in the program. A group of hockey players are guzzling bottles of Cristal like it's water. Yeah, I know. Why are they drinking champagne? Obviously no clients among them, or the Rangers would have the Stanley Cup as well. An SNL alum is sitting alone, eyes dilated and glazed.

Rolf appears, my favorite martini in his hand, and strikes up a flirtatious conversation. It's a meaningless PR exercise, but Nathaniel is not wise to the ways of the meaningless world. He stands behind me, a protective gesture, which is nice, but considering that my Level 3 powers could knock anybody senseless, it's not really necessary. However, I let him do it because the security of Nathaniel behind me is delicious.

Rolf is in the state of nervous sobriety when you notice that everyone around you is either way cooler than you or else so drunk they don't care. I don't envy him his insecurities. "It's a crush tonight," he says. "So crowded you can't even breathe." I know what that means. He's going to stay all night and make sure the papers get some mention of him copping a feel with a member of the female persuasion. Considering the way he's eyeing me, I think I might be the top contender. When it rains, it pours. I flash Rolf a smile of consolation because he ain't getting any from me and send him on his way.

"Why're we here?" asks Nathaniel when we're alone again, or at least as alone as you can be with eight hundred people nearby. The "something else" in his eyes is changing to suspicion and wariness. Suspicion and wariness I can handle. This is progress.

"I thought you'd enjoy some of the hot spots."

He shakes his head. "Let's go."

Life would be much easier if he were as impressed as he should be. Instead, I think I disappointed him. On the way out, two more male acquaintances come and say hello, which usually involves a lengthy kiss (more PR) and lots of touchy stuff. By the time we leave, Nathaniel is pretty well steamed, but I feel I have done my job. I have erased all traces of the "something else" from his eyes.

After Plaid, we take a cab to the park and walk. It wouldn't be my first choice, but I go along with him. I can't exorcise Nathaniel from my life completely. There is a life-preserver quality about him, and I feel the need to cling.

Nathaniel is quiet and introspective as we walk. I, knowing that introspection is not good for the soulless, choose to pry.

"Plaid wasn't your cup of tea?"

He shakes his head, and his mouth curves into a mocking smile. "That's your idea of fun, not mine."

We walk along the path that leads to my building, and my hand curls into his, which is about as close as I come to an apology. His is warm and strong, with rough calluses that speak of hard work. Most male hands that I come in contact with are manicured and soft. My female parts are intrigued by the idea of rough calluses, but I suspect that tonight is not going to end happily for said parts.

The city is never quiet, but sometimes late at night you can press a mute button and pretend you're alone. "You want to tell me what your idea of fun is?" I ask.

"V, why're you doing this?"

"Walking in the park? Well, it's a nice night—"

He cuts me off and backs me against a tree, which normally is a little more forceful than I prefer, but he makes me feel all girly, and yeah, I'm thinking a little somethin', somethin'.

"Is there a boyfriend, some Scottish movie star or underwear model you need to make jealous?" he asks, like I'm toying with his affections. My hips migrate to his affections, and his eyes turn smoky.

"There's no underwear models nearby, and unless there's a photographer behind that tree, I'd say we're all alone, or at least as alone—"

I don't get any further. Nathaniel has an effective way of shutting me up. His mouth is as hard as his hands, not smooth or cajoling, no, it's all just him. I've experienced desire, but I've never experienced all-consuming need before. I try and turn it into something I understand, a straightforward seduction, but he's not in on the plan. Longing seeps into my blood, warming me from the heat and chilling me with fear.

When I realize he won't be dissuaded, my fear rises fourfold, and I start to fight him.

Fear seems to work, and he pulls back, licking his lips, his breathing heavy. "Shit." Which isn't exactly what I want to hear. "I don't want to get involved with you." Which isn't exactly what I want to hear either.

"I don't remember me asking you to," I say in a prissy voice.

"You don't understand, V. Hell, I don't understand. I'm leaving in two months."

I fake a good laugh. "You're worrying too much."

"I don't trust you," he says, which cuts to the heart of the problem.

Normally such insults from someone whose hands are all over me would piss me off. However, I'm glad he doesn't trust me. It means he's not stupid.

I play the femme fatale, running my hands up his chest, feeling his muscles dance under my wicked touch. "We just go mild. No big whoop." I suspect mild is all I can handle from him.

He puts a hand on my face, pushing the hair back, leaving me feeling more exposed than I like. "You don't inspire mild in me. More like crazy."

Crazy? Really? I swear I'm not using my powers here. "We could take things one day at a time," I answer easily, like it's just another walk in the park. My heart is beating so loud, I swear they can hear it in Philly, and I wish I could just kick him out of my life. He's a complication I don't need right now. Unfortunately, he's become a need, too.

"I could do one day at a time," he tells me.

Slowly we walk back to my place. I know Mom is home, and I cast a peeved glare at my window, because I don't think she realizes what she's costing me here.

But what's wrong with being a little slow? Yeah, I know I'm the queen of instant gratification, but Nathaniel is a man who needs to be savored. Also, I have built up a fantasy in my mind of one night with him, a night where he can actually touch my soul.

At the door, he gives me a last kiss. I shoot him a wistful smile. "If my mother weren't visiting."

He looks at me like I'm the cherry in his dessert. "Another time."

I don't say anything else, but float up to the thirty-seventh floor.

I find myself wanting to be alone, just so I can remember everything all over again. My mother stays in her room, and I can hear the theme music from *Access Hollywood*.

I try to fall asleep, but tonight the hot flashes are worse than usual. I suspect it's me longing for things I can't have. Eventually I convince myself that it doesn't matter and fall into the precarious sleep of the damned.

Nine

In the battle of the tabloids, nothing is sacred. A certain West Coast editor from hell has seen the light and was spotted loitering outside the halls of the Beverly Hills Church of Scientology. So will this new-found conversion affect her hard-hitting journalistic techniques? Ha. Even God couldn't reform this devil-child.

Ouch, ouch, ouch. Political fund-raisers can be the death of a politician, especially when he's caught taking money from a certain Saudi national who is rumored to be "less than friendly" to the U.S. My prediction? Two female senators for the great state of New York by 2008. You heard it here first.

> *At the Time-Warner Center yesterday (or the Mall, as we city types call it), the first daughter appeared for lunch, Secret Service in tow. And apparently she's a charter member of the I Love V fan club. Her exuberant squeals were heard in Red Hook (did you know she was a squealer? I didn't). Get on the waiting list fast, because the Sonata bag is going to be hotter than hell.*

On Monday I go to my store, and yes, the lines outside are longer than at the annual Manolo Blahnik sale. I pull my Michael Kors fur around me and swish past the crowds, enduring the hushed whispers and a smattering of golf-link applause with true aplomb. As I make my way through, I remove my sunglasses and wave. "Please, stop," I say, with a "please-don't" wrist-flick, before finally ducking inside.

The glow of adoration is still around me as a man dances in from the back rooms, a purple cape draped around his neck. It is the designer formerly known as Paolo.

"I saw the item in the *Post* today. You are the Liza to my David," he says, then puts his hands in front of his face. "Ew! Don't hit!"

My cell phone rings, so I am saved being rude.

"*V, it's Meegan.*"

"Megs, are you okay? Did you bloom up three sizes overnight or anything?"

"V? I can't hear you."

"Megs?"

"V, are you still there?"

I walk over to the window, searching the Verizon for a clear channel. The crowd thinks I'm there to be friendly and they wave, *Today Show* style. I opt not to be a bitch and wave back.

"Megs? Can you hear me now?"

She has hung up.

The crowd is still staring at me, so for another three minutes I pretend to chat and then with a loud ta-ta, I snap the phone shut.

Fucking cell.

"Sweetie, Amy called and left a mah-ssage for you. She'll be here for lunch to chitchat about the auction. And then Regina Bassano came by. Cow city. Moo." Then he giggles, which is just too over the top.

I study him carefully. "Are you holding out on me?"

He makes a three-point moue with his mouth, which no man with a stubbly jaw should do. "Nothing."

"What did Regina say?"

He zips his lips. "Si-lence."

"Paolo. Do you *like* her?" (I swear, sometimes he acts like a schoolboy.)

"She doesn't have enough lunch meat in the deli case."

"Paolo, you are not gay. There is no one here but me. It's all right. You can be yourself."

He drops the swish. "All right. Yeah, she's hot," he mutters.

Here I am thinking the woman is très Baldwinesque, and he

wants to jump her. There is absolutely no accounting for tastes. I watch him as he putters around the display shelves, hand on hip, buttocks flexed. How sad to be trapped in a life that is a lie.

"You're a good man, Paolo."

"V, V. When did you turn into Dorothy? I'm a heartless prick."

I know that tone, so I humor him. "Of course you are," I say, patting his hand, and we don't say anything more about it.

Amy shows up seventeen minutes late, which surprises me, because as a rule people are not late to meet me, especially those people who are after my cachet.

"V!" she says as she makes her grand entrance. Then she does the euro-trash kiss on both cheeks. "You look fabulous! Ready to go kick some homeless butt?"

I now decide that Amy is truly a fun person, and we link arms, which is not something I'd ever do as a rule, but her enthusiasm is contagious. "Let's go!"

We slum a ride in a cab. The car service was not an option because my phone was out of range. However, in the forty-five minutes it takes us to get uptown, I bond with Amy. She is such a suck-up, but in an honest and caring way, which makes it work. I tell her that Regina and Calvin will be helping out, and her eyes glaze over because she has never heard of these people and could care less. When I mention Nobu and dinner, her eyes unglaze.

We end up lunching with every other New York post-Atkins blond at Payard Patisserie on Lex.

"So what drew you to charity and this do-good life-style?" I ask as I take my fourth bite of braised rabbit. I am curious about her because, from all outward appearances, she is a decent upstanding human being with an appreciation for those less fortunate than her. I knew that species existed, just not in Gotham.

"I was a soap opera writer, and I needed to find something a little more real. Every day it was my job to invent some new crisis, but I wanted to make a difference. I wanted to solve problems, instead of writing them up in a script," she says, and then shoots me one of those "know what I mean?" looks.

I nod wisely and keep my mouth shut.

After the waitperson takes our plates (Payard has notoriously bad service unless you're on the A-list, which, of course, I am), she takes out her pen and paper. "So what were you thinking about the fund-raiser? A fashion show?"

I've given this a lot of thought. I know exactly what to do. "Not a fashion show. An auction. We'll do divas, dinners, and dresses."

She leans back against the candy-striped banquette, catches her own eye in the mirrors on the walls, and grins. "Sounds divine."

I shrug. "Of course."

Next stop is the Lower Manhattan Women's Shelter, which is on the fourth floor of a small, nondescript building on Christopher Street. For a place where poor people hang out, it seems pretty nice.

"Have you been here before?" I ask, for no other reason than to make polite conversation.

"No."

"Why this place?"

"I picked it out of the phone book. I just decided that I was going to let fate take over, so I opened the book to "Charitable Organizations" and let my finger fall."

Alrighty, then. I take a deep breath.

The owner/manager/person in charge, Tamsin, is a very, very young girl who seems idealistic, yet world-weary, like a reader at the Bowery Poetry Club. I'm sure she doesn't eat red meat or shave under her arms, either. She is excited about the auction. After looking at the shabby furniture, I can understand the thrill.

Tamsin takes us on the tour, and then Amy wants to speak to some of the women there, "just to get a feel for the place, and how best to position the evening's festivities."

I'm impressed with her energy, which I suspect may be Ritalin, but I should not judge. . . .

We first meet Sandra, who is an older black woman with very sad eyes. Amy, who has only one gear, is immediately enthused and starts clapping. "Can you tell us why you're here and how LMWS has helped you?"

Sandra talks about her first husband, who was a one-night stand who beat her up, and how she is trying to kick a bad heroin habit.

Amy frowns, and then her eyes light up. "What about a broken arm?"

Everyone stares, but Amy continues on into oblivion, her hands laying out the scene for us all. "Her first husband, Alfonz, beat her horrifically for a period of two years, while she tried to escape. Eventually, she shot him in self-defense but was acquitted in the trial, where it was revealed that the real killer was her long-lost yet still devoted brother. And we need a kid. Do you have a kid?"

Sandra, who now looks depressed because she is *not* a single mother, shakes her head, so Amy turns to me. "We could hire an extra for the show."

"I just do fashion," I pipe in, but Amy's not ready to concede.

After we finish arguing over child actors, we meet Svetlana, a mail-order bride who hails from the old country. She doesn't speak English, but Tamsin translates the Russian for us.

Amy furiously takes notes. "How long was she married?"

After a brief foray into words I don't understand, Tamsin says, "Seven years."

"That's a long time," says Amy, frowning. She walks around Svetlana, a gleam in her eyes. "What if her husband was gay? Or maybe a father who she never knew and there was incest. Oh, yeah, that's much better. Of course, we'd have to do that in a flashback, but it could be done tastefully. . . ."

Tamsin looks appalled. I see the fight brewing, and I pull her to one side. "Tam, look, you want to do what's right for these women, right?"

She nods reluctantly, and I continue. "Here's the deal. Amy can make you a shitload of money that will keep these women in pork and beans for a helluva lot longer than you're going to be around. You have to step above your personal code of ethics and sacrifice yourself for the cause. You believe in the cause, don't you, Tamsin?"

Tamsin is digging in her crepe-soled heels. "I don't like it."

I shot her my "no shit" look. "Who does? But you can't argue with success. It's bigger than you. It's bigger than your morals. You just have to work within the system as dictated by the American media conglomerates. Trust me on this. I know what I'm talking about."

Eventually she comes around, and by the end of the afternoon, I am convinced that Amy will make a fortune for the poor, star-crossed women of the Lower Manhattan Women's Shelter. With a little creative PR, I can see a reality TV spot for some of these ladies. What Lucy could do for these lost souls . . .

I remember the two souls I promised Shelby, and I'm thinking that Svetlana and Sandra would actually move a gazillion steps up in the world if they were introduced into the program. However, this soul-recruitment business has gotten me in a bit of a bind, and I'm currently putting the brakes on it until I determine (a) if Meggers is preggers, (b) if the answer to (a) = yes, does that mean the end of the world is an imminent threat, and should I be concerned? and lastly, yet most importantly, (c) why am I feeling bad about taking souls? These people get everything they want. For instance, Meegan is getting her baby. I am the It-est of New York's It Girls, so why should I worry? Svetlana and Sandra could live life beyond their wildest dreams. I frown, because no matter how fancy I trim it out, I still feel bad.

*   *   *

The following two weeks are good. Sales are brisk, Nathaniel is attentive, and Mom is staying out of my way. Other than Meegan and the possible vindication of the prophecies of Nostradamus, I can't complain.

Finally it comes down to PG in Dumbo day. After Meegan visits her therapist, she's going to take her at-home pregnancy test. I run over to her place to hold her hand (metaphorically speaking only—you have to pee on those sticks, and handholding's just not in the realm of things I want to do).

Meegan, of course, is a total wreck. She is sitting in her gliding rocker, knitting booties and listening to Eminem. "I shouldn't listen to you, V. I'm so nervous, I think I'm going to pee."

"Save it for the stick," I tell her. Then I paste a confident yet cheerful smile on my face. "We're in this together, Meegan, whatever happens." I figure loyalty is the least I owe her, since I'm the one who brought her to Lucy's attention in the first place.

Carefully she stows her knitting in the little Lambsy Divy bag at her feet and stands.

I open the instrument and hand it to her. Her chin lifts, she looks me in the eye. She wants this kid so badly. It tears out my heart to know that she's in a lose-lose situation and doesn't even know it.

I give her a nervous smile, which is about as good as I get, and then send her into the bathroom with a large glass of water.

I stare at my watch, counting the seconds. It's times like

these when I should reexamine the things I've done, look back on my actions, and maybe learn something. But sometimes you can't look back. Sometimes the brain won't let you, because it knows you can't handle the absolute horror of the mess you potentially have made. So I sit there, watching the second hand limp across the numbers, until Meegan returns.

The stick's in her hand, and I mark the time. We sit in silence, staring at the little insubstantial strip of plastic—Meegan, hoping against hope that she is. Me, tilting at my windmills that she's not. Just then the little blue line starts to appear.

Well, shit.

Instantly Meegan morphs from zombie woman into party girl. She starts to grin and screams and then turns to hug me. Like a trooper, I endure it all.

There is no pointing out the error of her way. She is in a place of elevated hormones and hope for the future that I have never seen. If she weren't going to go down in the history books as the woman responsible for the demise of civilization, I could envy her this happiness.

"Do you think it'll be a boy or a girl? Oh, and I need to get the nursery ready. I like yellow. Do you think she'll like yellow? Oh, God. What am I thinking? It's a false positive. I can't get pregnant. Oh, V, I can't be pregnant."

"Go to your doctor. Get tested again." I give her a really big smile, with lots of teeth. "But I bet it comes back positive, too."

"V, I'm glad you're here for this. My own little miracle." Yeah, little does she know.

Meegan wants to go see Shelby and share the joy. After a pregnant pause, I offer to take her drinking instead.

"V! I can't drink anymore."

I look at her, pretending confusion. "Really? Because of the baby?"

"Yeah. I'm going to be careful. Very, very careful. This is my chance."

"I don't see where a shot of tequila, or even forty-seven, would do any harm. Just to celebrate."

She thinks I'm joking and ignores me. "Let's go tell Shelby."

"How about after dinner?" I say, and then go into the kitchen to find a glass of water for her. After I pick out a plastic Yankees cup and fill it up, I begin to work my magic. This baby can't see the light of day.

Pennyroyal, cotton bark, wort of mug, douse this spark. Purest water, ever clear, make this baby disappear.

"Here. Drink this."

Because Meegan is basically a good person, and trusts me way too much, she drinks quickly.

There is a stoned smile on her face, which lasts until the effect of the chemicals wear off. Before she comes out of it, I get rid of the evidence, washing the cup out in the kitchen. By the time I sit down next to her, she's way less stoned, and she's curious.

"What did I just drink?"

I smile tightly. "Prenatal water. It's got all sorts of stuff that's good for you."

I wait around in her apartment for a couple of hours

watching the Baby Channel. Eventually it dawns on me that the spell didn't work. Knowing Lucy, this is the only egg in the world that can't be broken.

I go home to my apartment, and Mother is there, smoking like a chimney and watching TV.

"You want a martini?" I ask her.

She taps her cigarette on the ashtray. "You drink too much, V. I've told you before."

"Lay off me tonight, Mom."

She looks like she's about to say something and then stops. "I talked to your father today."

Suddenly things are looking up. "That's good news. What did he say?"

"Laurie's pressing him to get married." She looks away because she doesn't want me to see that she's hurting. When I was growing up, I always saw her looking away, but I never thought about her hurting.

"I'm sorry," I tell her because somehow Mother always seemed invincible.

"Can I stay with you for a while?"

"Of course," I answer, knowing it will give me great pains. However, Mother is no more invincible than me. And to be fair to the little shrunken dwarf-person (not meaning to offend little dwarves, only my mother), it hasn't been that bad.

"I'll find a job."

"I can help you. You could work at the shop if you wanted."

She shakes her head. "I think we'd kill each other. Bad for business. Maybe I should move into a hotel?"

This time I shake my head. "You can stay here, Mom. It's okay. And I'll try not to kill you." I give her a weak smile. "I'm tired. I think I'm going to go to bed."

"You had a bad day?"

"Nah. Nothing I couldn't handle. See you in the morning."

I poof another martini, but even the hard kick of a double martini doesn't ease the pit of fire in my stomach. There's a part of me that really wants to save the world. A small part that wants me to be somebody better than who I really am. How did this happen? I don't know.

Unfortunately, that's just me tilting at my windmills, because the only thing I've been able to save is—well, nothing actually, unless you count the damned dog, and he could swim.

I sit on my bed in the dark, watching the sunset turn the city skyline into fire. Trust me when I say, It's not pretty. You know how most mothers will tell their kids not to play with the stove? Well, my mother told me to touch it, so I'd learn not to. That's been my motto ever since.

However, this time I'm the one who touched the stove, but it's Meegan who's going to end up getting burned.

Just as I'm about to nod off, the phone rings. It's Shelby.

"V, can you believe it?"

"Megs?"

"You betcha. She got knocked up. She said 'she knew.' I think it's weird. Glad I'm not pregnant, I barely have enough time to take care of my own life without someone else."

"Yeah, Shelby," I mutter.

"I'm thinking of starting a dog accessory line. I think I could go really far with it."

"Sounds nice."

"But there's like ten thousand things to worry about. I think I need some help. Do you have a personal assistant?" she asks.

"Yes, my mother."

"You think she'd work for me, too?" Shelby, who has never met my mother, asks.

"I don't know," I say. "She's really expensive."

For Shel, money always equates to quality. She's never met the Donald in person, I bet. "That's okay. I can afford her."

"Let me talk to her and get back to you."

"Good, you can tell me tomorrow."

"What's tomorrow?"

"Harry is on me about the plastic surgery; he called me turkey-throat. The nerve."

I could have told her about Harry. His mean streak is no surprise.

She continues: "I called Lucy and explained my sitch. She wants to meet me at your store tomorrow at one. It's time for you to ante up the two souls, sweetie."

Ten

According to sources, the previous first daughter (code name Energy) is not happy about the party press that seems to accompany the second daughter, Twinkle wherever she lights. Overheard at her London Terrace Towers apartment: "You know, she always makes the papers, but I'm a fun person, too. I can party just like the next First Kid. I've been drunk before. Honest."

The cat-claws were drawn and dripping blood when two West Coast teen queens happened upon each other at Triple X. Numerous sources have paired Johnny Midnight with a certain young teen queen, who seems to enjoy smoking his cigar. As he began to serenade H, "L," in a bit of pubes-

cent-girls-gone-wild rage, jumped her main-screen rival and began to pull her hair. Mr. Midnight said nothing, but did watch the whole melee with a devilish smile on his face.

The revival of South Pacific will be hitting the boards this summer, and the tickets are going fast. However, Nellie's part is being recast. The first name being bandied around is a certain Hairspray torch singer. It'd be new, it'd be daring . . . is it going to happen? Sadly, no.

Tuesdays are never my favorite day of the week. Knowing that Lucy and Shelby will be waiting for me when I arrive at my store is going to be one of the high moments of my life, right up there with watching *The Brown Bunny* in the theater. I consider what to wear for the start of soul-hunting season. Perhaps something in traditional Ascot black and white, or a more patriotic/war-mongering camouflage? I conjure up a darling little white Valentino number that is innocent, yet dramatic as well. I'm still in the middle of my soul-recruitment moratorium, and I am determined not to be steamrolled today. It will take cunning and brains to stay one step ahead of Lucy, but I'm going to try.

The store looks like Times Square on New Year's Eve (without the drunken revelry, party hats, and sodden confetti). My staff is busy busting their little butts just so that I can make a fortune today. For a moment I am lost in my inner mogul and forget my own troubles, but then Lucy comes through the door, sporting her newest Satanista-in-training, Shelby. My troubles are remembered.

"V! Darling!" Lucy is all huggy-kissy, and Shelby is watching my customers with the gleaming eyes of a professional shopper with somebody else's plastic. My eyes leap to her throat, but she's wearing a scarf to hide the throat-dongle.

Paolo, the coward, stays in the back, hiding. Lucy wanders through the crowds, doing what she does best (I swear, she works a crowd better than Oprah). In less than ten seconds, she returns, with an East Side nanny under her wing.

"V, Shelby, this is Monica, and she'll be having dinner with us this evening." She turns to Monica. "I'm assuming you don't have plans."

Monica, too starstruck to know better, shakes her head. I stand quietly and keep my mouth shut, which is not normally something I do well. Monica is a college student, pursuing a degree in childhood education, but hates her job (Welcome to America!).

Shelby steps in and handles the particulars, reciting the credo from the soul-free handbook. Everything is couched in terminology you'd hear on a 2:00 A.M. infomercial. And I quote:

"We at Life Enrichment Enterprises believe in the superiority of the human intellect over the transfiguring mumbo-jumbo that has been promised by other big names for centuries. And where are the documented results? There are none. The Life Enrichment Program is simple and successful—because it works."

Monica buys it all, hook, line, and sucker.

After Monica, there is Caroline, then Candy, then Mandy. My corner gets smaller and smaller. At this rate, Shelby will be a Level 9 before my shop closes, and I will still be considering whether I should be participating in this at all, in light of my previously steadfast soul-recruitment moratorium.

Lucy keeps her eye on me, and I think she's doing the mind-reading thing again. I keep my judgments to myself and stare at the floor, stare at the ceiling. Then a spark of an idea hits me.

I wait till Lucy is occupied and go find Paolo in the back, surfing Web porn.

"Paolo!"

He jumps.

"You scared me!" he says, trying to block the screen from my view.

"I need matches. Do you have matches?"

He holds out his hand, and matches appear. "Hello? Spell. Magic. Remember?"

I have a short *duh* moment, which tells you how flustered I am.

I pull out the wastebasket and start dropping matches in as fast as I can.

"Uh, excuse me, not the best way to meet firemen, V."

I look up at him, and he's scared. I don't blame him, but I'm done being used like some soul pimp. In my soulful days, I never liked being used. Not by Johnny Petrocelli behind the junior high gym, nor by Helga, the bitch-secretary in my accounting office, who wanted me to cover for her two-hour lunches. Since I sold my soul, however, it seems like I'm getting used right and left.

"Get off your ass and help me," I snap.

He still doesn't want to participate in my hara-kiri, but by now I have the flames well in hand. I look up, waiting for the sprinklers to turn on.

And wait.

And wait.

And wait.

I use the morning paper (the *Post*, of course) to fan the flames. The trickle of smoke begins to blossom into a full-fledged cloud, that is slllloooooooooooooooooowly rising to the ceiling.

Paolo, who thinks much better on his feet, just runs into the front, screaming, "Fire!"

I'm here to tell you, everything you've read about yelling "Fire" in a crowded bag store is absolutely true.

Instantly the women run for the door, stilettos flying, elbows gouging, trampling one another. It's a warehouse sale at Barney's gone bad.

The little trashcan that could is now puffing wildly, great cumuli of smoke billowing everywhere, tiny flames licking at the walls, the ceiling already starting to turn black.

The back room's ceiling is pretty much totaled, but all the souls have flown the coop. Pocketbooks are strewn everywhere, belt displays toppled—all in all, it's a mess.

I've temporarily ruined my store, but no souls were taken in the making of this movie. It's a small stand for my principles, but it counts.

Lucy looks my way, and I hide my look of satisfaction. Not stupid here. I know Lucy is pissed because she swears, and that's not something that she normally does, but then she recovers. She waves her hand, and it starts to rain inside the store, the flames fizzling to nothingness.

She can do weather? I am amazed. That is so cool. Then she turns that dark hellfire gaze in my direction to determine the cause of my smallish disaster, and I quake, but only for a moment. One hand sneaks behind my back, and I conjure up a burning cigarette. Then, in a masterful bit of drama, I bring it to my lips.

"I didn't know you smoked, V," she says, her voice like velvet over steel.

I inhale, feeling my lungs start to decompose. "Of course," I croak, still working to keep the nicotine inside me. One poof, and my charade will be exposed. "That's how the whole fire got started. Butt. Trashcan. Sparks."

She just watches me, waiting for my mistake.

I clear my head of all random thoughts (harder than you'd think) and pray that Lucy will leave soon.

Shel starts to cough from the burning leather smell in the air and then runs for some water.

I'm going to owe Shel big-time for that, because Lucy gets distracted and I breathe.

Then she looks back at me, and I suck it back in. "The damage isn't bad. You can open again before the week is out."

I swallow, and the world turns a little woozy, so I fan my face. "I think I must have inhaled some smoke. I'll probably get asthma now."

"I thought it was going well before the chaos effect took over."

"You were awesome," I say, because sucking up is never a bad idea, and I think I may have fooled her.

Unfortunately, I am wrong. "You're back to a Level 2, V. Don't try it again." Then she starts to walk away.

Oh, yeah. So what's she going to do? Ground me?

She wheels around and fixes me with a glare that has probably turned lesser women into stone. "Don't piss me off, V. You're not smart enough; you're not brave enough. And most of all, you're only a Level 2. With big hips."

Fuck.

Slowly I feel my butt expand, and my Valentino skirt pulls tight. Why is she torturing me like this? Why can't she leave me alone?

That seems to amuse her, because she walks out the door, laughing.

Bitch.

Less than thirty minutes later I'm sitting in an anonymous bar in Soho, getting drunk. I can't go home (depressed mother from hell), I can't go to work (burned to hell), I can't call Meegan (the mother of hell), and I can't call Shelby (who's going to hell).

Fuck.

Outside, everyone seems to be enjoying the sunlight, enjoying the fresh air.

Fuck.

Fuck, fuck, fuck.

A little girl looks at me and reads my lips. Her mother is horrified and hurries her away. I laugh because I think a little corruption is good for the soul. I mean, look where it got me. Across the street I see Caroline, one of the possible recruits, peering into the posh window of Prada. She turns around and sees me and waves.

She is soulful, because of me.

I don't feel like company, so I don't acknowledge her. Eventually she looks embarrassed, like she's made a mistake, and moves away, never knowing how close she came to being damned.

I raise up my martini glass in a silent toast to the soulful of the world. Cheers.

"'Nother round?"

The bartender is tall and hunky. Another wannabe actor. Why is it that everyone in New York is a wannabe? Are there any be's in New York at all? That's only a rhetorical question; I know the answer is no.

"You're an actor, right?" I ask.

"No. I'm studying to be an accountant."

I start to laugh. "You should be an actor. You'll get more respect in this town."

He gestures to my previously pristine Valentino. "Have you been playing in ashes?"

It hits me that I am covered in soot, and I'm just about to do my clean-up spell when I notice the approval in his face.

Tall, hunky, not-a-wannabe guy is okay with my wet appearance, and even my larger-than-usual ass.

I practice a little self-discipline and survey my ashes (okay, I have another martini, too).

After my third martini, my cell rings, and it's Lucy. Of course, when the devil calls, the reception is crystal-clear.

"V, I'm having a dinner party next week. The best of New York's literati. I need you there, of course. And bring Meegan, will you? I've got a baby present for her."

I mumble something that could have been, "Eat shit and die, you demon cunt," but came out sounding more like, "Yeah, I'll be there."

"Boyfriend?" the bartender asks.

"Boss," I answer.

He nods in agreement, like he has the boss from hell, too. You haven't seen anything, buddy.

I cut myself off after one more martini, and leave Mr. Not-a-Wannabe a fat tip to help him through accounting school.

Outside, no cabs will touch me in ash-covered Valentino, and I'm thinking it's impossible to survive in this city without either magic or money, ideally both.

Resigned to my perfect life, I do my clean-up spell and add the sparkle of Tiffany at my neck and earlobes. The cabs are soon lined up three deep.

There's a lesson to be learned here, and I quote: "The Life Enrichment Program is simple and successful because it works."

* * *

I call Meegan, and she is thrilled about the dinner party. She fills me in on her latest. She went to see the doctor. And the verdict? Surprise, she's got both a healthy uterus and a healthy baby.

"You were right, V. I should listen to you more often."

Oh, yeah. Words to live by. I don't tell her about the baby present. Knowing Lucy, it's a scarlet christening gown from Versace.

I hang up and wander into the living room, where Mother is sitting on my couch, smoking and watching the Psychic Channel.

"Look what I got today."

She holds up the most butt-ugliest *objet de crap* that I have ever seen. It is a squatty little bowl with naked people on the side. "What is it?"

"It's a scrying bowl."

(Do you know what scrying is? It sounds both painful and sexual at the same time.) I look at my mother with new eyes. "You've been scrying lately, Mom?"

"I bought it from my psychic."

And my day just gets better. "Why are you seeing a psychic?"

"I thought it'd be good to know my future, whether I'll win the lottery, or maybe get that new mink hat I saw at Bloomingdale's. I need to move on. I like New York. I'm going to stay. Permanently."

(That scream of agony you just heard was me.)

"A psychic can't help you. No, you need a travel agent. Maybe someplace warm with the ocean."

"I live in Florida, V. I get that warm ocean stuff all year round. Besides, I have to start a new life without your father."

"You've got to fight for him, Mom. Why, just yesterday he was asking about you."

"Really?" she says, so hopeful and happy that I feel a teeny, tiny crack in my titanium heart.

"Of course," I lie and sit down next to her. I wish I were a Level 7, and capable of actual behavior modification, 'cause then I'd poof her and Dad together again. The separation is starting to take its toll on her, her skin sagging a bit around the eyes. That's me in twenty-five years (only I'll be taller). "Psychics are nothing but con artists, Mom."

She takes a long drag on her cigarette and then blows rings, which is a sure sign that something is wrong. When she turns to look, I'm surprised to see that there's a glimmer of something in her eyes. She's crying. "I don't know why I wanted to look into my future."

"Then don't."

"It's too late, V. I can't believe it."

"Mom, it's all superstitious nonsense," I say, but Mom's not moving. "What did she tell you?" I ask.

"That you were going to die soon."

Her voice is shaking, and you'd almost think she was human. But I understand her fear. I'm terrified of dying, too. I try to be practical. "Mom, of course you're going to die, but if you'd quit smoking, you'd add a few years to your life span."

Then I realize that the *sujet de mort* is not my mother. . . .
It's me.

Suddenly the yawning jaws of hell are opened just a bit too wide. Somehow I manage a laugh. "Do I look like I'm about to die, Mom?"

"With all that drinking you do . . ."

I don't tell her that my liver has long been pickled and is safe for many millions of years. "It's better than smoking."

"Don't preach to me on my vices," she says, but I do notice that she puts out the cigarette.

"You're the one who started the lecture, Mom."

"I don't want you to die, V. I know I haven't been the best mother to you . . ."

No shit.

". . . but you're my only daughter."

"Let's not talk about death today, hmm? Instead, let's talk about scrying. What is scrying? You know I've always wanted to know, but stupid me thought it was a Taiwanese food source."

She starts to sob, and I hope it's only theatrics, but eventually she's still crying and I'm sitting here like a bump on the couch, feeling more bumpish with each passing wail.

I reach out and pat her hand. Nothing overt, but the wails lessen.

Oh, fuck it. I give her hand a little squeeze. *A very small squeeze.*

Then she pulls me into a little person's version of a bear hug, and I endure it. Okay, maybe secretly I like it, but I'll never let her know it because she'll hold it over my head for a gazillion years and I'll never be able to win another argument again.

She must sense my return to normalcy because then she gets up from the couch, and sniffs. "Thank you."

"Don't mention it," I say, and knowing me and Mom, we won't.

Eleven

Nabokov said of critics, "It's a short walk from the hallelujah to the hoot." Apparently, it's an even shorter walk from the hoot to the hors d'oeuvres. At last night's New York Public Library literacy fund-raiser, there was an all-out brawl between a certain book reviewer from the Times and a certain famed New Yorkish lady scribe. It started as a simple protest at the lack of coverage for lady authors, but then turned dishy when she stuck his hand (his pen hand, mind you) in the dim sum dumplings. Her next book hits the shelves in August. We're guessing the Times will pan this one.

The latest rage hitting the surgical beautification offices are brow lifts, biodegradable hooks that truly get under the skin and keep the gloomy droops away. Unfortunately, the patent resolution on this case is starting to get very bloody as two of New York's top face men are battling tooth and nail to claim sole rights to the procedure. We're just waiting for the plaintiff to subpoena the client list, just to see if the rumors about you-know-who are true. . . .

And what daughter of the statesman from the Constitution State is eating for two now? Rumors of the baby's paternity include a well-known NASCAR driver, a New York chef whose wife might disapprove, and a little blue man from Mars. We'll be on top of this story as it develops. . . .

I spend Wednesday in a flurry of activity, getting the store cleaned and opened up. I wonder why I worked so hard, because by the time that Friday rolls around, no one has come through the door. It bothers me that we have no customers in our store, and I suspect this is Lucy's doing. This is the home of the Sonata bag, the hottest bag in New York. There should be demand. There is none.

I spend the morning mulling over my empty-store puzzle, since it's easier than contemplating what to do with Megs's baby.

My butt is fat, and my protégé (Shelby) is zooming past me in the soul-recruitment ladder of powers. I have decided that I'm going to talk to Lucy about my soul-recruitment moratorium. If she wants to make me a lifetime Level 2, okay, I can live with that, but she's got to stop jerking me (and my body parts) around.

Surprisingly, it's Paolo who provides a potent panacea to my pain. I hate all his wiseass remarks about my butt, but it helps to bond with someone whose depraved tendencies surpass even my own. I bother him in the back room, where he is glued to his computer monitor, on which two desperate housewives are seducing the pizza boy. You see why Paolo fits the bill nicely.

"Maybe we should do more branding. Like Gucci," I tell him.

"We have a brand. We make fucking good purses. That's our brand."

I'm not convinced. I have begun to read the papers. We lack marketing, and if I continue in my downward spiral of powers and coolness, then we will actually begin to need it. "They're doing Murakami fingernails at Warren Tricomi. Maybe we could have Sonata toes."

"You were never *in* marketing, were you?" asks Paolo.

I tilt my head. "No, I just kept the books."

Paolo turns around, and his eyes get wide. "Oh, my God, the sun, you're blocking the sun!!!" Then he turns smarmy. "Oh, sorry. Just your butt. You know, polyester's not a good look for you."

I move strategically to hide my poofy ass. "Very funny, Paolo, and you know that polyester makes me allergic.

Rounded butts are very stylish, and it's not huge, just—" I search for a non-depressing adjective—"*zaftig.* I'm starting a new trend."

Thankfully the door chime sounds, interrupting the moment.

"Customer!" I say.

"Don't scare her away, V," he whispers into my ear, following me into the front showroom.

Alas, the "customer" is my mother.

"What do you need?"

"I had Henry take the clothes out for cleaning. I hope it's okay."

"Who is Henry?"

Henry walks in, a hottie with peroxide blond hair, an orange spray-on tan, and a capped white smile. My mother has hired a gigolo.

"My chauffeur-slash-personal-assistant."

Paolo gives Henry the once-over, but Henry knows who butters his bread. He heads over to Mom (she's bought him one of the English driver uniforms) and takes her arm.

"Mother, you're supposed to be heartbroken. Fire him."

Henry looks nervous.

Unfortunately, my mother stands committed. "I'm trying to make your father jealous."

These are my genes. Oh, God, please don't let it be hereditary.
"I talked to Daddy. He's coming up here in two weeks." It's not exactly the whole truth; I talked to my father yesterday and he told me he'd take her back when hell froze over. Being

in the program, such as I am, I realize the odds are not good, but I'm an optimist.

She presses Henry's arm against her breast, and everyone looks away, including Henry. "That's good, then. See, already my plan is working."

I look around at my empty store and stand as firm as Paolo's sexuality, which is actually very firm, but masked behind the whole nouveau gay persona. "I'm not paying for him."

Mother raises herself up two inches (not hard when she's wearing these glorious five-inch diamond-studded strappies: Stuart Weitzman). "V, you need someone to help you out with things around the house." Very smart, how she's going for the All about V angle, which usually works well. She waits a beat before grinning. "I took a job with Shelby. She's paying."

I give Mom a high-five, and we share a rare moment of familial chicanery. "That's so bad, Mom. You're tearing me up here."

Mom just winks at me. "And by the way, I've been taking your messages. Rolf, Eric, Jamie, and Nathaniel. I told all of them you were out on a date with Tony Danza."

Paolo frames a belt display between his hands, needing to flaunt his preferences in front of Henry. "Tony Danza? Oh, God, as if she's not a public pariah already. He's just too Omaha . . . " He trails off shaking his head. "He's not even in V's league. What do you think? It should have a little more color, hmmm?"

Mom picks up a bright pink attaché case and puts it dead

center. Actually, it looks kinda nice. "Next time I'll say Frank Sinatra. That'll really wow 'em." Then she walks out, parroting the Upper West Side mince-step, her hand holding the bag (Sonata, of course) and the metronome hips clocking back and forth in precise movements. Henry rushes in front of her to pull the door open. Just before the door shuts, he flashes a quick smile at Paolo and then winks.

My mother has hired a gay gigolo. Why am I not surprised?

That evening I have dinner with Regina, Calvin, and Amy at Nobu. I invite Paolo because I am a nice person. (Actually, I need him in case a transitory emotion emergency arises, and I, the lowly Level 2, am unable to perform.)

Regina and Calvin are late.

"We were next door," she says, like that means anything to me.

Calvin is a large sans-a-belt man who has the open face of a man from New Hampshire. Not that I've ever been to New Hampshire, but if I had, I would think they would look like Calvin, or "Cal," as he wants everyone to call him.

There is an interesting dynamic between Regina and Cal. They seem happiest when they're ignoring each other, which fits right in with my definition of familiar interaction. Imagine having a father like Cal. I pity poor Regina. If I were her, I think I'd disown him. Of course, Mom is the pits, and I haven't disowned her, so maybe there's something.

Cal spends long (thirty!) minutes poring over the menu and interrogating the waiter, and I'm left to wonder if this man has any redeeming qualities. However, I have no redeeming qualities either, which is why I shouldn't throw stones.

"What is the name for the sticky green sauce? Puts my taste buds on fire, but man-oh-man, it is some dee-lightful hoodoo."

Oh, but I really want to throw stones, or at least a spell to stop the insanity. I look over at Paolo for transitory emotion support, but he is ogling Regina and is of no help. Amy has not noticed (and no, she's not in the program, nor have I put her name down on my marketing plan. New York needs more ex-soap-opera writers turned charitable patrons, don't you think?), she's busy looking for boldfaced names. I would not have pegged her for a celeb stalker, but there you have it.

The waiter is patient with Cal, probably because he is sensing a fat tip. Cal continues his questions, and I really wish I were a Level 3. I could stop this shit. I kick Paolo under the table, but he doesn't register the "zap-him" hint; he is too busy making sake eyes at Regina.

Eventually the ordeal of ordering is over, and everyone breathes a sigh of relief. I have to be nice to Cal, because I am doing this all for Blanche. I don't have a clue about how I'm going to help Kimbers and Marv yet, but today I'm determined to hatch a solution.

In light of my moratorium and the extra junk I'm carrying in my trunk, I've had lots of time to think more about this good-and-evil thing. I don't mind being called selfish, or bitchy, or even vindictive, but I don't want to be evil. It's a personal choice. I think I screwed up things for Megs and possibly the rest of the world as well, but there's still some hope for

Kimberly, and by default, Marv, not that I care personally about either one of them.

Cal drones on, but I tune him out. I get a momentary reprieve when the waiter delivers a plate of the black cod in miso and waves it under Cal's nose.

Immediately Cal takes a bite. "Mmm. Mhh-mmm-mmmm-mmmm-mmmm," he says, *loudly*. Amy's face turns an unattractive shade of purple. Cal continues to eat, sucking on his fingers at odd intervals.

"Slow down there, cowboy," I say in a joking voice. I'm not a fan of *Fear Factor,* and I most definitely don't want to eat dinner with it.

Regina and Paolo are oblivious. Some conversational tidbits I gleaned from the twosome, while trying to keep my eyes off Cal's rapidly diminishing plate:

"I really love your designs, Mr. Paolo."

Paolo starts to blush. "You can call me Paolo."

"I was worried when I read about the fire at the store. You could have been hurt."

"Paolo will never die," he says, his accent heavier than usual, which means he's trying to impress the ladies.

Regina looks as if she wants to say something here, but then she stares down at her plate, her fork making little curlicues in the rice. I bet she puts hearts over her *i*'s, too.

There is no help in that corner, so I try and distract Cal from his food (not easy). "So, what do you do, Calvin?"

"I prosecute securities fraud and insider-trading cases for the SEC," he says while still chewing.

"Sounds thrilling [lie]," I say. "I followed the Martha Stewart trial [lie]. It was so exciting [lie]."

Calvin stops eating and wipes his fingers on the napkin. Must remember to avoid finger foods when eating with Cal.

"We try and root out corruption wherever it strikes."

"I bet those insider-trading cases are really tough to prosecute."

"No, they're usually straightforward. Collusion is wrong. It's my job to set things right."

"Marshal Dillon of the SEC?"

"You got that right, little lady."

"Do you ever see innocent people caught up in the process?"

"Lots."

"How do you feel about that? I'd be heartbroken [lie]. Can you even sleep at night?"

"Nope. Apnea," he says, then snorts with laughter.

My face muscles strain to make a smile.

"So, what case are you working on now?"

"Some stripper is dating a broker, whose boss's wife's hairdresser's cousin works for a Parisian fashion house. He tells her that the *Times* is going to feature a certain trench coat in Style Review that week. She passes on the tip to another customer of hers, who passes it on to his mistress. The stock jumps 67 percent on Monday. Then, not a week later, the *Post* runs an exposé on the designer. He's Republican, heterosexual, and believes in WMDs [CNN Factoid: WMD=Weapons of Mass Destruction. I did not know that]. The stock tanked, and stores were left with Taiwanese boatloads of pink trench coats. Our weasels dumped the stocks the day before the *Post* article. Damned journalists never could keep their mouths shut. I got 'em"—he slaps a greasy fist in his meaty palm—"dead to rights."

"So the broker was the mastermind?" I ask, pretending fascination.

"Yeah, sad to see Old Al go. He was my broker for more than twenty years. Now I'm going to have to put him away."

I file away the information in my head, not finding anything worthwhile. This is not going to be easy. If Cal were somewhere on the scale of men I'd do, I'd opt for a mind-bending fuck. However, the thought of a naked Jabba the Hut is horrific in its proportions, and I have no mind-bending powers anymore, so I must use my brains.

"So he never passed any tips to you?" I say, the beginnings of an idea starting to gel.

Cal tucks his thumbs in his pants, and I avert my eyes, just in case there's something carnal going on down there. "Nope. I think the stripper was the one who did him in and lured him over to the dark side."

Poor Cal, probably never had a stripper try and lure him anywhere. I shake my head in a narrow-minded, judgmental way that I think will appeal to Cal. "You never can tell about people, can you?"

"No. It's all about greed in this world. I thought the eighties were over, but the ghost of Gordon Gekko lives on."

"You must love what you do."

He nods. "It's good work. V, I gotta tell you, you're good people, you know that?"

If it'd been anyone else, I would have sworn they were sucking up. But Cal? Nah, the man's just one shit short of a load.

As we're leaving, I realize that I have no choice. "You can help out with the auction, can't you?" I ask.

"Well, I be dingle-dangled," says Cal. "I'd be delighted."

I pick up the check, and he slaps me on the ass. "I think that's the prettiest little tushy this side of Kansas. Love a woman that's got some booty in her call."

I suppress my whimper, and "Dueling Banjos" plays in my head.

I talk to Nathaniel on Saturday, and he wants to go see a movie on Sunday night. I decline because as much as I adore Nathaniel, I'm determined to hide from him until I get my perfect ass back, Cal's opinion notwithstanding.

"We'll do something soon," I say, trying to be chipper. He doesn't sound convinced.

I spend Saturday intellectualizing my Level 2–ness and my thirty-seven-inch hips, and discover that I hate them both. I go for tea at the Plaza with Amy, and the waiter ignores us. If I were a Level 3, I would zap him into subservience, but instead I must put up with it. When I take my mother to Prada, I pretend they are ignoring us out of professional jealousy. I try on some pants, and the uppity salesperson wants to know if they need to let them out for me. She's just lucky I'm not a Level 3. We walk out.

That night I go to Suede and party like it's 1999 and my

butt is still small. Actually, I must admit, I get a lot of attention, and I'm happy to note that when the *Post* comes out on Sunday, I've been linked to four different men. A hint of promiscuity is always good for sales, and our current sales levels could use all the help they can get.

Sunday is chess with Blanche, and I'm ecstatic. She is the crème anglais on the fallen soufflé of my life.

I meet up with her at the park, and she's not hard to spot. She's the only little old lady dressed in widows' weeds, a row of black quartz bracelets covering her arms. Today all rings have disappeared.

"That's a very autumn look for you, Blanche. What happened to pink?"

She shuffles her way toward the chess tables with springless steps. I think she's aged ten years in the last week. "I can't believe he's gone."

"Think of the ten bucks you'll save from the table."

She cuts me with a "go to hell" look. For all intents and purposes I am, so I don't respond.

We trudge up the bridle path, past the carousel, all those little kiddies having a fine time.

"You don't know he's dead, Blanche. Maybe he went to Boca."

"In the spring? Eh. You don't know men, V."

As the tables rise into view, Blanche falters a bit, and I catch her elbow, just in case she's tilting for a header. Her head raises, and I see what she sees. Yuri is there, the sun glinting off those heavy brows, and he's smiling.

Immediately Blanche walks over (step definitely more

springlike) and whacks him with her bag, which is a Sonata courtesy of *moi*.

Yuri holds up his hands to block the assault. "Crazy woman! Why you hit Yuri?"

"I thought you had died, you Commie pinko Cossack," she says between whacks.

"And you care that much, that you would kill me now?"

That makes her stop. She gathers her little clutch to her chest and takes a prim step back. "I didn't say that."

There's a wonderful Hallmark moment, and I step in before the violins start to play or the two crazy lovers kill each other, whichever comes first. If Mother had one-tenth the heart of Blanche, Dad would be home, Mom would be home, and I'd be a Level 4, thank you very much.

Blanche really deserves this, though. I scribble on a card and hand it over to Yuri.

"Here's her phone and address. You call her tonight, or you won't be running tables in this town anymore. Do we have an understanding?"

Yuri's face cracks into a smile, exposing two missing incisors. "Da."

I grab Blanche by the arm, and we take our usual table. She seems slightly dazed.

"Didn't I tell you he wasn't dead?"

She's blinking uncertainly, but there's no masking the joy in her face. "I was so sure . . ."

"You're an old woman, Blanche. You think everyone's dead."

"Everyone dies sometime, V. None of us are immortal."

Just what I want to hear, words to die by. But I shrug it off.

"How are your troubles going, V?"

"What troubles?"

"You know, your business problems with Lucy."

"Oh, those problems." I rub my cow hips. "Not so good. We had a fire at the store."

"Was it serious?"

"Nah. You know, I've been trying to do the right thing in my life, but it's not going well."

"Doing good is never easy. I remember one time, when I was"—she looks up at the sky—"about eighteen, I think . . ." She trails off, and I'm left hanging.

"What happened?" I ask.

"You going to set this thing up?" she says, pointing to the board.

"No. What happened when you were eighteen?"

Blanche starts to laugh. "V, am I supposed to remember what happened when I was a teenager? Now tell me about this Lucy."

Her black hole of a memory is really starting to worry me. "You've been forgetting more stuff?"

She waves a hand at me. "All the time. Wait till you get to be my age."

"I hope I see seventy-three, Blanche. I really do." The way things are going, I'll be happy to see forty-three. I pull out the chess pieces and pick my usual color. Black.

"She's really got you spooked, huh. This Lucy lady."

"I thought I could stand up to her, show her who's boss."

"What happened?"

"I gained an extra three inches in my hips."

Blanche points a finger at me, blinding me with the glare of her ring. "You're eating all the wrong things."

I only wish it were that simple, but I don't really want to spend the afternoon bitching to Blanche. I finish setting up the board, and we shift into the usual routine.

"How's it going with Marv? You think he's going to prison?"

"I'm doing my best, Blanche. It's not going to be easy for me. He did a very bad thing," say I, the Queen of the Damned.

She waves a hand, musical bracelets tinkling with the movement. "Bad is all relative."

I eye Blanche with new appreciation. "You really think so?"

"You get as old as I am, and you learn there's no such thing as absolute good or evil. We're all just humans, V."

I like her way of looking at things. That's a transcendental-ism I can sink my teeth into. On a day like today, when the blue clouds are steaming overhead (they're actually a smoggish yellow), I'm thinking I can scam at least fifty off Blanche. She's watching Yuri out of the corner of her eye, with a satisfied smile on her face.

Fifty? *Hehehe*. Today I can take her for two hundred. Between Marv, Kimbers, and Yuri, she really owes me.

Twelve

What is spring without the annual Easter parade? And what is the annual Easter parade without controversy about bonnet regulations? This year's *verboten haberdashery*: the NRA's assault-weapons bonnet (who knew the Easter Bunny was so cute with an AK-47?), R. J. Reynolds' Joe Bunny bonnet, complete with cigar (apparently Joe Camel was unavailable), and the Fab Five's Queer Eye on the Jesus Guy bonnet.

Tonight, I'll be holding my annual Readers for a Literary New York fund-raiser. Dave Eggers will be signing his newest novel, Another Heartbreaking Work of Staggering Genius, *and that* mediatista, *Anthony Lupinus, will be regaling us with more "on-the-spot" anecdotes from last year's Martha Stewart trial.*

The Sonata girl has certainly been making a lot of music recently, with a lot of different men. There's been some rumors of drugs, but I don't buy it. Unfortunately, customers aren't buying her bags, either.

And because I would be remiss to let it go unmentioned, the Shelby/Harry (Sharry) duo is no more. Shelby has been seen on the arms of New York's most eligible: The Derek, The Johnson, and that chef-all-about-town, The Rocco. Harry was last seen crying in his beer.

Nathaniel calls on Tuesday and asks me out for the day. In a moment of audacious bravery (he hasn't seen my hips recently), I say yes. He makes me forget a lot of things that I currently want to forget, so I agree to go and then promptly cancel the drinking jaunt with Rolf that I had earlier committed to.

When Nathaniel shows up at my apartment, he's wearing a pissy look on his face, and it doesn't take a Sherlock to realize that I'm the cause. I pick up my bag and keys, hoping to postpone any unpleasantries.

"I've been reading the *Post* recently," he says, starting in on the unpleasantries immediately.

Oh, this is not going to be good. I put down my keys. "It's a rag. Ignore it."

"You kiss a lot of guys."

He's upset about who I kiss? Geez. When you don't have a soul, chastity is the least of your concerns. I sit down, because this can only get worse. "It's meaningless; don't let it worry you."

Giving in to his worries, he starts pacing around the room while I sit and wait to see if my excuses are making a dent. "That's the problem. Everything is meaningless to you."

I open my mouth, but his face stops me from making a joke.

"Almost everything," I say, which is closer to the truth than my usual lines.

I don't think that's the answer he's looking for, because he heads for the door. "I'm wasting my time here."

However, I'm even faster. "No, you're not. Please." I crack a smile. "What happened to one day at a time?"

He stares me down, trying to get beneath my rock-solid veneer, but I won't let him. Actually, I'm afraid he'll find nothing beneath my rock-solid veneer. Eventually he nods, and I begin to breathe and go off to gather my keys.

When we get downstairs, he leads me over to a motorcycle. A big, hulking motorcycle. There are some women who consider motorcycles sexy; I however, consider them death traps. After a heated argument, which he wins, I agree to go, albeit with heart-stopping concerns.

"I thought you took risks," he tells me, strapping the helmet under my chin.

"There are risks, and then there are *risks*," I say, and then realize that I must mount the beast.

Nathaniel takes in my flouncy skirt and quirks a brow. "You can change if you need to."

I consider running upstairs and putting on pants, but I'm still butt-full V, and the skirt is infinitely more flattering. Throwing caution (and my not-exactly Victorian modesty) to the wind, I climb aboard.

Soon we're zipping through the Holland Tunnel, my legs wrapped securely around 100 percent U.S. Prime Army Ass. My cementlike grip is partly due to the aforementioned necrophobia and partly due to the tinglies that I get from feeling up his pecs.

It's a strange experience to see the New Jersey state-line marker in the tiles of the tunnel and feel—God don't strike me dead now—excitement.

At the moment, with my skirt whipping around me, my arms holding on for dear life to Nathaniel, and the roar of a gazillion horsepowers between my thighs, I can almost believe I'm not wasting his time.

Almost.

The Garden State is just as annoying as I remember—trucks, swamps, construction, and tolls—but we do eventually arrive at Belmar. I do one quick spell to get rid of helmet hair, and then pop off the bike like the professional motocross rider I'm not.

It's early in the season, but the locals are out in force, working on their tans and taking advantage of the beach before the summer crowd hits. The whitecaps are rolling in along the coastline, and out on the horizon there's a few fishing boats and one hulking tanker. The long ride has seemed to cool some of

Nathaniel's jets, because he grabs my hand and we start walking down the boardwalk. Somewhere between Exit 137 and the Asbury Park tolls, I gained a reprieve, and I'm not even sure I deserved it.

"You ever come down here much when you were a teenager?" he asks.

"Nah," I answer. Mom didn't want to go anyplace but Southampton; not that we could afford *that*.

"Too bad. We rented a summerhouse here every year."

I'm taken with the image of a younger, more optimistic Nathaniel in the typical masculine uniform of summer: no shirt, shorts, and a Vinnie Barbarino strut. "Were you a musclehead?"

He shrugs, which I take to mean, "Yes, but I don't want to admit it."

It strikes me that if I had ever wandered down here in my wild youth, our paths could have crossed, and I wonder how things would have turned out for me.

"I love being near the water," he says, and there's a peace in his voice.

"Not much water where you're going, huh?"

"That's why I wanted to come." Interesting point, that. Neither one of us is looking forward to the future, but today's kinda like our own little time-out.

He buys me a hot dog, and we eat on the beach, the seagulls yapping and flapping their wings in hopes of landing a crumb. Nathaniel feeds them. I, understanding that well-fed birds only become more annoying, do not. Just one more ideological difference.

After we finish with lunch, we sit in quiet and watch the waves. It's a pretty place, far, far, away from Fauslhamabaad. "Have you ever killed anybody?" I ask.

He nods, but doesn't say any more.

"Don't you think that makes you a bad person?" I ask, which is probably tactless, but he was supposed to go into more details, so I would know that I'm not alone in my inner devilment. Currently my offenses are too numerous to list. My quest to find something redeemable inside me is becoming more and more futile.

"I don't fall into that trap. You don't think that, do you?"

I don't tell him that I want him to be a bad person. Or maybe a little more morally indecisive—like me. "No, you're not bad at all," I say, with only a tinge of sadness in my voice.

As we walk farther, the teenagers and old folks are out in full force, cruising the drag. There's a mix of cute houses and rip-off shops, which just goes to show, there's no such thing as paradise. Later on, the sun officially sets and night falls in, and the shore turns to magic. The sound of the ocean is soothing and anesthetizing, and for a moment I can wrap my brain around the consequences of Meegan's baby.

"Can I ask you something?"

"You can ask anything you want."

"Do you ever think about the end of the world?"

He shakes his head. "I've seen Armageddon more than once."

The way he says it, I know he's not talking about the movie. "Are you going to heaven?"

"There's no such thing as heaven. This life is all we got."

I think about telling him that he's wrong and I can prove it, but I've already introduced one friend to Lucy. Fool me once, shame on you. Fool me twice, shame on me.

The moon floats over the water, a huge ball of light, and we walk back to his bike. "Can we stay here for a minute?" I say.

"In Jersey?" he says, raising his eyebrow at me.

"It's not so bad," I answer, and then sit down on the padded seat. He gets behind me, his hands locked around me, as if I'd actually go somewhere. It's so easy to lean my head back against his chest and rest. He tells me stories about his youthful summer adventures, and I realize how much of life I missed out on.

"Do you have regrets, Nathaniel?"

He stays quiet, but his chest rises against my back as he breathes. Finally, he answers.

"Some. I screwed up a lot when I was a drunk. My dad died last year, and I never got a chance to make things right. If I could go back and see him, I would. Make peace."

"You squared things away with your mom, though?"

"Yeah. They moved to the Midwest after I enlisted. And I've been back a couple of times. Especially after Dad was gone. Taking care of stuff for her."

"I'm sorry," I say, because I understand that no-going-back problem.

"What about you?" he says.

"Yeah, there's been one or two things I've done."

He doesn't ask, smart boy that he is, and I don't volunteer the truth. "So tell me about this reunion. Army guys. Sitting around the poker table, drinking beer, and making up stories about women, right?"

He laughs at me. "Some are like that. Why don't you go with me? It's a dinner and then a dance. It's not Plaid, though."

I'm tempted much more than I should be. This is what makes Nathaniel so much more dangerous than any other man in my realm. He wants to pull me back into a world I left behind. And it's a world I can't go back to, no matter how magically he kisses me, or how his eyes glimmer when he looks in my direction.

"Oh," I say, wrinkling up my nose, "you know that's not my style." When the warmth in his eyes cools a bit, I twist my head back and temper my loss with a kiss. He climbs on the front and starts the engine. The darkness hides the cold in his eyes, but I know it's there.

"Yeah, don't know what I was thinking," he says, his voice just as cold.

I know exactly what he was thinking, but no matter how much I think about it, too, my future's already been decided. The ride home is not nearly as much fun, and by the time I get home to the bright lights of Manhattan, I almost hate it. I sold my soul for this city, and now it's Jersey that I miss.

Thursday night is Lucy's dinner party. It's a hard choice between watching *American Idol* with Mom and having dinner with Lucy, the goddess of the underworld. I, bearing the weight of the world on my hips, depart to the inner sanctum of the devil.

When I step over the threshold of Lucy's apartment, I'm instantly thrown into some subterranean world with lots of unkempt hair and . . . brown. Everyone is wearing tweed or corduroy or—I start to back away in fear—khaki. There is an aura of intellect and arrogance that envelops the room in a fog of philosophical twiddle-twaddle. I can feel it sucking the fuchsia right out of me, but then I take control.

Meegan is completely in her element. Perhaps it's the repressed Bohemian in her, perhaps she has no taste. I don't know. The room is pretty much as I remember, although the cute bartender is gone. A long dining room table is set up in the middle, very classy, possibly Chippendale. Along the walls are those little plasma TVs—there must be a hundred—all playing different videos. I look to see what's playing on the devil's Cineplex. No *Exorcist* here; it's nothing but talking. There is a clip from *Sixty Minutes* featuring some little dude who is a dead ringer for the one who is holed up in the corner. Whoa! That *is* the little dude in the corner.

The next TV is showing an interview about Hobbes. I don't know who Hobbes is, nor do I care. So why are these people talking about him? Just as I'm ready to move on, Shelby glides into my vicinity, and I'm glad to be back in my own element. Her skin looks fab, and the scarf is tellingly absent. Elementary, my dear Watson, plastic surgery's afoot. I look closer, checking behind the ears.

"There's no marks. It's all me," she says, her eyes twinkling.

"You're a Level 2, aren't you?" I whisper, noticing the perfect golden highlights in her hair, the slight glow to her skin, the extra cuppage in the bust. Can I say I hate her? I've spent more hours than I want to confess trying to get my butt back, but even at Level 2, I can't unhex Lucy's pound of flesh.

She whisks a hand down her body, model-style. "In another thirty-six hours I'll be a Level 3, so if you're not nice, I'll give you satanophobia."

(That's a little Life Enrichment Program humor.)

"Speaking of demons, I need to talk to you."

"Certainly. What about?"

"It's Mom."

"She's a gem," she says, which I think is pretty whacked, but it's a win-win for me, so I'll go with it.

"I've always thought so," I say. "However, if you want to keep her in your employ, there's a couple of rules."

Shelby nods. "For a friend. Anything."

"Keep your hands off her soul, Shelby. You have to swear."

"You're so bad, V. I don't do family."

"Really?" I hadn't pegged Shel for the scrupulous type. But she really is blooming. "Me, either."

Shelby looks down her perfectly shaped nose at me. "But don't think this means I'll forget about the deuce you promised. You can't scam me, V. Those will get me to Level 5. Mind alteration, including selective amnesia and memory implants."

I immediately backpedal because I admit, the whole Meegan-birthing-the-Antichrist thing has taken over my mind, and maybe I don't want to think about my own soul-taking right now. Maybe I'm avoiding. Maybe I'm turning into a chickenshit. "You're killing me here, Shel. I'm a mere Level 2—"

"V, you are the iconic emblem for the all things 212. Why do you think I signed so easily? Because I wanted to be like you." There she is, looking at me with all that respect in her eyes. I've come a long, long way in two years.

"Thanks, Shelby."

"About those two souls . . ." She spreads a hand wide, gesturing to the veritable smorgasbord of souls laid out in the room. It's like the lunch counter at Carnegie Deli. I feel some of my resolve weaken. I don't like these people. I have never liked the ones with superiority issues. Do I really care whether they go to hell or not? Then a new and even better thought occurs. If I fail in my plan to save civilization (which now seems to be the most likely scenario), will it really matter? Something tells me that it will.

"I don't know anybody here, Shelby. You have to manage the relationship very carefully in order to implement the life-enrichment objectives—Life Enrichment Rule something-or-other—and you know my personality . . ." I shrug my shoulders, hopelessly inept.

"I've been practicing. Watch my technique and learn."

She undulates over to Brown Guy Number 437 and starts to flirt. She's cooing, rubbing her hand down her shirt, and I'm thinking, Damn, she *is* good. Am I this good? Of course I am. Eventually, she whispers in his ear, and then they wander hand in hand over to Lucy. I watch, completely fascinated, witnessing the fast food of soul-taking. Three minutes and forty-seven seconds. It's a new world record. The crowd goes wild.

Shelby returns, sans Mr. Soul-free Brown, and smiles. "You just have to know what people want, V."

I used to know what people wanted; now I think we're all confused shits. "What did he want?"

"What does every man want?"

Okay, it doesn't take a rocket scientist to solve the equation here, but I have my doubts. Sex is not something that should be tampered with, in spite of what I said earlier (standard Life Enrichment Program sales smokum-hokum). After Brown has three years of blond twins, threesomes, and the entire college campus of Beaver U, his doo-dah is going to lose the zippity, and at that point, you might as well be flossing.

"You're a shrewd businesswoman, Shelby."

"You're too soft, V."

Sad to say, she's right. I've grown soft and confused and beaten-down, and I don't like it at all. There was a time when nothing could have stopped me. When I was just as successful as Shelby, who has now leapfrogged me in the program, because I keep falling back a level because I'm being too soft. This is the life I chose. I should make the best of it, like Shelby's doing. It's not necessarily a bad thing, because these people don't really mean anything to me. These people are the reason that I sold my soul. "Soft?" I scoff. "I'm hard as nails. Watch the master at work and learn."

I go over to Mr. Brown's friend, the khaki with paisley tie. And loafers. It's enough to cause a refined woman to make vomiting gestures.

"Hello, I'm V." I touch his hand, but can't force myself to retain contact. My hand falls away.

"Gordon Kovel." He scrunches his nose. "V? I don't believe I've read any of your work. Whom do you write for?"

I raise myself up to my full height. If this peon thinks that he can intimidate me, well . . . he's doing a damn fine job of it. "What do you do, Gordon?" I ask, determined to put Dr. Seuss in his place.

At that point, Lucy strolls over, the epitome of a perfect hostess. "Gordon creates fiction that overlays a universal truth." She laughs. "We have a lot in common."

Lucy thinks she can just laugh, and all will be forgiven with me. Well, no. It's going to take a little more than that. Getting my butt back to normal would be a step in the right direction.

"You must write horror, Gordon," I say, sweetly.

Lucy, ever the professional purveyor of all things evil, throws her head back and laughs. "I've been trying to get him into the program, but so far—no luck. Why don't you try, V?"

I look at this man, a nondescript novelist with a long fall of hair that would make fine nesting material for most species of New York's rodent population. If ever there was a man crying out for Level 2, here he is. And as a bonus, his career will get a nice bump as well.

Gordon blithely ignores me, that arrogant, dismissive gaze that I've seen my whole life. I snap. Could I take this man's soul? In a New York minute.

"What's your dream, Mr. Kovel?"

His eyes drift away from me, following the others in the room. I'm not exciting enough for him. When he finally answers, it's in that faux intellectual ennuized tone. "Dreams are a yolk-like yearning from a materialistic world. Creativity must break free from the chains of humanity in order to truly aspire to greatness."

I'm not fooled for a minute. "Cut the crap, Hemingway. Everybody wants something."

"You bore me." He turns to Lucy, cutting me out of the conversation. "Did you invite this tripe-headed nit?"

It takes all I can do not to kick him in the balls, assuming that he has some. If I were a Level 7, I'd freeze 'em right off. Then Lucy comes to bat for me. Nothing more than a flicker of her eyes, and I see the change in him. The ennui is gone. *Now*, I'm worthy.

"What do you want?" I ask him again.

"A quote."

"What's a quote?"

"A cover quote for my book. I want a quote from J. D. Salinger. The trademark of approval from a literary genius."

"Is that all?" I ask. God, these men are too easy. Has the world forgotten how to dream with style? What happened to world peace and treasure troves of riches? Now all anyone cares about are handbags and cover quotes. "He's alive, right? I mean, if he's dead, we could have a slight problem, but nothing insurmountable."

"He's alive, but he never gives quotes. It's part of his image."

Lucy looks over at me and smiles. Like she knows what I'm thinking (because she probably does). She's testing me again.

Dammit. Gordon is a first-rate ass, not even worthy of a soul. Would it be so hard to take it? Get my Level 3 powers back, my über-model hips back, and have him rhapsodizing in iambic pentameter about the pimple on his ass? After all, what am I going to do? Spend the rest of my natural life fighting with the devil?

"Gordon"—I put an arm around his shoulder, feeling Lucy's measured gaze on me—"you're totally screwed. Your writing sucks, and if you're lucky, you'll end up a beaten-up old man, living in Kansas. Mr. Salinger ain't gonna give you the time of day. Sorry."

Kovel stomps off, ask me if I care, thus leaving me and Lucy alone.

There. I did it. I pissed Lucy off, royally. I wait for other body parts to expand, but for the moment, all is svelte. That's it. I've made my choice. She's just going to have to accept it.

Lucy gets this really sad look in her eyes. "You shouldn't have done that, V. Why can't you be what I want you to be?"

"Do I look like fucking Play-Doh? No. I'm a human being. We're all human beings. I may not have a soul, but I do have a brain. Sorry, Lucy. Find another minion that you can shape and mold in your image."

"That's what you want?" she asks, still being Miss Nice, which worries me, but I feel too good. I did right, and I know it.

Shelby, not sensing the tension in the moment, comes up, probably wanting to see if I've gotten the souls I owe her. Bitch.

Lucy grants her one of those most-favored-minion smiles. S'all right, pass the title, I'm okay with that. "Shelby, why don't you show V your talents? Bring Mr. Kovel back over here; our talk's not over."

I shake my head after Shelby leaves, because Lucy wants to see how far I'll go. I won't take his soul, but will I keep someone else from doing it?

"Don't make me stick up for him, Lucy. He's a walking penis, and I really don't want to lose another power level."

"You're scared of me, aren't you?"

"No."

"V, he's not worthy of you."

"You're right. He's not."

At that moment, Shelby and Kovel come back. Lucy whispers something to Shelby, and then Shelby starts her engines. I swear, the woman is such a ho. "A Salinger quote?" she says to Kovel, and he nods.

Shelby is all business. "We can arrange that. Lucy's got some papers for you to sign, and I'll have your quote within thirty-six hours."

Gordon looks unconvinced. "You don't know Mr. Salinger."

She lifts her chin. "Mr. Salinger doesn't know me." Then she holds out her hand. "Do we have a deal?"

"If you can do this, you're a miracle worker."

Lucy looks over at me. "Miracles are always possible. You just need the right tools," she says.

After Kovel retreats to his other book buddies, Lucy stays to chat. "Have you forgotten your dreams, V?"

"I dream about a lot more than getting a quote from Salinger."

"I know. That's what I love about you, V. You're so much like me, it's like looking in the mirror."

That's not Lucy being polite; she means it. There's a throbbing pain inside me, like a rotten tooth that's situated in the middle of my solar plexus. "You always say just the right things."

She nods to where Meegan is rubbing her somewhat pouchy belly. "She's glowing, isn't she? A baby is just what she needs to make her life complete."

I look her in the eye (scarier than you think), and try and decide if Lucy is being altruistic, but Lucy is such a cool customer, she doesn't give anything away. Two can play that game. "Nine months is a long time. Anything can happen," I say enigmatically, throwing down the gauntlet.

We sip our martinis in silence, and eventually my curiosity just gets the better of me.

"You could really be a nice lady, Lucy, and that's not just me sucking up. It's the truth."

However, this seems to piss her off. "Why is it so hard to believe that I'm not nice? I'm always the fall guy for everybody else's problems. Some jerk-off kills fourteen schoolkids, blame it on the devil. Some power-hungry tyrant makes sushi of his people, he must be one with Satan. I get blamed for *everything*. How would you like to be vilified and hated for millions of years? And not all deservedly, thank you very much. Did I threaten to destroy the world? Famine, pestilence, plagues? Was that me?"

I consider calling her on the whole threaten-to-destroy-the-world thing, but she really hasn't committed herself to total destruction, and besides, I think the timing would be bad.

"Maybe you need a new image. Something more . . . upbeat."

Lucy looks at me and smiles, and this time I see the weariness in her face. "I shouldn't be bitching and moaning while I have guests, should I?"

At that moment I feel sorry for her. It's only momentary, but it's there. I give her a smile. "You wouldn't be a woman if you didn't."

After that, dinner is a big yawner. We spend the time discussing the latest editor at the *Gray Lady*, who is not present at this dinner, and I can't figure out why we're discussing her. Everyone knows that gray is passé. Such fascinating tidbits include:

"It was narcissist and pretentious, a heady tribute to me, me, me. Far too overblown for the critical praise it's received" (Perry on *The Diary of Anne Frank*).

"An interminable diatribe against modern politics. Poorly structured and tedious" (Taylor-Smith on the Bible).

"Depressing with a meandering story line, trite phrasing. Shit. Absolute shit" (Bakersley on *To Kill a Mockingbird*).

The room is full of such vindictive jealousy that even I, super bitch extraordinaire, take notice. Choosing not to hear any more of these sour grapes, I eat my food quietly. Meegan picks at her salmon.

"You need to watch the fish," I say. "Mercury."

"How do you know all this stuff?"

"CNN," I reply between bites.

"How's your mother?"

"We haven't killed each other."

"Oh." Meegan takes the hint and moves the conversation elsewhere. "Shelby looks great. Do you think she had plastic surgery?"

I steer Meegan away from any hints of soul business. "Nah. She's into some of that homeopathic flower-grinding business."

Meegan nods, appreciating this. "I should ask her what she's taking."

"You can't. Baby."

"Oh, yeah. Right." Then she stares down at her plate, and I notice the way her hand is gripping the fork.

If she's not careful, she's going to break it in two. "Meegan. Sweetie? You all right, here?"

She doesn't talk, but shakes her head.

"Do you need to go home?"

Then she looks up. "The emergency room. Now."

Thirteen

Sunday is usually a day of rest, but today there's no rest for the antagonized. There are three protests scheduled for the steps of City Hall today. At noon, the needled tapestry workers rise up and protest the new WTC design. Apparently the Freedom Tower's resemblance to a large sewing needle is causing the group all sorts of identity confusion. After the seamsters unravel, the anti-Hummer conflagration roller-skate in to demonstrate the evils of the gas-guzzling, tax-loopholed übertank. Lastly, at 6:00 p.m., just as the sun goes down, the Citizens for Vampire Awareness will picket against cuts in the VA hospital budget.

The Tribeca Film Festival, in its fourth

star-studded year, is just around the corner, and all the buzz concerns the indie film written by an unknown Delaware film-maker. The sharp-witted scribe has been labeled a "more Cartesianistic" Sofia Coppola. The name of this hysterical romantic comedy? I Think, Therefore I Cry.

In other news, in day 666 of the Fauslhamabaad–U.S.–Spain–France conflict, the U.S. congressman from Connecticut will be heading overseas to help in the oversight of the Fauslhamabaadian elections. George Will will be moderating the debates of the presidential candidates, and the ever-popular Billy Bush will be on hand to provide on-the-spot commentary. Can't wait to see how this hornet's nest gets resolved.

Hospitals are not my favorite place. Actually, I think only weird people would list hospitals as their favorite place. All that sickness, that fluorescent whiteness and pale jaundiced yellow that seems to be everywhere you look. Gives me the heebie-jeebies.

After I drive Meegan to the hospital, they check her in for observation, which probably isn't a good sign. Her father is supposed to drive in from the Hamptons tonight, but for now, I'm all she's got. Yeah, yeah, that's me: Chicken Soup for the Soul.

The nurses and doctors wander the halls, their heads in clipboards, their feet operating at one speed—really, really fast.

I wait in the waiting room with a little old woman who's snoring with her mouth open and another man who looks slightly psychotic. I am not of their kind and choose to stay far away.

After waiting three hours, I'm tired, and the coffee is really bad. I corner the nurse at the station. "Excuse me?"

"May I help you?" she asks.

Nurse Ratched-san is a tiny Asian woman with a bad complexion and those 1950s cat-eye glasses. It's actually a good look for her.

"I brought in Meegan *bleep*. Can you tell me how much longer we'll be here?"

"What? You got big party to go to?" She starts to laugh, and I'm thinking, Been playing in the nitrous oxide again? However, the new, wiser edition of V keeps that to herself. "I just need to know that she's okay," I say instead.

"You family?"

"Of course. We're sisters."

"I need to see ID."

I stare her down. Jeez, if I was a Level 3, I'd just poof the information right out of her. "My driver's license doesn't list the family tree."

"You be bitchy and I no help you at all."

I start to argue, realize that I am here for more important things, and flash my ID.

Nurse Ratched-san doesn't even look. "You can see her in another forty-five minutes. Doctors with her now."

"Did she lose the baby?" I ask, trying to display adequate amounts of sympathy, but inside I'm thinking, Please, please,

please, because it would solve a *lot* of problems. I'm thinking this is my happy ending. I'm out of the soul-recruitment business, Shelby can have it. If Lucy's kid is gone, the world can move forward, and with all that off my plate, I can finally figure out how to ship Mom back to Florida. Except for Megs losing her heart's desire and the V-going-to-hell part, it's not a bad scenario.

"I can't give you information. You ask your sister."

"Forty-five minutes?"

"Maybe more."

"Gee, thanks."

"You're very welcome."

I spend the next *two* hours watching *JAG* on TV. I hate this fucking show. I tried to get them to change it to anything else, but I'm guessing the hospital tunes in to this schmaltz for a reason. It's a scam.

Eventually Nurse Ratched-san tells me that I can see my sister.

"'Bout fucking time."

Her glasses slip down her nose, which looks to be the Chinese equivalent of shooting me the finger. However, I have no time to engage the dragon lady in warfare. I have a patient to comfort.

Meegan looks tiny in her hospital bed. She's sitting up watching CNN, and her already pale complexion looks ghostly white. My stomach drops about eighteen feet. I had thought this was going to be a walk in the park. I was wrong.

"You get the good channels, huh?"

I sit down in the white plastic chair next to her. It's not great hospital accommodations, but at least there's no one in the other bed. Actually, I think it's nicer than the waiting room. "Private room, aye? Moving up in the world, aren't you?"

"Oh, yeah. The Ritz."

Ah, now she's showing a little spirit. That's my girl. "How ya doin'?"

She's watching the commercials really carefully, and I have no idea what that means. "Good," she finally answers.

"What about the baby?"

At that, she clicks the TV remote, and the broadcaster disappears. "What do you care?"

"I'm sorry, Meegan. You're a nice girl, and you don't deserve this. I guess this means you lost it, huh?"

Her head pops back, and her eyes look really pissed. "You don't have to sound so relieved."

Okay, I'm relieved, but I don't think I'm completely out of line here. The kid would've meant trouble for Meegan and for the rest of the undamned (everything I know about Revelations, I learned from the *Omen* movies). However, I can see that's not the best way to play this one. "You're young. You got your whole life ahead of you," I say, continuing to be the optimistic yet comforting friend.

"Just to let you know, I haven't lost the baby—"

Oh.

"—yet."

Her voice drops to a quivering whisper on that last part, and I forget about the rest of the world. Go save yourself, bub, I've got a friend who needs me. As the person who introduced her into Lucy's world, I'm not sure what help I can be, but I'll try.

"What's going on?"

"They don't know, but my body is rejecting the fetus."

"You just gotta trust that everything will turn out okay," I say, which probably sounds really stupid to her, but I don't think I'm ready to tell her that she is birthing the child of Satan.

Her hair flips back; the perfect gold highlights are the brightest color in the room. "Can you leave me alone now?"

I fumble around for words. I'm a Level 2. I can poof up a set of Cartier baubles, with an Armani dress to match, but I can't poof up a normal baby to give her. "If I could do something to make it right—"

"You can't do shit. I'd give anything to keep this baby. When I found out I was pregnant, I thought: Finally, something that means something in my life. Somebody who thinks I'm wonderful. Somebody to hang out in the park with and watch the pigeons."

"I'd watch the pigeons with you, if you want," I say in a quiet voice that is not my usual style.

She looks at me, and her eyes are sad. "V, you're kidding yourself. If it doesn't involve the beautiful people in this city, you're not interested. And God forbid, you might get shit on. I don't even know why you started talking to me that day in Elizabeth Arden. It was fun, but I'm not in your orbit."

I sit quietly because she's absolutely right, and it doesn't sit well with me. Before I gave up my soul, would I have been willing to sit in the park with her? I don't think so.

"We don't get everything we want, Meegan," I say, because I would like to be one of those people that would just sit in the park with their friend. But I'm not.

She shoots me a look. "Are you trying to help? You're really not helping."

"What do you want me to do?" I ask, because I have no experience in helping people pick up their life-pieces when they're scattered out around them.

"Help me keep my baby," she says, and she's looking at me with crazy eyes. Desperate eyes, the eyes of someone who would do anything.

That stops me for a minute, because she doesn't know why my life is so perfect, she doesn't know who Lucy really is, and I look Meegan right in the eye, because I know she's desperate. I know the exact moment when someone would sell her soul, and Meegan is there. "I can't work miracles."

Her mouth starts to wobble, and I stop looking in her eyes.

"I just want someone that wants me to be me and loves me because of it. Why does that have to be a miracle? I have tons of money. Why doesn't that help?"

Now this one I know the answer to. "It takes more than money to be happy." That's why Level 1s are so eager to get to Level 2. And why Level 2s are so eager to get to Level 3. Lucy's got a great scam going. There's always more. We always want more.

Meegan fists her hands in the sheets and starts winding them around like spaghetti. When she looks up at me, she's crying. I don't want her to cry. I hate it when people cry.

"Can't you make it right?" she asks. "You told me once that you could do anything. You want to help? Do something."

She's expecting Superwoman here, but she doesn't know that Superwoman gets her powers from evil rather than good. I don't want Meegan to hurt, and I know I can fix this.

It'd only cost her soul.

"Meegan, sometimes you've gotta believe that things turn out the way they do for a reason, and we don't always know what that is."

"THAT'S SHIT!"

"I'd help you if it could," I lie, because I'm not going to do this. I'm not going to take her soul. If there's anybody in this world that deserves a soul, it's her. Most of the people in my orbit don't deserve theirs.

I get up to leave before I change my mind. I like to think I'm really strong and that I'm some superhuman superstar, but I'm a good liar, even to myself. "I'll be outside in the waiting room. Your father should be here soon."

Meegan's head is buried in the sheets, and she's crying her heart out. She never notices that I leave.

Sometimes the devil is in the details; sometimes the devil is in the waiting room. Literally. Lucy is there, looking absolutely fabulous for having been up for most of the night. Quickly I do my morning-after spell. It helps to look your best around Lucy.

"Some party," I murmur politely.

"I thought it was perfect," she says, looking happy, smug, like I'm back in her good graces. I even feel my hips shrink.

Normally this would cause me to cheer, but now I'm just nervous.

"You did marvelous," she continues. "I think Meegan will be signing over in about"—she checks her watch—"one hour and forty-seven minutes. You're going to be a Level 3 again. Happy?"

Lucy should be torn up about this. This was her kid. What's wrong with this picture? "Why are you so cheerful?"

She shrugs. "Life goes on."

"Wait a minute. This was your kid that she was carrying. She couldn't have kids. What was all that shit about wanting a daughter? *The Omen.* Why else would you make her pregnant?"

"I would love to have a daughter, V, but the poor lamb she was carrying was just an ordinary zygote, just like every other embryo in the world."

Immediately I latch onto the operative words "was carrying." And she dismisses it like yesterday's garbage. "She's going to lose it, isn't she? You bitch. You just take it away from her. Because you feel like it? Oh, I want another soul, so I'll kill a baby."

"I didn't do that, V."

Yeah, right. "Oh, it just happened, huh? At your dinner party? Just like the pregnancy just happened like you said it would. The timing's just a little too convenient."

She waits a beat and then shrugs. "Actually, it was your special herbal remedy that she drank. That special little baby-be-gone potion? It'll do it every time."

I stop. Everything gets a little cold.

"No way. No fucking way."

"I can't kill anyone or anything, V. It's my own little curse. I can only give."

She sounds so rational, so logical. "I still don't believe you. She should have lost the baby right then if my spell worked. I would know."

"Did you check the fine print on the instructions, V? There's a delay. The worst sort of magic takes time. Why do you think I wanted to have my party tonight?"

I rack my brains trying to remember, but so help me, I can't. That seems like a lifetime ago. Did I do this? Dear God, I killed a kid. I reach around for a chair and collapse. I close my eyes, but Lucy's grin is there, lit up in my mind. I did this.

Oh, God. I did this.

I did this.

I make a sound, a cry, a plea. I can feel Meegan's pain. Eating inside me.

I did this. To her.

Sorrow freezes my blood. The room chills, and I'm shivering and can't stop. It's so cold.

I did this.

Lucy puts an arm around me, and I brush it off. I don't need to be comforted by the devil.

"Don't worry. You'll get over it," she says.

I rock back and forth in the chair. *No. I didn't. This is a dream. A nightmare.*

I don't want to get over this. My most offending sin is that

I wanted to turn myself into something good; I did, I truly did. Instead, I've turned into a reflection of her.

I take a deep breath and try to focus. There is a landscape on the wall, and I stare at it until it begins to blur. Mountains. Trees. Flowers.

I did this.

"What about Meegan? What happens to her?" I ask.

Lucy shrugs. "She's got a completely overhauled uterus. She can get pregnant again." She smiles. "With a little help from me. I've got the paperwork with me. You saw her; she's ready to sign over. And you'll get full credit for her soul, of course."

I sit there, rocking back and forth in my chair, staring at the stupid picture, the cold turning me into ice, my stomach churning with nausea. "What's so special about Meegan?" I manage to ask. "Why is her soul worth so much to you?"

Why is her soul worth so much that you destroy me for it?

"It's not about her. It's about you, V. You haven't figured that out, yet? You've been working so hard to change your own future. Working so hard to find something good inside you. *It's not there.*"

There is a quiet click in my brain, like someone just turned off the lights, and I recognize that sound. It's when all hope dies. "I thought I was supposed to save the world from little Damien."

"I know. It was tremendous fun to watch you work so hard in vain. You've been punk'd, V." Lucy just stands there and grins like she knew exactly what I would do.

I've been punk'd? I *hate* the look in her eyes. Like I'm the Bonnie to her Clyde. Like I'm the guillotine to her Madame Defarge. I was trying. I look down at my hands, and I can see the blood there. I wipe them on my legs, but the blood won't go away.

She knew I would do this. "I think you've proved my point nicely," she says.

I slap her in the face—hard, trying to erase that smugness, that absolute certainty that I would destroy an innocent life. Her dark eyes turn sad. "Feel better?" she asks, even as the red mark disappears, like it never existed at all.

"No."

"V, just accept who you are. You'll be much happier. Trust me. I fought it for a long time, too."

"I can't be evil, Lucy," I say. *But you are*, I think to myself.

She breathes a weary sigh. "Yes, you are, V. What do you call taking the life of a baby? That's right up there with the worst things I've ever done. In fact, I think it is the absolute worst." She takes the chair next to me and leans in. "You've been doing all these things, and you think I don't know. The charity auction. Helping Kimberly and Marv. Now you're trying to save the world. Why? I don't understand you. You have everything. Why do you want to throw that away?"

"I didn't want to help Kimberly. I wanted to help Blanche."

There's an echo of a smile on her face, and then it flickers away. "Poor dear. Sad about her Alzheimer's."

I raise my head and stare. At that moment, the full consequences of selling my soul crash down on me. You think you can isolate yourself from the world, but you can't.

"You did that?"

She shakes her head no, but she's looking at me with a question in her eyes. It's Pandora's box, and she wants me to open it. The solution is there, right beyond the realms of my heart. And I think to myself, what do I have to lose? I don't have anything left.

"You can fix her, can't you?" It's not a question. It's a statement.

She snaps her fingers. "Like that. Say the word, V."

Slowly I nod my head, and she smiles like she never doubted my decision. How do we do this to ourselves? When do we start to need the devil?

Fourteen

Speaking of best, or second-best as it were, is there a new It Bag for the spring season? Since the rubber Sonata bags have been popping up all over the streets of New York, the lawyers for bag designer par excellence, V, have been plugging a sagging dam with lawsuits, just as fast as the paralegals can type. Is this the end of an era, even before it begins? V isn't worried. "There's only one Sonata bag. Cheap imitations can only increase the value of a true original," she said in between heated conversations with Mirkin, Birkin, and Law.

And in today's media news, the mayor has announced the creation of three new shows for the small screen, all shot in New

*York. The new Bruckheimer thrill-a-minute,
CSI: The Bronx, the latest in the Law &
Order franchise, Law & Order: Devilish
Intent, and a new HBO production, Sexless
in the City. Written by Gotham's own Married Queen of the Single Scene, Sexless follows four divorced friends as they deal with
the eternal question, is there sex after fifty?
If only this was commercial television. I
imagine the little blue pill would pay big
green bucks to garner some airtime on this
one.*

There is nothing worse than when a damned person gets suicidal tendencies, thinking that hell can only be a reprieve from life on earth. I leave St. Luke's and take a cab to the park, where I spend some time sitting alone on the dewy grass of the Great Lawn. I don't like being alone; when you're alone, you have to think. I was so positive that protecting Meegan and protecting the world was my mission. My true calling. It sounded so noble—and good. Instead I ended up committing the unforgivable. The wind picks up, the night air turns cool, and I lock my arms around my knees. All around me, the city's alive, full of noise and lights, but inside I'm dead, and I don't know when that happened. You'd think that I would cry and yell and rage, but there's nothing in me to give. I clench my hands into tight fists, curling my nails into my palms, forcing pain to come, but still there's nothing. I should be horrified, but I'm not. I'm just dead.

A fire truck screams its way down Central Park West, and I wonder what other disasters are occurring right now in this world. This is the way my mind works. If there's another disaster out there, maybe it's worse than my own. Maybe I can concentrate on somebody else's screwup and forget what I did. Then the sirens fade away, and I'm left with no other disasters but mine. I'd like to think that Lucy's to blame for this, and don't kid yourself, I do hold her responsible for a good bit, but she just set up the stage. I'm the headliner who was handing out the purple Kool-Aid. And I can't run away from that.

When the devil is in your own head, there's nowhere to go. For all my suicidal drama, it's not in me. Hell scares the shit out of me, and as much as I hate Lucy, I've still got a wicked-cool life. Never surrender, never forget.

No, I won't run away. The doing-good thing is not for me. I'm a better person when I'm bad. Some people's talents are music, or art; mine are selfishness and hubris. I wish I were a person who could just sit on a bench in the park with a friend, feeding the birds and just talking, but I'm not.

I take a deep breath, reveling in my inner wickedness. The air smells a little smoggier, the noises are a little junkier, and the moon leers down on me.

For the first time, I discover pure, unadulterated hate. It makes me burn hotter than a tequila shot ever could. Hate is a very strong emotion for me, a person who is usually relatively emotionless, but I could kill Lucy with my bare hands and not even worry about my nails. However, I realize that killing the devil is an exercise in futility, and I'm done with futile exercises. I want something with some red meat in it. Something I can sink my fangs into. Something I can ride to successful completion. Lucy was right about this one thing. There isn't anything good inside me, and I shouldn't try and fight it.

I breathe in again. Yeah, I can do this. *Revenge.* I can forgive what Lucy has done to me, because I deserved everything I got, but I won't ever, *ever* forgive what she did to Meegan. And that's *her* unforgivable sin. She may be the coolest person I ever met, the most fascinating snake I've ever seen, but that's not gonna help her now. My smile rivals the light of the moon as I think how best to make the devil pay.

The next few days pass in a blur. I skip chess with Blanche on Sunday because, to be frank, I don't want to know that her memory is suddenly "fine." My mother is now dividing her time between Henry (her gigolo in name only) and her psychic. I dodge calls from Kimberly and Amy for a few days while I sit in my apartment and plot my revenge. It's not a soul, but it keeps me occupied.

On Tuesday, I get my Level 3 powers back. Hallelujah! A day without powers is like a day with fat thighs. I spend the day zapping everybody in my path. So far, *Vanity Fair* has called to do a profile on me, the New York Women's League wants to honor me as Woman of the Year, *Vogue* is doing a spotlight on the Sonata line, and I have hired my own publicist. There is no doubt inside me anymore. I was born to be bad.

Today is Thursday, so it must be lunch at the Grill Room.

As I walk in, a hush descends. Philip waves to me from his table, and I duck behind my hand (it's a faux move, but hints at humility).

Shelby is waiting for me, and she looks divine. Level 2 has really done so much for her. After we sit down, she giggles like a little girl.

"Isn't it to die for?"

"What?" I say, thinking, No, there is nothing in this life worth dying for.

"Well, Level 2, silly. And it's just an expression."

"Shel! You tease. You're a four, aren't you?" *Oh, God, I've got to watch my thoughts. She's got the ESP powers, she can read me.*

"Oh, come on, I was just playing. I'll tune you out. Can you believe it? I got them yesterday. It's like I'm sixteen with a driver's license all over again. Hold me back, V, I'm zooming down the autobahn of life."

Now here's the true test of a good person. If, upon hearing that a not-really-a-friend-who-has-sold-her-soul has acquired another level of power, ergo, someone else is walking around on the highway to hell, do you:

(a) experience sadness and loss in knowing that the snake of the devil has gotten her fangs into some other poor schmo, sending them into the flaming pits of perdition; or

(b) feel jealous and petty because the not-really-a-friend-who-has-sold-her-soul is more successful at sending schmos happily down into the flaming pits of perdition?

If you guessed (b), you'd be right. Which actually makes me happy, because it means I'm a bad person, and should never feel guilty about not having good thoughts again.

I take a moment and savor my bad jealousy. Next thing you know, Shelby will be planting fake memories (Level 5), and poofing up studmo escorts for the Met (Level 9).

A few Sonata fans come up to chat and schmooze, and I'm touched. The attention starts to get to Shelby, and when we finally get a moment of peace, she grouses about it.

"Look at all the notice that you get. I need a sideline, too. I tried the dog business, but it's not me. Dogs? Who needs dogs as a fashion accessory? What do you think about lingerie?"

"Shelby, you're not me, you got to make your own way." I smile at her because she's never going to be as cool as me, which is why she is my friend.

"What about baby stuff? I was paying attention when Meegan was pregnant. There's dollars there, and babies are very in."

"Have you talked to Meegan?" I ask. I have called her three times, and she doesn't answer the phone. I try not to let it bother me; guilt is not fun, guilt is not happy, and mostly, guilt is not me.

"No. I haven't tried. I read that she's been seeing Jamie, though. The power of the Life Enrichment Program strikes again. Lucy said that she's in the program. Have you called her?"

"No," I lie.

Shelby drops Meegan from the conversation like last year's Versace, and I wonder if she'll ever discuss Meegan again. People seem to just disappear from her life like they never existed. It's a quality that I wish I possessed. Of course, she finds a new topic: "I've been invited to next week's opening of Scratch, over on the West Side. You going?"

"No." Scratch is a pool hall cum dance club that is owned by the two former boy-band members who were trying to make it big in New York's club scene. Considering the write-up that Lucy gave it ("Darlings, you HAVE to go to experience its blissful, silvery luster"), I'm thinking they're clients. "I've got a date," I lie, all casual-like, mainly because I don't want to go clubbing, but still have an It Girl image to maintain.

"Tell!"

I don't have a date. The truth is that next week is Nathaniel's reunion at West Point. The date I turned down. Looking back, I can see that was very wise of me, because I don't want to see him again. That's actually a lie, because I'm dying to see him again, but I spent the week dodging his calls as well because he gives me false hope. He makes me want to be something I'm not, nor will I ever be. So dating is not a good idea, except with jackasses and assholes, and Nathaniel is neither. "Nobody you know," I say, because Shelby would never give Nathaniel the time of day. He doesn't wear the right labels, and he carries a MetroCard.

"Oh, too bad. I had you pegged for a foreign oil sheik or some Hollywood type."

"Wrong on both counts." As the waiter approaches the table, I wiggle my nose. By nature, I'm a show-off.

"V, how delightful to see you today. Just for you, you must

have the fresh tomatoes lightly covered in pesto. It is absolutely fabulous. Tell me that you'll try them and give us your verdict."

Shelby starts to grin. "Somebody's off the shit list. Lucy's such a softie."

No, Lucy is not a softie. Lucy is the world's most insidious bitch, and even though I haven't figured out exactly how she's going to pay for what I did to Meegan, I haven't forgotten. I smile politely at Shelby. "I know. What's not to love?"

The next week, Mother has her first séance. She's as excited as a little girl. Oh, yeah. Talking to dead people. That's how I get my jollies. But I smile at her because she's taking an interest in something. She's even been looking at co-ops. Her and Dad have talked some, but there's no progress being made. I argue with Dad on the phone myself, but he doesn't listen to me, nor should he, really. I mean, what do I know?

I think they're headed for the Big D, which, all things considered, is not a surprise. In fact, I'm secretly relieved because it means I come from a long line of emotional failures, and should not be surprised at the magnetically challenged void that is my moral compass.

"So tell me about the séance," I say, wondering if she's going to be bilked for an arm and a leg. I hope not, because it's her darling daughter who will end up paying.

"It takes three days, V. I won't be home."

"Three days? Are you crazy?"

"I thought you'd be happy to have the apartment to yourself."

That stops me. I should be happy. "That's very thoughtful of you, Mom. But why three days for a séance? What if she murders you?"

"She's not going to murder me, V, but thank you for your concern. She's very well-known in the city, and she makes the papers all the time."

I shake a finger at Mom. "Those are the people you've got to watch out for, Mom. I want a number where you're at."

She gets a big smile on her face. "You love me. You really love me."

My finger stops in mid-shake. Do I really? After forty years of bad blood, I'm turning a corner with my mother? Nah. Hell has not frozen over. I would know. "Just be home on time. If you're one minute late, I'm calling the cops."

The apartment is quiet that night. Deathly quiet. I consider going out to Plaid, or Pandemonium, or Bungalow 8, but my energy level is sapped. I smile at people all day because I have such a wonderful life, and by the time I get home to my apartment, my teeth hurt.

Out of the silence, my cell rings. "V, I'm downstairs. You're home?"

Nathaniel's voice sounds like he's a lifetime away, but there's only thirty-seven floors between myself and heaven.

"You missed your reunion?"

"I left."

I stay quiet. I haven't wanted to see Nathaniel; I think it would hurt too much. He expects me to be good and kind and soulful, and I twist up my life trying to be good and kind and soulful, but it's not going to happen. I try to be good and kind, and people get hurt, or damned. I think it's smart to just stop trying.

"We need to talk. Can I come up?" he asks.

He wants to talk. I don't want to talk. I want to play games, What Could Have Been being the most dangerous game of choice.

"Sure," I answer, because I always succumb to the lure of temptation.

Quickly I do my most powerful magic. In these days of Hollywood effects and *Harry Potter,* most people confuse magic with reality. Trust me when I say that magic is all about the illusion. When he appears at my door, I am the woman he's always fantasized that I was.

His eyes take in the sheer white robe—an innocent, virginal look, of which I am neither—and a deep growl sounds from his throat. There are so many things I want to forget tonight, and I can see one night of absolution in his eyes. The door slams, and we don't get very far, which I suppose is the story of this relationship. He pins me against the wall, and his mouth devours mine, using his teeth and tongue as a weapon of war. His anger suits my mood as well. We have fought and loved in equal turns, and I'm not even sure he was aware of it.

The first time he takes me against the wall. That's the revenge fuck. My body works to accommodate his size, but patience doesn't seem to be the mood of the night. He drives inside me, and I let out a hiss of pain, the world turning dark.

This sex, this wicked, wicked sex, is the penance I need. There is no love here, only the desperate mating of two very lonely human beings. He pulls my leg up higher, nearly splitting me in two, but I welcome the burn. For the first time in a long time, I feel alive. I hurt. I ache. Things can touch me where before I felt nothing. The room fills with the smell of sex and sweat and anguish. I can hear my own breathing, my chest rising in time with each thrust.

His eyes lock on mine, and it's not loneliness I see, but determination. He's looking for things that don't exist inside me, and even though I know they're not there, I love that he never gives up on me. Hope is an addictive drug for the damned. Like a junkie, I keep coming back for more.

I whisper his name, softly and reverently, my lone moment of truth. I know that he's lost in passion's rage and will never know. His face turns taut, his body still and sated.

For a moment, we're locked together, and everything stops. Time stops, and I don't want it to start. But who listens to me? Nathaniel looks at me, and there's shame in his eyes, which hurts more than the sex ever did. I give him a well-pleasured smile and bite his lip gently. "I never dreamed," I murmur, needing to make a joke, needing to put this evening in perspective.

"No more fighting me, V."

"No," I say, which is a lie, because he needs to fall for someone who owns their soul free and clear, but we have one night, and for one night I can pretend.

His eyes get dark and deep, the look of a man intent on seduction, which is still much better than talking. He kisses me, slowly, intimately, tenderly. It is the tenderness that makes me panic. I rub against him, and my hands scramble to find his cock. Nathaniel laughs at me, locks my hands behind my back, and continues to kiss me. Legend says that a French kiss can steal a woman's soul. On a night like tonight, with this man, I can believe anything.

We start out on the classic leopard-print couch, where his mouth makes fine work of my breasts. His hands are hard and rough and as strong as I knew they would be. He wants to atone for his earlier sin, but in the big scheme of things, a little rough sex is chump change. Just one more ideological difference.

His tongue is like a whisper on my skin, a sexy tickling feeling that makes me shiver with heat and cold. He notices my shiver and laughs softly, and this time his mouth moves to my neck, toying with me, nipping in slow, languorous bites. My thighs clench together, my pulse starting to race.

Then he whispers in my ear, vibrant suggestions that, as a bad girl, I am intimately familiar with, but for some reason this time there's an electric current buzzing inside me, pulsing between my thighs. His fingers walk down my skin, playing and circling, teasing me.

I squirm under him, the rough fabric of his shirt a nipplicious torture. Oh, my. I squirm again.

His finger slips between my thighs, still more teasing. Slut that I am, my thighs part with nary a protest. The butterfly touch goes back and forth along my slit, and I moan, the room starting to tilt. He takes my mouth in a kiss, his tongue playing the same stealthy game that his finger is playing between my thighs. My blood pounds so thick and fast, I think it's all going to burst out of me. My hips go up a little higher, and I rub against his cock.

And does he pay attention to my request? *Mais non,* the devilish man slides his finger inside me, finding my clit and starting to circle.

Please, say I, who never begs.

No, says he, who never listens.

The circles are driving me crazy, and I know I am getting closer, and just when I am ready to hit the ceiling, Nathaniel stops.

"What are you doing?" I ask.

He doesn't answer but gives me this slow grin, and then slips down to take me in his mouth.

I swear I've died. Honest. I begin to mutter nonsense, my voice going higher and higher with each sure stroke of his tongue, and eventually I explode.

Some time passes before Earth and myself return to the same orbit, and when I do, he's watching me.

The look in his eyes terrifies me. He wants to see inside me, wants my heart and soul laid out naked before him. My heart is already there, and I suspect he knows it.

I make him undress for me, liking to look at his warrior's body. Scars run across the golden skin, the puckered flesh a testament to the injuries he's received. My fingers are fascinated by the smooth flesh, but my warrior is impatient and doesn't let me look long. We tangle together, and he loves me.

I had always heard that sex as a Level 7 was worthy of paradise, but I think they're wrong. Sometime during the night, he pulls me close, stroking my hair. I have found my paradise here. There are no more could-have-been's for me. Has-been is all I have left.

The next morning, when the sun comes up, Nathaniel opens his eyes and gives me a sleepy smile. "Good morning."

"Mornin', sailor," I say, sipping my morning coffee.

"What are you doing dressed?"

"Some of us are not on vacation and must go to work."

He rises up, so strong, so capable, so steadfast. For a moment I think anything's possible. "I'll take you to lunch, then."

Just like that, the moment's gone. "We need to talk about a few things," I say, sitting down on the edge of the bed. "I know that things were said last night in the heat of passion, and I just want you to know that I'm not going to hold you to them. I mean, you're leaving, when? Tomorrow?"

"In four weeks," he says tightly.

"Soon enough. Times like this, things just get messy, you know?"

He looks at me with disdain. I know that Nathaniel's opinion of me has never been very high, but I need to make sure to cement that opinion here. I can't repeat last night. After all, meaningless is what I do best. There's a long, awkward silence, and I can see him digesting the truth. Finally he speaks.

"You don't have to worry about messy, V. Nothing's going to be messy but your sheets."

He gets up and pulls on his clothes, and I keep my face to one side, because I can't watch this. After he's done, he tweaks at my hair. "Hey, sweetheart," he murmurs, his voice husky and soft.

He's going to make this hard. Please, God, don't let him make this hard. God doesn't listen, because then Nathaniel shoots me a wink.

"Thanks for the fuck."

Fifteen

The sex-for-stocks scandal is going to get ugly. The arraignment is scheduled in Manhattan court in two weeks, and already the rumors have started. There will be names named, as Tawny Feathers, the most actively traded Scores stripper, is scheduled to testify on receiving tips from Wall Street broker Big Al D'Franco. Miss Feathers, who was pursuing a Princeton MBA by day, has a client list that reads like the S&P 500. It seems that already the suits are shaking in their briefs.

And today's society darling, Meegan, was seen at Capitale, trying desperately to avoid being recognized, but my sources noticed the man who was paying lip service

> to her neck, none other than Jamie "I Can't
> Go On without Her" MacGregor. True love,
> or just Meegan being charitable? Stay
> tuned, darlings. I think this story is only be-
> ginning.
>
> In Tony news, the daring revival of my fa-
> vorite show, Damn Yankees, was nomi-
> nated for best musical, and the ever-divine
> Dee gets the nod for best actress in a mu-
> sical. Get your tickets BEFORE the June
> awards ceremony because this one is a
> sure thing. After the win, you won't have a
> chance in hell for tickets.

Mom returns home with trinkets from her "otherworldly" experience. I would be happy with snow globes and T-shirts, but
instead I get candles and voodoo dolls that look like a four-
year-old's art project gone wrong. However, in deference to my
new state of calm and peace and acceptance of my badass self,
I do not throw them out the window as New Yorkers are prone
to do. I smile and say, "Oh, how pretty." I think that's
progress.

I've recruited another soul, a cabdriver from Ethopia. He
was taking me to Brooklyn via Staten Island, so I showed him.
I damned him. Another thirty-six hours, and I'm going to get
the ESP powers, and I can't wait to show up Shel. She's getting
so uppity that I can't stand it.

We're scheduled for lunch at Davidburke & Donatella. It's

not usually on my list, but considering the recent changes in my life, I'm wondering if fusion cuisine is just what I need. Can food really solve most of life's crises? I'm thinking that's a yes.

When I get there, Mom is at a table alone, waiting for me.

"Why are you here?" I ask.

"I take my job very seriously."

"For Shelby? You've got to be kidding."

"It takes a lot to be a PA. I'm responsible for handling all of her social engagements," she answers.

"So where is she?" I snap, peeved that Shelby is pulling this crap on me. I hate waiting on people. And to make it worse, while I'm sitting here waiting, I bet she's out recruiting some crank addicts in her race to be a Level 8. Okay, that was snippy, but I'm sorry. She's turning into a true soul-ho. I myself have standards.

Mom's fingers tap on the table, like she's having a craving. Behind my back I poof up a piece of nicotine gum and then slide it across to her. "Big B had a business meeting. Said she'd meet me here."

"Big B?"

"Yeah. Shel-B. I think she needs a nickname. Something with some flash, you know? I think I need a nickname, too. What do you think?"

Most of my nicknames for my mother are unprintable. However, in the interests of keeping my restaurant peaceful and free of blood, I change the subject.

"What business meeting?" I ask, wondering if Lucy is cooking up something with Shelby behind my back. Probably. Ask me if I care.

"I don't know. Lucy something or other. I haven't met her."

"She's a trannie, Mom. Stay away."

Mom isn't listening; she's looking around impatiently, and I realize this is more than a nicotine fit at work. "What's with you?" I ask.

She lowers her voice to a whisper, checking out the fellow patrons. "My psychic tells me that I'm going to meet the love of my life today."

"What's the matter with you, Mom? You were married for forty-four years. You just hired a gigolo. Don't you think that at least *one* of those should be the love of your life?"

"Oh, coulda shoulda schmouda. I don't need to limit myself. I'm not dead."

"I talked to Dad again," I say, which isn't true. Dad's now started screening his calls, and until I get to Level 7 (actual behavior modification), I can't actually make him pick up the phone.

Her eyes sharpen, and the fingers still. "What did he say?"

"He misses you, Mom. You should go home."

"Not while that floozy is still warming his bed."

Fortuneously, at this moment Shelby runs into the room, her hair mussed, her heel broken. It's a bad look for a Level 3.

Then she collapses into a chair and takes my drink. "I nearly died."

"Well, yeah. Look at that heel. I'd die, too."

She looks up, her eyes wild. "No. I mean, I was nearly killed."

Mom is now all agog. Apparently this is better than Prada in the afternoons. "What happened?"

"I was walking down West Fifty-seventh Street, passing under this great red awning, and it came out of nowhere. It missed me by *this* much," she says, holding out fish-story hands.

"What missed you?" I ask.

"A bowling ball."

I start to laugh. "Oh, Shel. You had me going."

"I'm serious. I was nearly beaned by a number-ten ball. One of those big flashy ones with blue glitter. It took a chunk out of the sidewalk that could have been my head." She puts a hand over her heart. "I saw my death passing before my eyes. Ehuck. I need a tissue."

I summon the waiter and order her a shot of whiskey. I believe there is not an ill that alcohol cannot cure, even death.

Then Mom decides to pipe in. "You're so lucky. Don't get me started about the stuff that falls from the sky in this city. A gargoyle. Can you believe it? Crashed down right next to me. You need to go see Madam Fortuna. She's the best. She told me that cancer was eating up her insides, but then one day— poof. It just disappeared. The doctors said it was a miracle, but Fortuna, she doesn't believe in miracles. She says we're all meant to die, and now that you've cheated death, you're going to have another death experience to, you know, get it right. She can tell you these things; she knows."

My mother, the messenger of good tidings and great joy. I wonder, what are the odds that the gargoyles will strike twice?

"Do you think so?" asks Shel, staring at the glass of whiskey in front of her. "Did you ever think what happens when you drink this stuff? Cirrhosis of the liver? I should stop."

I take her drink and down it. "Get out of here. You've got to raise your head up high. You want what you want when you want it. So you take it."

My mom scrunches up her face. "Pardon. I'm going to go outside and take a smoke." I watch her march off to the smoker's limo that's kept outside.

Shelby continues in her whine, and I'm tuning her out when the waiter arrives with our food, making a big deal of hemming and hawing for Shel. And what am I here? Chopped liver?

"Angry lobster in nails," he announces to her, like she's the pope. My plate of fish is plopped down in front of me without any announcement at all. I'm tempted to use my powers just to show her up, but Shelby would see through it. "How do I know where this has been?" asks Shelby after he leaves, staring at her plate, which I'm happy to say looks neither angry nor nailful.

"It's dead. Its past experiences no longer matter."

"V, I came so close to dying, you know? And all I could think of, when that ball landed—splat—in the concrete, was that I could be dead, with pots of fiery lizards melting on my face."

"Can we cut the imagery?" Those are visions that I have avoided. For good reason.

"No, think about it, V." She spears the lobster with a fork and starts shaking it at me. "This seafood. Mercury. Lead.

Toxic waste. It could cut my life expectancy by twenty-five years."

"So become a vegan. But don't be hanging out with me. I didn't sell my soul just so I could start eating rabbit food for fun."

She lowers her voice. "Do you ever think about the blood dripping off your face as the flames melt your skin?"

Out of the corner of my eye I notice that the next table is getting cherries flambé. My skin starts to tickle. "I think that's a little extreme," I answer back. (Yes, that's me, the pragmatist, talking.)

"Maybe, but do you actually know what hell is like?"

"It's probably dark." I'll be damned if I'll let myself slink any further into her doldrums, so instead I take a bite of sole, lightly buttered and perfectly seasoned. "You'll be dead. Who cares?"

"What is death?"

"Shelby, eat your lobster so you can die and report back in."

"Can you be serious?"

I am being serious, but I don't tell her that. "You're not going to be roasted over a pit, Shel," I say, with more confidence in my voice than I'm feeling. The truth is that I suspect hell is a scary place, and I want to avoid it for as long as humanly possible. Unfortunately, not one of the nine powers lets you live forever. More Hollywood.

"So what's the meeting with Lucy about, Shelby?"

She dodges my eyes. Something's fishy. "Amy called me and

told me you ditched her. She needs my help. I'm taking over the auction, V, and Lucy's working with me. Did you meet those women at the shelter? I'm figuring I can hit Level 9 easy."

The auction. I get an idea.

A horrible, terrible idea. It would take brilliant maneuvering, steely mind control, but I can handle that. Most importantly, it's the perfect fucking way to get back at Lucy. I snap a superior look on my face. "You can't do it. I'm your mentor, I say no."

"Amy came to me first, V. You stole my idea, which Lucy thinks is brilliant, by the way. If you're going to back out, then I have no choice."

No way is she going to rob me of this. It's my one shot. "I'm the bigger name, Shel. Develop your lingerie line, and maybe something will come of it, but for now, get used to the shadows, 'cause I'm back in."

Shelby glares, and I can tell she's not happy with me, but considering the student has already passed the teacher in powers, she can just suck it up.

"You're such a prima donna, V," she says.

"I know."

I was saved from further arguments by the appearance of Mom, fanning her face. "It's hot as Hades outside."

At this, Shelby turns pale and puts down her fork. "Oh, God."

Mom looks at her plate. "Is it the lobster?"

"I can't live like this anymore."

Mother looks at me. *What's wrong with her?* she mouths.

Menopause, I mouth back. Mom nods and dives into the salmon.

"I'm serious, V. That's it. No more drinking, no more seafood, and I'll start going to gym."

Now this is beyond the pale. "I can't be friends with someone like that. God, you'll end up as a Lloyd Grove subject, and even Lucy won't touch you. Next thing you know, you'll be sipping gin from a paper sack with the Tenth Street trannies. And who will I have to party with after that? Nobody."

Shelby runs a hand through already mussed hair. I suppose that's what bowling ball backdraft does to it. "You're right, I don't know what's the matter with me. I just need to stay calm and concentrate on getting to a Level 5."

Mom butts in. "What's that?"

I change the subject. "QVC, Mom. Nothing to concern you."

BANG.

The room shakes for a minute, glass rattling. I swear to you all, no matter how I might wish for a grenade to drop on Mom, it wasn't me.

Shelby drops to the floor. I look around, notice everyone else is still eating and talking, and so I peek under the table. "What the hell's wrong with you?"

"We've been bombed."

"A car backfired, Shelby. Nothing more."

Eventually she climbs back into her chair. I don't want to tell her, but the bowling-ball hair has just gotten worse. She doesn't eat any more of the lobster. Instead she sighs, very dramatic. "I'm going to turn over a new leaf. I swear."

The next day Kimbers shows up in the store.

"V, please tell me you've talked to Cal again."

I piddle with the display, putting the pink bags behind the yellow bags and then back again. I have no design sense, but sometimes I like to look busy. "I'm sorry, K, I've been swamped."

"I can't believe you're doing this to me. It's because you still hate me, isn't it? You were just leading me on, letting me think you were my friend, and all this time you were planning on stabbing me in the back."

Actually, I never planned on stabbing Kimbers in the back; that would interfere with my pursuit of all things selfish and hedonistic. I have no time for doing good, no time for contributing to the betterment of my fellow man, or woman as the case may be. I put the pink bag back in front and turn around. "Kimberly, I'm not a lawyer. I can't do anything for you."

Her mouth falls open. "But you said . . ."

"Why do you listen to me?"

She hits me on the arm. "Because you're V! Look at you. Everyone listens to you."

"Kimberly, you need money? I can give you some money. Go hire F. Lee Bailey or something."

"You've got connections, V. You told me about them. What about Cal, Regina, the auction, the whole plan? I can't do this on my own. And I can't go to prison for thirty-eight dollars and forty-seven cents."

"It happens all the time. They have those state-run acting programs where you can learn to mime while doing time," I say, moving the red bags to a lower shelf

She stares at me, unimpressed.

"I'm sorry, Kim."

"Please. You're the only one that can help," and this time I hear the fear in her voice. Why do people think I can do anything? I can't do shit. "V, I made a mistake. Okay. I'm sorry. Haven't you ever done something that you regretted?"

"Never," I lie. I want to tell Kimbers that she's putting her trust in the wrong hands, that I'm the one who ends up damning people, not saving them, because my list of damned friends is growing ever longer. However, she seems intent on this, and who knows, maybe we'll get a miracle after all.

Yeah, right. I killed the last miracle that happened.

She just stares me down.

"Not recently," I answer this time, studying the newest designs for summer. They really do look nice.

She raises her eyebrows. "I know you better than that, V. I fucked up, okay? I admit it, but you can't hold it against me forever." Then her look turns a little uncertain. "Can you?"

I sigh extravagantly and put the lime green bag behind the yellow. Much better. "Okay, I'm back on the case. But very, very reluctantly."

She gives me a hug and picks up the lime green clutch. "I love this one."

"Twenty-eight hundred, and it's yours."

Sixteen

It's opening day, and all around the city, people are donning their Yankees caps and heading to the Bronx. Today's opponent? Why, the World Champion Red Sox, of course. I had the most entertaining evening last night, telling tales with George S. He's a class act; a man that knows how to win. With seven banners under his reign, there's no end to the Bombers' dominance, at least in my foreseeable future.

There was an interesting sighting on Tuesday night at 40/40. Jamie MacGregor and the daughter of the senator from Connecticut are out and about again. What sort of spell has he put on the bluestocking in order to give her the new look she's sport-

ing? Could there be a Scottish bun cooking in the oven? There are telltale signs. I don't know for sure, but I'm happy to say that whatever it is, she looks darling.

And over at Elaine's. Ah, what is New York without Elaine Kaufman presiding over her dining room like a Soviet diplomat? Late last evening, after all the doors were closed, there was a séance to raise the spirit of Jackie Kennedy. Apparently some of the old guard at the Upper East Side eatery are distressed about the latest Kennedy book and want to get a tu quoque direct from the dead first lady's mouth. The Merry Medium is playing coy after the evening, but my sources say a book deal about the heavenly tête-à-tête is in the works.

Tuesday afternoon, I'm visiting Cal at his offices in the shadow of City Hall. It's an austere building with those marble columns and marble floors that make your heels sound like gunshots. The halls are lined with statues of naked people holding up torches, scales, and all sorts of icons of justice that you never see in the real world. In this country, we fall over backward to provide equal justice, but it's all a scam. O.J., Lay and Skilling, Michael Jackson, the Tyco scion, Michael Jackson Part II.

Martha was an aberration because she spent her days teaching people about cleaning. If she'd been a funner person, I'm telling you, she would have dodged that one.

Anywhoo, I end up at Cal's office, his secretary giving me the eye, like I don't belong. "Is this business?" she asks, in her hoity-up-my-toidy voice.

"Social," I answer, giving her my polite "noneya" look. You can never show fear. It's very important.

She taps at some keys on her computer. "I don't see you on Mr. Bassano's schedule."

"Who are you? His fucking mother?"

"You don't want to use that tone in this office. We'll have you tossed out of this building so fast even the cabbies can't catch you."

I will not be engaged by the peons. Instead, I pick up a magazine and hold it in front of my face. I don't have to put up with this crap. As I scan through the table of contents, I realize that I'm reading *SEC Today*. I make a small moue of distaste and let it flutter to the ground.

Wanda the Wicked glares.

Suckage, muckage, eye of bitch, get some manners, get 'em quick.

And miracle of all miracles, she smiles and punches her intercom. "Mr. Bassano, Miss *bleep* is here to see you, sir."

"Well, come on in!" Cal's voice booms through the speaker.

His office is a tribute to the beauty of glass. Everywhere I look, I can see myself reflected in a thousand prisms of light. And there's Cal as well. Oh. Not pretty.

Must . . .

look . . .

away . . .

No, I can't weaken. I'm on a mission, so quickly I regain my bearings. "Cal, wonderful to see you. And your office. It's so . . . deep."

"Yup. I've heard that glass is the ultimate power tool, and it certainly seems to throw people off when they visit. Whatever it takes to gain an advantage."

"Wily. Very wily."

Cal preens, and I notice his hands creeping down under the desk, out of my sight. "Glad you came by. After our talk, I've put together a list of Justice Department who-haws who want to help out with the auction and the donations. Regina's going to play hostess for a little dinner party at my country place in Chappequa to start the ball rolling."

"That would be lovely." And I could slip some incriminating evidence onto his desk at the same time. It's an ingenious solution. Devious, sneaky, and unprincipled. Just like me.

One of Cal's hands slips back on top of the desk, the other firmly hidden in private spots. I focus my attention on the wide forehead, determined not to look, not to wonder.

"We're right behind you, V. One hundred and thirty percent," he says while looking at me—excited, enthusiastic, energetic.

"Doing good works is a great form of deep satisfaction," I say, repeating one of Amy's favorite lines.

Cal winks. "I know exactly what you mean."

* * *

I call Amy and tell her I've been out of the country because I just discovered a twin sister of whom I had no memory. She bought it, telling me that she was delighted I had returned, because, and I quote, "You're the boldfaced name that I need for this project."

I nearly cried.

It takes me another four days to gather enough courage to call Blanche and return to our regularly scheduled Sunday chess match. It's time for me to start getting back into the old routine and on Sunday we play. Okay, I confess, I'm a little nervous. Part of me wants Lucy to have fixed Blanche's memory, and part of me understands that when Lucy does something good, something bad is lurking nearby.

Her response when I call? "It's about time. I need the winnings to pay ConEd, and Marv said he was tapped out. You're good for my pocketbook, V." You see why I love this woman?

On Sunday I get there late, and Blanche is already sitting down. I notice she's wearing pink, which is a good look for her; love agrees with her. The bracelets are there, making music just like always.

"Where're you been? I was worried," she says.

"I've been busy, Blanche. Out of the country."

"You're lying to me, aren't you, V?"

Blanche is nowhere near as gullible as Amy. "I've been thinking over some things. How's your memory? Still forgetting stuff?"

"Not a thing. Yuri says it's because I've been eating more fish," she says, then waves over to the big Cossack, who is watching her possessively. I try to be positive and happy right along with her. I try and smile. It's like cracking cement.

"I bet Yuri's right. Fish is the brain food," I say.

"You look like death warmed over, V. What's eating you?" she asks, opening with the King's Gambit. An aggressive plan, even for Blanche.

"I'm fine."

"You think I can't see? These glasses are very powerful. I can see better than most people your age. Look, see that tree over there? There's a knothole on the fourth branch. Do you see that? I bet you can't see that."

"I see the knothole, Blanche."

"Good, so what's wrong with you? You're not saying two words. That's not healthy."

"I'm fine."

"All right, you don't want to tell me, I won't pry."

Two minutes later, and she's prying again. "How's your mother doing?"

"Better. She's trying to get her own place, so we won't be in each other's hair so much, but the co-op boards keep refusing her." Now I'm sure you're asking, V, why don't you use your powers to get your mother in? And I've given that much thought. The answer? I'm a masochistic lunatic. She grows on you. Like a fungus.

"A place of her own would be good. So she's not going back to Florida, huh?"

"No," I answer.

"Good, you've got your family nearby. Family's important. And your father?"

I shrug. "They're better, but I think he's going to marry somebody else."

"Getting married? At his age? What's he thinking?"

"I don't know."

The bracelets start jingling again. "This is what's eating you, isn't it? The divorce. It's the young that pay the price. But it'll work itself out, V. Go get yourself a therapist."

I smile politely, because the only thing a therapist could get me is another level of power. I move my bishop, and for a while Blanche plays in peace.

"What's happening with Lucy?"

"Everything's fine."

"You backed out of that agreement with her? Sounded like bad business to me."

Bad business? Blanche is the master of the understatement. "No. It's binding."

"Are you sure she's not with the mob? Those Guidos are everywhere in this city. Wouldn't be surprised if they're recruiting ladies these days."

I think for a minute. Lucy's heartless and conscienceless, but she's not in this for the money. "She's her own woman. Sort of a self-made businessperson."

"Well, you gotta do what you gotta do, and I think it's good your standing by your commitments. Marv's been giving me updates on his situation. He thinks you'll get him out of trouble."

I really wish people wouldn't paint me with the saint brush. I have my own motives, V-centric motives. I found it's what works best for me. "I don't know that I can help him, Blanche," I say, because I don't want to disappoint her.

"Well, at least you're trying, and you're a woman of your word. I like that about you, V. Wouldn't play chess with you otherwise. People start welshing on their bets, takes the fun out of the game."

We play on, and Blanche wins the first match. I guess my heart isn't in it today.

I notice the way she keeps looking in Yuri's direction. "I'm glad you found somebody, Blanche. Yuri's a good catch for you."

"You should find yourself a guy, V. It'll perk you right up."

"I already found one."

That brings her head up. "What? You're holding out on me. What's his name?"

"Nathaniel."

"What sort of name is that? It doesn't sound Italian."

"It doesn't really matter. I already lost him."

She whaps me on the hand. "What? Can't you learn anything from an old woman? You've got to go after what you want, V. If you want this Nathaniel, you have to go get him."

I wish I could. I really wish it was that easy, that I could just go after him and tell him I love him. Except that it wouldn't change shit. I suppose I could try and be a better person. I mean, there's nothing that says you have to be an awful person if you're damned. "Maybe I'll do that, Blanche. Maybe I will. Can I ask you something? Do you think I'm the sort of person that could just sit in the park? Feed the birds, crap like that?"

I know I can't save the world, nor can I really do much for my friends, such as they are, but I think I could be a person that would sit in the park and feed the birds. That seems attainable to me.

Blanche thinks for a minute, her lower lip disappearing as she ponders and I await her verdict. Finally she shakes her head. "Nah, you're too busy. Got a high metabolism and can't sit still. My uncle Leonard was just like that, God rest his soul. Always had to be on the go." She points to her head. "You have to keep your brain occupied. You're just like me."

"Yeah, you're probably right."

We finish the game, going double or nothing on the last few moves. Blanche's pocketbook is two hundred dollars heavier.

ConEd's gonna be pleased.

The next day is D day—lunch with Lucy. It's my first real test since I came up with my plan, and I can't just blow her off. No, it's very important to play the devil's devoted bobblehead. I don't think it's a huge acting stretch for me.

She meets me at St. Ambroeus, where I eye the chocolate cakes with the eye of a woman who knows that the road to hell is not paved with good intentions. No, it is succulently lined with chocolate and thin thighs.

After lunch (veal Milanese, pure ambrosia), Lucy gets down to business. Soul business.

"Five souls in less than two weeks. I think that's a record."

"It was a piece of cake," I say, before biting into chocolate ganache with a marvelous raspberry sauce. As far as accomplishments go, I'm not sure it'll get me on the *Today Show,* but I can't help it. It's what I do best.

"You've turned a corner. I knew when I first met you that you would be of special service to the organization."

"I bet you say that to everybody," I murmur in my faux-humble voice.

She leans in on the table, and smiles. "Where do you want to go? Do you want to stay in fashion? Branch out into politics?"

Politics is the world's biggest Snoozapalooza to me, but Lucy's got a tension in her that almost hums. Since when does the devil mingle in politics? This piques my curiosity. "So what's up with that political sideline?"

"You think this has something to do with Meegan?"

I shrug. "Don't know, that's why I asked. Did you make her pregnant again?"

Lucy looks at me. "That's what she wants. Her greatest desire. What would you do?"

This is why Lucy is so dangerous. She doesn't go around turning people into farm animals or curse the world with locusts—no, she gives you the tools to hang yourself. "I think you should give her what she wants. If she's damned herself, it seems to a shame to not make her happy. After all, that's why the program works. You get unsatisfied clients in the program, and the whole thing could go up in flames, metaphorically speaking of course."

She studies me for a minute. "I really wish it was you. You would be absolutely perfect."

"What?"

"I wish *you* were my daughter. For real."

Daughter? I think back on all the stuff she told me about wanting a daughter, all the hell she's put me through, and scary thought this, it actually makes sense.

I lean back and censor my thoughts, which is a basic self-preservation tactic. She wishes I were her daughter. *Her daughter . . .*

Once you get past the ick-factor, I could even be flattered. She (being the devil) actually wants me for her daughter. As compared to my biological mother (also being the devil), who, until I sold my soul and became rich, famous, with more style than Chanel—didn't.

"Why me?" I ask.

"We work so well together. Think about it—we could dissect the fall lines, laugh at everyone's bad plastic surgery, and all those girly things that a mother and daughter are supposed to do. I have a lonely job, and a lonely life."

"You could get married. Couldn't you?" I don't know what rules the devil has to live by. If any.

She waves her hand in the air. "Men. That's another crisis all by itself. Women rule the world. You know it, I know it, the American people know it. If I found a man, he'd just want all my power for himself. Their egos just can't handle it. It's better to put them in the toy category. They're good for pleasure, but that's about all."

"I know what you mean. The ideological differences can be a real relationship killer," I say, thinking about Nathaniel.

Lucy takes a sip of her mineral water. "You haven't told me what you think, V."

"That's very perceptive of you. You know, Lucy, I have a mother already. Now she's no saint, but we're getting closer."

"Tell me something, V. How can a woman who has recruited nine souls into the program think she's going to pass a character test?"

Sometimes it's very difficult to argue with the devil. "I don't have any illusions that I'm gonna be passing any test."

"Yes, you do. And it's those illusions that are keeping you from being happy."

I hold tight to the table, keeping a rein on my thoughts. Careful, V, very careful. "I wouldn't want to be your daughter, Lucy. And it doesn't have anything to do with my illusions."

There's disappointment in Lucy's eyes, but she nods. And quickly I change the subject to her: "When did all this start? This wanting-a-family thing."

She picks at her cake, shaking her head. "It's something that's been building inside me. God has his kid. I want one, too."

"So do you know God, then?"

Lucy takes a long sip of coffee before answering that one. I didn't know it was a toughie. "I used to be in heaven, but it's a limiting place, and God said I was too ambitious and unsettled and that I was disrupting the troops. So, rather than have me prove him wrong, I got kicked out."

"Yeah, I bet you were a disruption." Lucy has that effect on people.

"I told him that man would always need to be better than anyone else. He didn't like that, but it's the truth. He's a little idealistic about man. I'm not." She shrugs, as if she didn't just diss the whole human race. But that's Lucy. She likes to see what she likes to see, and I'm not going to argue.

"What's he like? George Burns, Morgan Freeman, Charlton Heston?" (My money's on Charlton Heston.)

"Arrogant, a bit of a know-it-all."

I hear it in her voice. Lucy is jealous, jealous, jealous. Well, welcome to my world, honey.

"Do you miss it? Heaven, I mean."

"Sometimes, but I have New York. It's close."

I can't believe she's actually talked to God. That God and the devil might actually sit and chat over—chocolate ganache. I look around the room, just to check and see if Charlton Heston is anywhere nearby. All clear. Maybe I'm a little disappointed. "So you want to show up God, don't you?"

"Well, of course."

I watch all the faces of the people at their tables, all watching each other with little beady eyes. This is why I sold my soul, to know that I am too cool ever to have beady eyes. But there's always someone better, soulless or not. I can deny it every which way from Monday, but the truth is that I get the beady eyes too. Even now. How can you fight the feeling? I think God's a sucker. "You're going to win."

She nods. "I know."

And we wrap up lunch. The waiter comes by and whispers in her ear, and she turns and waves to the former mayor of New York.

"What was that about?"

"He just picked up the check."

When in New York, never bet against the Yankees. And don't bet against the devil, either.

Seventeen

What Connecticut good girl gone wild is planning a March surprise? As spring rolls forward into summer, it seems the birds and the bees weren't the only ones getting busy. The proud papa has turned over a new leaf as well. Seems that both have been seen hitting AA meetings religiously.

And the rumors, oh, the rumors!!! I swear we couldn't make this up. What hot, homo haute couturist has been turned down for the cover of Outré? It seems the designer wasn't quite gay enough. We've all heard the stories—the supermodels, the late-night disguises at Scores—but has he finally moved out of the closet?

After skirting through my first test with Lucy, I'm ready to move forward with the charity auction. V, what are you doing? you may ask. Forgive me if I don't share all the details for my Lucy revenge plot, but her spies are everywhere, and I need the element of surprise. Suffice it to say that the auction has to be beyond successful in order for me to get back at her. And for that to happen, I have to bring in the greediest, vilest, and basest citizens of New York, the most likely candidates for the Life Enrichment Program. And you say, Why would greedy, vile, and base citizens go to a charity auction, V? They will because I have just the bait: the auction pièce de résistance—the inimitable gift bag.

Those of you not wise to my way of my life would say that I'm deluding myself, and gift bags are a benevolent gesture.

Oh, have you got much to learn, my friend. No one cares about raising money for a "worthy cause." No, the true lure is the swag. The circling buzzards you see at these events are not hovering near the bar, nor the stage, nor even the disturbing pictures of starving children. No, they are eyeing the loot to determine how much they can carry out, and if anyone would notice if they took two.

It's a twisted, perverted system of bribery and kissy-ass, and today it is my mission to show Amy just how it all works. You see, Amy has a keen eye for drama and human suffering; however, she knows squat about fashion and what impresses people in my circles. I divide the task into three subcategories: cosmetics, services, and bling-bling.

"Who would donate to the cause?" she asks, her eyes blinking guilelessly.

"Everyone," I answer, because the secret is that it's all about getting the right people to want to be you. "Let me explain. Say that Bulgari has committed to donate twenty-five pairs of their newest diamond-drop earrings."

Platinum, silver, posts of gold, good bling-fairy, bring them to hold.

I pull the black Bulgari's bag from behind my back. "Now I go to Harry Winston and say that we've got Bulgari on board, but we need to add that H. W. cachet. What do you think they'll tell us?"

Slowly the beauty of it dawns on her: the complete one-up-manship that is totemically Manhattan. Amy begins to smile. "We could play off MAC against Clé de Peau."

"Now you're talking."

"What about services?"

"Fake bakes, spas, and catering. Possibly some chocolates from Jacques Torres, dinner at Spice Market. A PDA from Blackberry."

"Oh, I love those things. Digitally geeky with style."

For the next two hours, we're making phone calls from my office at the store. We've just gotten D&G on board when Kimbers runs in, out of breath. "They've moved up the grand jury date."

"Don't worry, you'll be fine," I murmur while adding up the hour's philanthropic mega-millions.

However, Amy's ears have picked up the magic word. She puts line one on hold. "Trial? You're going on trial? Did you kill anyone?"

"Insider trading."

Apparently, insider trading doesn't rate with Amy. "Oh."

I do the intros. "Amy, Kimberly. Kimberly, Amy. Amy is helping me with the auction. And by the way, Cal is having a party at his house to get some of those Wall Street types on the bandwagon."

"Really? Oh, I knew you would come through." She gives me an almost-hug and then pulls back, embarrassed. I'm not a hugger, and the world knows it.

For a split second I feel a thump-thump inside my chest cavity where my heart should be, and ruthlessly I squash it down. I've made this mistake once before, and I'm not gonna repeat it.

"Don't get your hopes up," I tell her.

"Are you kidding? This is the best news I've heard in weeks," Kimbers says, her face flushed with happiness. "You've saved my life, you know that don't you? I could have never gone through this on my own."

Amy ignores the blinking red light on the phone to look up at Kimbers. "Have you considered a career in daytime drama?"

Oh, no. See, I know Kim's dreams. For me, it was purses; for her, it was acting. Ever since she saw Shirley MacLaine at the Ninety-second Street Y.

"Are you kidding?" she says. "I would love to act."

"You're too curvy for drama. Daytime's where you should be. I have friends on *All My Children*."

"Really? You think I could?"

"Can you do dramatic readings?"

"Romeo, Romeo, whereforth art thou Romeo. Oh, that this too, too solid flesh would melt. A horse, a horse, my kingdom for a horse."

I'm figuring that this crap is actor-code for "yes," and nod wisely.

Amy is yelling good-bye into line one, and then turns back to Kimbers. With my luck, it was Cindy Adams she's pissing off. "With a little practice, you'd be good. You know, start out with a small walk-on role—the serial-killing dental assistant, or the babysitter for the capricious child that gets kidnapped by his evil father who still loves his wife and is using the kid for leverage. You'd get strangled, of course, maybe even raped. But death is really the best shot to fame and stardom."

As they pass the time discussing Stanislavski and Juilliard (do we really care?), I make calls to Sephora, the Garden Spa, and the Plaza. Before the afternoon is over, we have more than $3 million in donated goods and services, not counting the $2 million worth of poofed-up merchandise that I used to start the bidding. It's still not good enough. I want more. By the end of the week, I'm figuring we can log $10 million in donations, and I'll go down as the hottest fund-raiser since Jackie O.

Never underestimate a Level 7.

I throw myself into the auction because it's a good outlet for all my currently unused sexual energy. Have I mentioned my Nathaniel dreams at night? Actually, they're really more replays, but they're starting to keep me awake.

I consider talking to Shelby about my problems, but she is no help. She has invested in some ancient Indian (Native or Eastern, I don't know, nor, frankly, do I care) art designed to ward off death, and I think that's just stupid. Death happens. However, I do feel sorry for her, and so I don't laugh about it to her face.

The final straw occurs when I come home to a dead chicken. I don't mind dead chickens, but I want them on a plate, sautéed, preferably covered in cheese and a light yet zesty tomato sauce. This one was hanging from the ceiling.

Mother is blasé. "It's gonna protect you from the evil spirits, V. You've got a dark cloud hanging over you."

Translation: "I worry about you."

"If my dark cloud would move back to Florida, where she belongs, I wouldn't need rites of sacrifice in my living room."

Translation: "That's very sweet, Mother, but get rid of the dead chicken."

"Don't mess with the dark side, V."

"You don't know who you're talking to, Mom." I stare at the offending fowl. "How much did she pay you to do this to me?"

Mother looks shocked and then she pounds on her chest. "Pay me? This is from my heart, V. You need this protection."

"Why can't you be like all the other mothers, Mom? What happened to fresh-baked chocolate-chip cookies?"

"I'm allergic to chocolate."

I sigh. "Cut him down."

"Shelby says he has to stay up there for forty-eight hours."

"FORTY-EIGHT HOURS?"

Wisely, Mom moves back a step.

I look up at the chicken. Then look at her.

"I'll be back."

"Where're you going?"

"To kill Shel."

I find Shelby in her apartment. The doorman casts me a funny look and buzzes me up. When I walk through the door, I am knee-deep in Saint Thomas on a budget. There are beads and candles, and crosses, which tells you how desperate Shelby really is. I walk over the pieces of straw lining the floor and wait for a cow—or some other piece of large livestock—to emerge. None appears. But Shelby does come out in this robe that is embroidered with dragons, and yes, I think it's zombies. Not her best look.

"Shelby. Fire your designer. The pits-of-hell look is so five minutes ago. You need something more upbeat."

She looks around. "It's protection. The spirits surround us, they are everywhere. Today I was nearly run over by a taxi. I was crossing the street and"—she holds out her arm to show the bruises—"somebody pulled me back out of the way. I never even got a chance to thank him. It's happening, V. I can feel it. Fortuna says the spirits of death are stalking me."

I look around and see no spirits. "Shel, there's no such thing as spirits."

She hunches her shoulders. "How do you know? I bet you didn't think the devil existed before you met her, did you?" She waves a hand through the air. "They're out there, waiting to harm us."

I use my powers to raise a lamp (Level 6, elementary levitation) and fly it across the room. "Like that?"

Shelby pulls her robe tighter. "They're out there, V."

"Shelby, I did that. It's nothing more than a parlor trick. I think your psychic is part of the Life Enrichment Program."

"Madam Fortuna does not deceive. She only exposes the truths we are not willing to face."

"What did she tell you?"

"That I'm going to die a violent death. That the ball of fate has dropped, and I cannot escape my doom."

A breeze slips through the apartment, and even though I laugh in the face of danger, violent death is only funny when it doesn't concern me or, alternatively, someone I know. "You're not going to die."

"Yes, I am. This is twice, V. How many times do I have to stare death in the eyes before you believe me?"

"If you don't shut up about it, I'll kill you myself. Do we understand each other?"

She glares. "Yes."

"Good. I want you to keep your voodoo out of my apartment."

"It's your mother, V. Not me. She's her own woman."

"Shelby, save the excuses. If it keeps up, you're going to lose your assistant. I'll make her quit. And you know how much I like having her out of the house."

"I need help."

"Well, yes, you do, but trust me, Mother is not a licensed therapist, nor does she play one on TV."

"Get over it, V. We're practicing our *asentados* together, and

I'm considering a franchising deal on the supplies. Candles, incense, animal parts."

"What happened to lingerie?"

She shrugs. "It's been done to death. I just can't compete, but this—"

"Fine. Just keep the dead chickens out of my living room."

"It's necessary. There's just so many dark forces at work," says the woman whose apartment is far from cozy. The endless shelves of burning candles alone are enough to strike incontinence into the heart of New York's Bravest.

I can't reason with her when she's all hoo-dooed out like this. It's freaky. I decide to try and bring back the old Shelby I knew and hated. "Oh, enough of the death talk. We could go out, walk in the park."

"We would get mugged. Are you nuts?"

"Okay, strike the park. Come with me down to the store. Let's go find some souls, or go shopping, whichever comes first."

She looks around the room, seeing ghosts that I refuse to acknowledge. "I shouldn't go out."

"Shel, if you're going to die, they can get you here just as well as out on the street. Hell, you sneeze wrong and this apartment will go up in flames. What did you sell your soul for if you're not going to live a little, huh?"

My words sink through her subconscious. For a moment she does this trance thing, and then she walks over to a candle and lights it. "All right. I've put a layer of protection around us that will last for a few hours."

She's out of there in thirty minutes (snuffing out candles: twenty-seven minutes), which I'm glad because I don't like these dark, eerie places. There are things I don't understand, things that I don't want to understand, but I know enough to realize that after I die, I'm in trouble.

I've heard the rumors. Having your tongue pierced, not with a cute diamond stud but with scalding spikes. Or taking a full-body wrap in an ocean of blood. It's not in the V repertoire of things I want to do after I die. Still, I look at my choices: living the life of all rewards, or schlepping my way back to Jersey, with thighs that jiggle when I walk, and at the end of the day, I end up in hell anyway. Nope, it's damned if I do and damned if I don't.

We get our hair styled at Elizabeth Arden and then shop like two women possessed. Because, well, we are.

Eighteen

I'm sure you've heard about the grand fete auction that It Bag designer V is hosting at the St. Regis Hotel. The cause is worthy, benefiting New York's lost souls of the Lower Manhattan Women's Shelter. I'm planning to be there myself, because there, but for the grace of God, go I.

And speaking of lost souls, who has noticed that funky new religion that is taking Tribeca by storm? First it's the Material Girl breaking off her ties with nonaffiliated friends, and then Mr. Hollywood, Charlie Sanderson, fires his longtime agent because he's a Catholic. Interesting to see celebrities, who have long eschewed anything remotely God-like, now embracing the

latest metaphysical hootenanny, inspired by
the best-selling book The Life Enrichment
Program: Staying Focused in a Mad,
Mad, Mad, Mad World.

After suffering severe withdrawal symptoms, I consider many opportunities to track down Nathaniel. Coincidentally, two days later, I just happen to find myself in Central Park at the atrocious hour of 6:00 A.M. watching the natural beauty of the runners as they do their morning routines. It is poetry in motion watching their muscles pump, and the sheer concentration on their faces as they begin their morning constitutional makes me glad to be alive. And if you bought all that shit, then you are so not worthy. I'm not here to speak to him, or anything. I just want to *see* him.

I'm wearing cutoffs, T-shirt, and sunglasses, and my hair is tucked under a Yankees baseball cap. It's a brilliant disguise and makes me completely unrecognizable to all who know me: I would never, *ever* stoop to wearing a Yankees cap.

My heart stops for a moment when I see a broad, studly gentleman running my way, and I hold my breath. Alas, it is only one of the Afflecks. A moment later I am passed by Howard Stern and a Stern-esque blond. Joggers pass, all athletic and surgically enhanced. None are Nathaniel. My patience is wearing thin, but at last I spy a familiar figure. He passes and doesn't notice me. I consider calling out, but my intent isn't to start anything, I just want to remember. My feet start moving before I know it, and soon I'm jogging through Central Park.

It's a low moment in my life, jogging, anonymous, merely to get a glimpse of a man who is way too good for me, but a woman in love is pretty much an exercise in stupidity anyway, so I'm not gonna beat myself up for it. He's pretty quick (like I didn't know), and I'm pretty slow (like you couldn't guess), and in no time at all I've lost him. But I keep running. I go around the corner, prepared to see nothing, but it isn't nothing. It's him.

"What are you doing?"

Damn, he's seen through my clever Yankee disguise. I put a hand on my hip, going for cocky and self-confident. "Jogging. It's a public park."

"If you want to get laid again, find some other dick."

Okay, there's issues here, and I don't blame him, but he also doesn't realize that I'm a Level 7. "I've got a few things to tell you."

"Go ahead."

"First of all, I'm sorry. I wish I had met you a long time ago, but I didn't. And because of things that I've done, my life is a lot more complicated than most. There are things that I can't share, and because of that, a relationship between us is not in the picture. And unfortunately, when you take out the relationship, it just leaves the sex, which was really fantastic, by the way, I have absolutely no complaints, but I can see that both you and I have issues with only a sexual relationship. And you're leaving, too."

"What am I supposed to say, V?"

"You could say hello, for instance."

He cracks a smile at that. Ah, progress! "Hello."

"In certain foreign countries, a greeting is accompanied by a kiss."

"What countries?"

"How the hell should I know? Am I the world traveler here?" I answer, and he kisses me. Please note that Nathaniel is truly the world's best kisser. He makes an ordinary woman feel like she's extraordinary, and an extraordinary woman feel like she's exceptionally normal. I linger in one long kiss. A final kiss good-bye.

Again.

When I pull back, I tell him my second most deepest, darkest secret, which is something that I will admit only once. "I love you, and although I'm not fully cognizant of the various idiosyncrasies of this emotion, I do know that you give me hope and you make me want to be good, and you don't know what a monumental achievement that truly is."

He starts to stay something, but I can't have that.

Moments gained and visions drawn, memoria, remoria, time is gone.

It's incredibly easy to make a man forget you when you're past Level 5. If I were a better person, I would wipe his memory clear of me completely, but I'm selfish that way and only wipe out the last ten minutes. Before he comes out of it, I race down the path (much faster this time), and don't look back.

I stop, catch my breath, and replay the memory that I took from him. I collapse on a bench and teeter between laughter and tears. It's another memory that I can store away in my scrapbook for a life I wish I had.

Another jogger wings by and notices me sitting there. He gives me the once-over and says, "Go, Yankees."

I shoot him the finger. "Yank this, asshole." He gets the point.

The next morning, I'm drifting in a nirvanic state, caught in that perfect moment before you wake up, when life as you know it, with all its problems, doesn't exist. You know they're going to catch up with you, but right then, with my eyes closed, and my dreams filled with thoughts of lying in my bed with Nathaniel, I'm at peace.

Then, as all things good must turn to crap, the phone rings.

It's Marv. See what I mean?

"V, look, I've stayed quiet, letting you pull your strings with the SEC, not wanting to rock the boat or interfere, but I can't stay quiet any longer. I went to sleep last night watching Court TV and woke up this morning in a cold sweat."

Thoughts of Marv in a cold sweat wipe away all traces of Nathaniel in a warm one, so reluctantly I wake up. It's time for the big powwow with Marv and Kimbers. I'm not sure it's a good idea if we're all in a room together; perhaps someone will die. Most likely, it would be Marv. Anywhoo, all that death business aside, I should let him know that yes, my plan to save his worthless ass is, of course, going splendidly. I invite him over to my apartment, because now is his only chance to see how the truly successful people in New York—like myself—live. Oh, but V, you sound so malicious and so vainglorious.

Yes, that's right. I do, don't I? Lest we forget, he is the infidel here, not I.

Ahem, my mother has been instructed to refrain from all ritualistic sacrifices (which are legal in New York, if used for religious purposes. I did not know that), and rather than face my ex-husband and his ex-mistress, she is heading out with her non-ex-gigolo, so I have the place all to myself, which means that Marv is going to see my showroom apartment, will be sneered at obligingly by Ed the doorman (who I gave an extra hundred to do just that), and will of course be blinded by my six-carat diamond, right-hand Bulgari ring.

Can I endure the punishment of the damned merely to see the abject misery in my ex's sad little face as he gazes on the wonder of my new existence?

Of course I can; why do you think I signed on?

Less than ten minutes later, both are in the V-Suite, and I'm happier than a kid in Dylan's Candy Bar.

"V, this place! It's fabulous!" Kimbers exclaims, her voice shaded with appropriate levels of jealous.

I give them the tour (thirteen rooms) and make a big show of the view (the sun setting on the Hudson). Kimbers gets louder and louder, and Marv doesn't say a word.

After we're settled in the living room, he sinks his hands low in his pockets. I know that look, and I paid attention to it for many years. Tonight it gives me great satisfaction to ignore it. "Let's get down to matters criminal," I say.

Marv looks down. "Yeah, it'd be a sorry-ass crime if we forget why we're here."

"If you could just keep it in your pants, we wouldn't BE here. Just once—" I snap back.

"Children, children, children." And now Kimbers is the voice of reason. How low can we go, hmmm? Well, considering I have sold my nonrefundable, no-returns, damned-forever soul, I can go pretty low without worrying about my future prospects in eternity.

She continues: "If you don't work it out, we're both going to jail. Marv, I don't want to be nobody's bitch, so behave."

"Things are going according to plan," I say mysteriously.

Marv, who knows my planning abilities well and never truly appreciated them, isn't buying it. "Whose plan?"

"I have connections with Cal Bassano. He's helping me with a charity auction."

"So what does this have to do with dropping the charges?" Marv gets up. "I don't know how this is going to work."

"You want to solve your own problems? The ones that I did NOT create for you, thank you very much? Once again, you take no responsibility for your own mistakes. Everything is MY FAULT. You want to leave, you go right ahead."

Marv heads for the door, and I'm there to open it for him.

"Both of you, sit down," orders Kimbers.

Marv hesitates, manly pride warring against common sense. He knows I'm his best shot. I have connections that he could never imagine. He plops back on the couch, arms locked across his chest.

Reluctantly I follow.

Kimbers smiles at us, that can't-we-all-get-along? smile that the East Side nannies use when they're out of options and Valium. "V, tell us what we need to do," she says, speaking very slowly.

"I told you both, I don't need any help. It's all under control." In fact, I do have it all under control. The dinner party is tomorrow night. Oops, the stock statement with those pesky boo-boo transactions will appear in Cal's hands, which Paolo will be there to witness and mainly act the outraged innocent. Then V will have a little talk with Cal on how he can't very well prosecute Marv and Kimbers for something that he did as well, and then Cal will cave. Poof, problem solved.

"Why do you think he's going to drop the charges?" This from Marv. He looks at me, and I tune in on his thoughts. *You're fucking him, aren't you?*

The idea that I will actually service a man to save my husband from jail is so repulsive (far more than the thought of actually fucking Cal) that I gasp. "No, I would never do something like that. And especially not for you."

You let Todd James fuck you at the Christmas party.

I set my jaw for serious fighting now. "I never slept with anyone but you, you jackass. Todd James was passed out on the bed for half the night, under the pile of coats. If you had been paying attention to the party, instead of spending half the night with your eyes superglued to his wife's cleavage, you would've known that."

Marv stops. "You didn't sleep with him? He said you did."

"Eww."

My horror must have seemed genuine because Marv looks at me with new eyes. "You didn't, did you?"

"DUH!"

He runs a hand through his hair and looks at me, confused (not a stretch for Marv). "Are you sure you didn't sleep with him? He said you did."

"And that just clinches it for you, doesn't it? Did you ask me, Marv? Did you even think about saying anything to me about it?"

"No."

"If you had learned to *co-mun-ni-cate*, perhaps we would have stayed married."

"I'm sorry, V. He told me, and I believed him."

I am shocked at this, because apologies were never Marv's forte. "Do you feel badly, Marv?"

"Yes."

"How badly?"

"I feel bad, okay?"

"I'm sorry too, Marv. Okay?"

Kimbers now just looks peeved (I guess Marv never apologized to her, either). "All this rehash of personal history is very touching, but can we get back on the case here?"

"Both of you will have to trust me," I say, looking them both in the eye.

They look unconvinced.

Now, I admit my track record isn't one to brag about, but

would it be so hard for somebody—just once—to have a little faith in me?

Probably.

Meegan has a baby shower two days later. I get the hand-engraved invitation by messenger, so I'm assuming I'm not on her shit-list, which is somewhat of a relief, because it means she'll never know the awful thing I did to her.

What do you buy for the woman you have first destroyed the baby of and then condemned to hell? The truth is that there is nothing I can give her to make up for my deeds, and I end up buying a Mercedes convertible (one of the mini ones, ages five and up) and a case of diapers. The car's a spiffy shade of blue, but it's not even close to what I owe her.

Her grandmother has rented out the Crystal Room at Tavern on the Green, and it's overflowing with ladies of all shapes and sizes and varying degrees of wealth ranging from "Going bankrupt in Manhattan" to "We bought four houses in the Hamptons with Dickie's year-end bonus." I went to baby showers in Jersey before (my cousin Carla had *seven*. We tried to tell her that anything over two was tacky, but would she listen? Nooooo), but nothing in Jersey was ever like this. There is an overabundance of Tiffany-blue packages, a reclining car seat with built-in massage, and last, but never least, a Lulu the Lamb rocker. Instead of balloons, there are topiaries in the shape of a bear in need of a diet, a tiny pig, and some jackass with long, droopy ears.

In the middle of each table is a little Maclaren baby carriage, and for place mats we all have cloth diapers with our names embroidered on them. I search the crowd for Meegan and see her holding court from the table in the center of the room. She's smiling, and glowing. Full of baby happiness. Anyone looking at her would think she had it all.

"V!!!!" She launches herself at me as if I were the best person in the world. I endure the hug and then take a step back. "Be careful, or you'll hurt the little guy—or girl."

"Oh, you're right," she says as she gingerly sits back down. "Sometimes I get so excited, it's like I'm just drowning in happiness. Do you ever get like that?"

"No."

She laughs, like I'm making a joke. "You're such a kidder. Can you believe it? Pregnant, again! Jamie has been the greatest. We've been going through parenting classes together. He's my rock. I don't know what I'd do without him. OH! And guess what??? We found this great Tudor estate out in Greenwich. It's too die for! AND WE GOT IT." Then she starts to squeal.

It's like I'm looking at a Stepford wife, but Meegan is no Nicole Kidman, even on a good day. "This is what you want, isn't it?"

"It's what I've always wanted. A house in the 'burbs. A family. A baby with a cute little christening dress."

"A christening, huh?"

"We've already picked out the church. Presbyterian. Serious, yet dynamic. Perfect for a family who needs to grow in their spiritual faith."

I lower my voice. "Uh, Meegan, you're still in the Life Enrichment Program, aren't you?"

She nods. "Level 3."

"Then what's with the Presbyterian mumbo-jumbo?"

"It's stability, V. A baby needs stability in the family life."

She points across the way to a tall woman with flaming hair. "There's Jamie's mother. She's a jewel. She flew in a week ago from Scotland. It's like the mother I've never had, V."

"You're really okay with this, aren't you?"

She thinks a minute, her hand rubbing protectively over the slight swelling to her belly. "Lucy gave me back the thing I always wanted. I feel like a whole woman now. The doctors think it's a miracle."

I force a laugh. "Yeah. I'm glad everything worked out for you. I'm sorry. Hey, look outside. Don't you love the weather like this? Why don't you ditch the crowd for a minute, and let's just go and talk. Catch up. I haven't seen you in a while."

Her smile hardens a bit. "You're okay, V, but I don't trust you near Jamie, I don't like your attitude on kids, and I don't have time to sit in the park anymore. I don't like the pigeons. They're shit."

It wasn't anything I didn't deserve, but that didn't mean it didn't hurt.

Nineteen

The heads are starting to roll in the Scores Sex-Stock Tip Scandal. First to fall, the chairman of the Second Avenue Stock Exchange, Walter Spears. Apparently, Walter never grasped that IPO meant Initial Public Offering.

And under the "You Only Thought I Knew Gossip" heading, did I not tell you all that Fauslhamabaad would be soon holding elections? The U.S. peace delegation was so pleased with the warm reception they received from the Fauslhamabaadian government that there is talk of granting Fauslhamabaad most-favored-nation status. Does that mean we may soon see the end of the war? Wait and see. I've been in-

vited to the soiree with the leader's wife, the charming Sahira, and I just can't wait. Of course, you'll be the first to hear all the details.

Already the critics are pounding the "still-yet-unreleased" summer blockbuster. According to sources, the movie's diva-licious star is spitting nails because her ex-lover (the director, but you didn't hear it here) never bought into the sweet directorial nothings she was whispering across the pillow. The studio has planned a press junket for the two, but I'm betting it's going to be canned because the life insurance premiums on having those two in the same room would cost as much as the movie. That's show biz!

The Bassano estate in Westchester is a nice place, with a helicopter pad out back and stables. There's a preponderance of purple azaleas and tulips aplenty. It's a pretty place, a little drafty.

Regina's dressed to the nines, in anticipation of Paolo the horndog, I'm sure. We gather in the conservatory, and their butler *(butler?)* serves drinks to all. It's the first time I've seen Regina in her moneyed element, and now I realize what Paolo must see in her. She's gracious, charming, and okay, I'm eating my words, nonboring. Cal has got his hair slicked back and a glass of whiskey in one hand as he wanders through the room, one hand tucked in his belt.

I'm introduced to Charles, Charles, Richard, Davidson, Biff, Davis, Jefferson, Bill, Bing, and Mahajabib-something-hoobie. If I was inclined to listen to conversations about the stock markets, interest rates, and the financial indicators, I would have been thrilled. For the next forty minutes, the only thrill I have is watching Paolo and Regina make cow eyes at each other (CAN SOMEONE JUST SHOOT ME AND PUT ME OUT OF MY MISERY? Oh, forgot. Eternal damnation. Strike that last rant, please).

At last Amy puts on a short presentation about the shelter, bringing Svetlana in for show-and-tell. As Svetlana tells her story, people get sucked right in, and the finance talk ceases. I can see Amy's handiwork as the woman starts to describe the day her husband came home from work to a burned dinner and knocked her around. As she fondled the steak knife, she swore that she would have revenge, and so she planned, and saved, and hid her secrets from him, until she had enough to get a new identity. There is even a quiet sound track playing in the background. *Flight of the Valkyries.* Very effective. The men are nodding, and the wives are wiping tears from their eyes. In less than two hours, the whole room is digging for their check-books.

And she's not even a client. Wow.

After dinner, it's time for the true drama to begin. Paolo has agreed to play the detective in my little tableau. On the flimsy excuse of needing to find the little girls' room, I sneak into

Cal's study. It is really fabulous. The giant hand-carved desk looks out over his man-made lake, and I swear I see a flock (bevy? group? gaggle? do we care?) of swans swimming in the lake. But I'm forgetting my mission, and we can't have that. In less than a minute, I have found his brokerage statements in the file cabinet labeled "Stocks."

I pick up one of the papers, and quicker than you can say "Ernst Young Lynch Lybrand Anderson Mulroney," I've got a poofed-up copy, complete with the purchase of 15,000 shares of Synron. And then, voilà, the sell order, which just happens to be on the same day that Marv sold his.

I take the papers and lay them oh so innocently on the desk. And then, oops, V spills her wine all over the desk. Bad, bad V. It looks like I'll need help (i.e., a witness to Cal's indiscretions).

I stick my head out the door. "Paolo! Can you come here for a minute?"

"V? You need some help?"

It's not Paolo. It's Cal. Okay, change of plans then. He saunters into the room (Cal is a really good saunterer) and sees the wine spilled over the desk. "Look what you've done! You don't get any of that on your fancy dress."

I start to blot it up with my cocktail napkin. "Cal, I'm so sorry. Red wine. It's a bitch to get out."

"Let me help," he says and pulls out a pristine white handkerchief.

"I can't believe I'm such a klutz," I say, and then I begin the spell.

Stocks of yesterday, stocks of old, remember how you bought and sold.

It happens really fast, the memory implant. Cal picks up the statements, his eyes taking in the numbers in front of him. His whole body freezes. "Oh, God."

"Is something wrong?" I ask innocently, like I don't know that his sense of justice is now about to turn wonky.

He starts to blot and read and blot and read, and his forehead sinks lower and lower. The truth (according to V) is starting to resonate. Eventually he looks up; I've seen that look on four-A.M. drunks, too.

"What is it?" I ask.

He stares into space.

"Cal?" I snap my fingers in front of his face. "What it is? We got a heart attack here?" Oh, God, I hope not. I'm not out to hurt anybody, I just want to keep Kimbers and Marv on the right side of the law. I expected shame, anger, you know, the usual suspects that I'm intimately familiar with, but not this . . . this . . . shock.

"I can't believe. Oh, God. I can't believe it."

"What?" I ask, my voice cracking.

"I did it. I did it. I did it." He buries his head on the desk.

"Cal." I touch his arm. "Cal, there's red wine there. It won't come out. Trust me, you need to snap out of this before it stains that . . . fancy white shirt."

"I know you're just being nice. What are people going to say? Me, the defender of justice in this town? And I sold them all out."

It's guilt. He must be a Catholic. I didn't plan for guilt. I think fast. "Cal, nobody has to know. It can be our little secret."

"But how can I live with myself? How can I look myself in the mirror every morning?"

Actually, I don't know how he looks at himself in the mirror every morning currently, but okay, I'm a hard-ass. "Cal, it's going to be okay."

He looks at me, stares hard, looking exactly like a six-year-old who knows his mommy is lying. "No, it's not."

"Let's think this through. You did something just a little outside the boundaries of what you consider right, but we're not a judgmental society." I sit down on the corner of the desk (carefully avoiding the wine—I'm not an idiot, I'm in Chanel). "After all, how else are we supposed to get ahead?"

He shakes his head. Damn. That line always worked when Lucy said it, why not *moi*? "Not by breaking the law. A man has to break a sweat to get where he wants in life."

I have not sweated in over two years, and by the gold-trimmed trappings surrounding me currently, I'm thinking Cal isn't a sweater either, just a damn good liar. "Look, Cal. Look around you. How do you think you got this house? Everybody cuts corners. Everybody."

"I bought Microsoft at $10, Intel at $7, and was part of the Google IPO. I've never cut corners."

Talk about your lucky breaks, but I'm not a believer. "But the reality is, you did. Once. Synron," I remind him, trying to figure out how to work in the "dropping the charges against Marv and Kimbers" angle.

284

"I'll have to serve time. It's the right thing to do. I can't betray all those people I put behind bars. I just can't."

"NO!!!"

I jump up from the desk, forgetting about my Chanel, which tells you how panicked I am. "You can't go to prison, Cal. Think of your family, your daughter, all those law-breakers out there that you need to catch. Marshal Dillon, right? What's going to happen to this one-horse town if the marshal gets thrown in the hoosegow?"

I can't believe the self-sacrificial tendencies of this man. I've seen goats that aren't this accommodating.

"I couldn't live with myself, V. It's time. I'll go turn myself in." He rises from the desk, and for the first time I see something that I overlooked in those pudgy jowls before.

Strength. Character. Why do I keep missing these things? Oh, yeah. I'm bad. I forgot.

However, bad or not, I'm not going to let him do this. I can't. I swallow something inside me, possibly pride, I'm not sure, but it didn't set well inside me (I've never been a swallower; I'm too self-aware). "Cal, let me see the papers."

He hands them to me, and I poof up a match. His forehead pops back into shape and he snatches the papers away. "You can't. That's evidence."

Once again, Mr. Martyr is determined to fall on the sword.

But before the blade hits his chest, Paolo bursts into the room.

"Excuse me? You're about ten minutes too late," I say, hoping Paolo'll keep his mouth shut about the plan.

Paolo, however, is in full Liberace mode (ever since the Page Six item, he's been hell to work with). He tosses his cape behind his back and throws back his carefully coiffed hair (à la Barry Gibb). "You fiend! You sit behind your big desk, deciding guilt and innocence on a mere whim, and yet here you are . . . guilty of the same crimes." Paolo pulls off a glove and slaps Cal in the face. (Gloves? That's *so* last year.) "I demand you let my people go!"

I grab Paolo's hand before the other glove comes off. "Ixnay on the lanpay."

Paolo does not speak pig latin, only 1970s John Waters. "I will not tolerate this. Think of your poor daughter, your darling Regina."

I stomp hard on Paolo's Italian kid leather riding boots and grab the papers from Cal's hand.

Before anyone else can screw up (including me), I light the match and start the papers burning.

Paolo looks at me in disbelief. "*Cara*, no! You cannot destroy the evidence."

Cal tries to pull them from my hand.

And then the fire alarm begins to go off, starting up the ceiling sprinkler system. My flames fizzle, but I'm undeterred. I stuff the papers (slightly burned and soaked) into the shredder. Anyone who's ever fed a crumpled dollar into a Coke machine already knows how this goes over. Hell. I start to rip up the paper, which will not die. Cal fights me for it. He's bigger, but I can do magic. I freeze him for a minute (behavior modification), and Paolo leaps into the fray.

"What are you doing? The bastard must pay!"

"Paolo, he didn't *do* anything. Remember?"

"V, you are so literal. Of course he's done bad things."

"I'm not going to let him go to prison for something he didn't do." Oh, God—scruples. Morals. Values. I can't believe the shit that's coming out of my mouth. Oh, how the mighty have fallen.

"Well, of course he's not going to prison," Paolo snaps, getting all huffy. "He's just going to drop the charges, and everything will just go away."

"You don't understand." I glance over at Frozen Cal. (The magic only works for a few minutes. Life Enrichment Clause Number 375). "He doesn't want to look the other way. He wants to be punished for what he's done."

Paolo gives Cal an appraising look. "Oh, that's so *kinky*."

"We're not going to do this."

"But Regina . . ."

"Get over her, Paolo, and find yourself a übermodel, with umlauts to match. You're too shallow and self-obsessed for someone so ordinary."

Nathaniel is ordinary. I'm shallow and self-obsessed. The truth eventually hits Paolo.

"I can't give her up."

I look at Paolo, and I know exactly the ache he's feeling. Exactly. "You don't have a choice."

After undoing Cal's memory plants, the rest of the evening passes quite successfully. Amy is in her element, and I'm unusually quiet. Introspection will do that to a person. After analyzing my life in that intimate minutiae that only women are capable of, I realize one basic truth.

I'm so fucked.

There's a certain grass-is-always-greener about me, and I suspect there's a lot of me's out there who have a starboard cabin in the little *Titanic* that is the world. I wanted to be cooler than all shit, show up Marv, and have a great bag, so I sold my soul. It's a high price, but I thought it was worth it. Somewhere along the way, I'm not sure exactly when, although I would suspect it was when I jumped in after the kid in Central Park, I began to want to be good. This from a woman who sold her soul to be cool, because she knew there was no chance in hell she was going to heaven.

And to be fair, I still want to be good. Today I'm willing to state it aloud. I want to be good. I want to be a park sitter, someone who not only can play the part of a good friend but can be one.

The question is, how badly do I want this? Badly enough to piss off Lucy and face no telling what purulent tortures she would make me endure? Yeah. I've endured fat thighs and big hips, what could be worse?

So do I want it bad enough to chance something like killing Meegan's baby-to-be (the first one)? No. See, Lucy knows my weakness, and I can tell she's going to keep making sure I screw up, so I'm not sure I have a choice.

That's a neat bit of rationalization there, which tells you something about me. I want to be good, but I'm still not willing to give up my lifestyle choice. I gave up my soul for it, and if I thought I could get it back, I would give up my lifestyle choice, or at least I'd like to think I would. But I can't get my soul back; the contract is binding.

I'm just fucked.

And tomorrow I get to explain to Blanche that Marv is going to jail and there's nothing I can do to stop it, although I would imagine that Lucy could fix this one. It would cost Marvin his soul, but I won't do that. Even for Level 9 powers. Not anymore.

I walk in the door, and Mom is still up watching *Lifestyles of the Rich and Famous* on the new plasma TV. Someone's been shopping. Again.

"Hi, Mom," I say, sitting down next to her.

"Did you have a nice evening?" she asks, as the little devil Viagra commercials commence. I swear Lucy's got her hand in *everything*.

"No. I want to go to the park, Mom."

"It's eleven o'clock. You'll get mugged."

"Come with me, this is important."

"Aw, V. I've already got my pajamas on."

I take in the FDNY nightshirt and the flannel bottoms. "S'all right. You can wear them. They look very nice."

"You really think so?"

"Yeah, Mom."

"You're going to make me miss Robin Leech?"

"Would you do it for me?" I ask, because tonight I really need this little victory. It's been twenty years since I've asked anything of my mother. You hear "no" often enough and you stop asking. But this is important.

"The things you ask of an old woman."

Ten minutes later, we're sitting on a bench in the park.

"So why're we here?"

I could tell her that I want to pretend I'm a different person, with a different life, but Mom is not insightful enough to understand. "I don't know. I just think it's something that we should do. You know, take time out, feed the birds, smell the roses."

Mom sniffs. "There's no rose smell here."

"You thirsty?"

"Did you bring some water?"

I poof up a sack from beneath the bench. "I got a bottle of wine."

"V, you know I don't drink. Much."

"We can make it a special occasion."

"You have something to celebrate? My life is crap."

"I'm sorry about Daddy, Mom," and I truly am. I could use my powers to earn Mom a temporary reprieve, but there's nothing in the powers of the nine that can make someone change forever.

"I found a co-op today. I'm going to move out, V."

"I think we'd get along better if we didn't share the same space."

"Yeah, I think so, too. I gotta say that you're not the evil daughter I once thought you were, and I'm not just saying that because I can now get fabulous clothes."

"Thanks, Mom. I don't think you're evil, either."

She puts an arm around me, and I curl up against her shoulder. It takes us a few minutes to get this right; neither one of us is very good at it. Eventually we go home, and nothing's really fixed. I went and sat in the park with my mother, and that was nice, but do I feel better about myself?

No.

Blanche and Yuri are in the park when I get there, and it looks like he's teaching her to play.

I smile at Blanche. "Don't be getting so good that I can't play you anymore."

"You don't have to worry, V. I've thrown games to you in the past, I'm not averse to throwing them again."

We sit down and play, and Yuri wanders away. I know he doesn't like me. Yuri is very perceptive, and I'm glad that Blanche found him. I let her take my rook and bishop before I start in on the Marv update.

"I've got some bad news."

"If you don't have cancer, life is good. What are you trying to tell me? Just spit it out."

"Marv's going to jail."

The bracelet jingling stills. "Oh," is all she says.

"I'm sorry, Blanche."

"You couldn't do anything? I was so sure you could do something."

"I know you may not believe this, considering all the bad blood between Marv and me, but I tried. It just didn't work out."

"I don't know what I can do for him. I suppose I could see him during visiting hours, but I really don't like prisons."

"Who does, Blanche? You do what you think is right. That's what important."

"I knew he was going to come to a bad end. That Marv, always taking the shortcuts. You learn a lesson from this, V. Don't take the shortcuts."

And it's a little too late for that word to the unwise.

Yuri, sensing the depressive pall that has descended on the game, comes over and puts a hand on Blanche's shoulder. Automatically she reaches up one braceleted arm and covers his. He glares at me, his brow one long slapshot across the forehead. "Do you need protection from the devils that take advantage?"

"I'm not taking advantage," I say. It is the first time those words have ever emerged from my mouth. (And okay, I have won a couple of twenties from her in the *five years* we've been playing chess, but I think you can cut me a break here.)

"You move pawn to black six," he says to Blanche, after I move my queen forward.

It is the first time we've had coaching from the peanut gallery, and I'm not happy, especially since everybody knows that Russians wipe the floor with American chess players. "That's cheating."

"Yuri, put a lid on it. V's my friend," says Blanche, taking my side, but sliding her pawn to black six, nonetheless.

I smile tightly at the abominable Yuri.

"She has no friends," he shoots back, with a look that

lumps me, Rasputin, Stalin, and a million other Soviet despots all in the same category. "Only those she uses for her own purposes."

He glares at me from beneath his single brow, waiting for me to refute the irrefutable. I look at Blanche, who is only jangling her bracelet impatiently, waiting for me to move. I don't like being judged (again, it makes a lot of sense if you examine the whole heaven-hell conundrum), and I would dearly love to tell Uncle Yuri to take a flying leap off a slow train to Siberia.

But Blanche loves him. And there is the possibility, however remote, that if I make her choose between Yuri and me, I will lose. I, me, my.

Blanche comes through for me, though. "Yuri, shush."

I stay quiet, because I think Yuri is right.

The next morning Kimbers tracks me down at the store, and she is very practical about the news. "Do you think Cal will take a bribe? I have $1,386.47 in my checking account. It's not much, but do government jobs pay that well?"

"He won't take a bribe, Kimbers."

"But I didn't *do* anything. Much."

"It'll come out in the trial," I say, trying to be optimistic.

Paolo comes from the back room, studiously ignoring me (he's still pissed because of Regina). "You have a problem?"

"Legal issues."

He looks meaningfully at me, quirking a brow. "I can take care of that."

Kimbers is instantly happy. "You can? How?"

Paolo transforms into full used-car-salesman mode. "Honey, maybe it's time for a little less talk and a lot more action."

I cough up a "Bullshit" under my breath, because Paolo is about to hit on Kimbers, and I'm not going to stick around for that. I'm ready to head for cover when I hear the his next line: "There's a special program we have, which can take care of some of life's peskier problems."

Hello??? I move very quickly, determined not to lose any more souls on my watch. I've done enough damage. I shepherd Kimbers straight to the door. "You can't listen to him. He's delusional, Bellevue."

She's holding fast to the inside wall. "I should listen to him."

"No, you shouldn't. He'll tell you stuff that you want to hear. Kimbers, it's going to sound great, but trust me, don't hear this, okay?"

She's still not budging. "I can't go to prison, V. It's not fair. I didn't make any money off that deal."

"Look, Kimbers. Life isn't fair. If we're good, it doesn't mean we don't get kicked in the ass every now and then. I don't know why, but it happens."

"Well, thank you, Dr. Phil, but I think I'm going to listen anyway."

"Kim, I know I'm usually a bit of a kidder, but I'm serious about this one. Walk away. Don't come back. Don't come near the store again. Don't come near me again."

"What's wrong with you? You used to be a fun person, V. I

never could figure out why Marv stepped out on you with me, because you were always so cool, and I was always so—not."

Please God, tell me there is ONE woman in New York that has self-confidence and some semblance of self-esteem. I don't think so. Everyone I've met is a basket case. *This* is why Lucy loves New York. It's the devil's playground. "Kim, this is your last chance. Go, sweetie. Run."

She takes a look at the street and then takes a look at Paolo. Do I know what she's going to choose?

Yup, because in her shoes I did the exact same thing.

Fuck.

I meet Lucy for drinks at Soho House (she's a member, but I think it's going downhill). She's in high spirits; I feel like hell.

"Why so glum, V? You should be on top of the world. I'm going to give you credit for Kimbers, so you'll be a Level 9! Isn't that fabulous?"

"Peachy. I think I'll just whip up some fawning sycophants right now," I mutter, all the while downing Pink Ladies (which tells you how depressed I actually am).

"You shouldn't be so beaten, V. Life is too short to waste it being sad. Do you know how many women would trade their souls to have your life?"

"At least nine," I say.

She laughs at me, a confiding, intimate laugh that draws you into her circle. "There's seven hundred thousand women in Manhattan. Any one of them would love to be you."

"I'm worse than cancer. People meet me, and they lose their soul."

"You're looking at life all wrong. The program isn't designed to suck life out of everyone. We're not vampires. I just want to bring some joy and happiness to the world."

For the first time, I hear what she's never said before. "If you want joy and happiness, then why torment me?"

"I'm going to tell you a secret, V. One I've never told anyone before. I need people like you. You're my testimonial as to why the program works. I can point to you and say, 'Look at V, she's got it all.' And people listen to that sort of true-life hype."

"But it's not like I'm leaving the program, and twisting the knife isn't going to make me happy."

"No, but it can make you accept what you have to accept. I used to be like you, V. After I got kicked out of heaven, I thought that deep down I was a good person, that God just misunderstood me. I've been the fallen angel. Do you know what that's like? To have heaven, and then have it taken away?" There's a hitch in her voice. A remembrance of the angel she used to be.

I murmur something meaningless and sympathetic, and she continues: "Eventually I realized that no, there wasn't anything good in me, and I would be happier if I could just live the life I was going to be forced to live anyway. You're going through the same growing pains I went through, and I like you too much to see you suffer for nothing."

"Wow," I say, carefully keeping my mind blank from all incriminating thoughts. "That's very nice of you."

We sit in silence, and finally I ask the question that's been on my mind for the last two years. "What's hell like?"

"Is that what's bothering you?"

"It's keeping me up at nights, yeah."

"It's my home, V."

This from the woman with the screaming fireplace. I'm not comforted.

She puts a hand over mine. "It's not all flames and pitchforks, V. I've done a lot with the old homestead."

"A regular she-devil of domestication, hmm?"

"I know how you feel."

At one time, Lucy was my idol. Now I'm just like her, and I hate it.

Her phone rings, and she's talking on the phone. Making her deals and sucking some other sap into her hell. Whoa. Gotta watch the black thoughts. I paste a smile on my face and covet the "Original Bad Girl" diamond brooch she's wearing. Much better.

Eventually she packs up her black Kelly bag to leave and I watch her go. Watch the heads turn as she passes. Lucy stops to chat with the bartender. Hands him her card. I want to be numb, but even the Pink Ladies can't quiet my conscience.

Before I leave, I sidle up to the bar. When the bartender turns his back, I swipe the little white piece of paper that promises it all and stuff it into my bag. Once outside, I tear it up into tiny pieces and drop it into the yawning mouth of the nearest "New York Recycles" can. It's only one soul, but I'll take my victories where I can.

Twenty

Out of the frying pan, into the soap: a defendant in the SEC sex-for-stocks scandal was granted a reprieve yesterday, and daytime producers, so excited by the charming image she presented in court, offered her a part as the newest long-lost daughter of Pine Valley's resident mogul. Shooting will start in a few weeks, but Kimberly has already been seen buying an apartment in the Trump STC (Space-Time Continuum). Already the prices have jumped 17 percent since word of her impending purchase leaked out.

And in a sad note, cops have closed down the Japanese tattoo parlor that has been inking celebs with "authentic Japan-

ese designs," after discovering that the de-
signs were not the "thousand-year-old dis-
course on Japanese artistic history." What
was the actual translation of the symbols?
Made in Taiwan, of course.

I spend the afternoon setting up the Versailles ballroom in the St. Regis. It's a great place, with huge chandeliers and a whole Franco-Napoleon thing going on. Amy has spent the last few days transforming it into this huge darkness where nightmares start. A fog machine is running, and there are black walls set up to cast eerie shadows everywhere, giving the whole far side of the room a look that reminds me of—hell.

I swallow, telling myself to get a grip. It's only a fashion look, not a lifestyle—yet. The other side of the room is much better, though. The runway runs the length of the room, and the plan is that the women will walk from one end to the other, ending up where the lights are brighter, and potted flowers and even a couple of dogwoods decorate the edge. It's very nice, this transition from darkness to spring.

"Well, what do you think?" Amy asks as she adjusts the black curtains that line the walk. "Do you think the effect is too understated?"

I remember the long "discussions" about the effectiveness of bodily injuries in promotional advertising, and I'm thinking that understated is a good thing. "It's perfect. Subtle, yet powerful."

She starts to smile. "We're going to raise tons of money tonight, aren't we?"

"A lot more than a one-star potluck dinner can bring in, Amy. You're getting the cream of New York tonight."

"I've seen the stuff that Lucy wrote in the *Post* about the auction. She really came through for you."

In my mind, I'm twirling my mustache, because I have big plans for tonight. I've been playing the role of the devil's faithful minion, but tonight? *Hehehe.*

(Assuming, of course, that I don't turn into a chickenshit, which is always a possibility for me.)

It's several hours later when the guests start arriving, and yes, speak of the devil, Lucy makes her entrance, lovely and elegant in a stunning black Zang Toi. I look good, I really do, but even as a Level 9, I can't outdo the devil. Well, maybe I can tonight. Whoosh. Gotta watch those thoughts, now moving into mind-censoring mode, but it's tough to keep satisfaction from my face.

Her dark eyes take in the stage, the ladies from the shelter, and Amy. I see the dollar signs clinking in her eyes, and quickly I whisk her away to give her some busywork.

"Are you excited about tonight?" I ask her, rubbing my hands together. "You're going to love it."

She smiles at me and takes in the decorations. "The room looks very dramatic. You went overboard on the hell theme, though. Not good for business."

We share a laugh. "Might I say that you look very lovely this evening?"

She twirls around. "You look nice, too, V."

And she's right. Tonight I'm spiffy. I'm wearing a blood red Dior that is cut down to Mexico, and a blood red ruby pendant to match. "You know I could talk clothes forever, but I need your help. The food hasn't come in yet. You're the Queen of the Underworld, all-powerful ruler of fashion and evil. Can you poof up some canapés and a few waiters?"

Flattery is the best way to get something out of Lucy, and she's off to the kitchen, and soon there's twenty hunkaroonies holding silver trays of canapés and hors d'oeuvres working the room. The bartenders show up and start to pour, and suddenly the party swings into full gear. Okay, this is good. I start to mingle as the crowd grows even larger. The mayor arrives, a few senators from New York and Connecticut, the delegation from New Jersey. I think we've got some Knicks players here, performers from Broadway, and lots of people I've never seen before. I spy the gossip crews from the *Post,* the *Times,* the *Observer,* and, ta-da—*USA Today.* Oh, my, this is better than I dreamed. Lucy really went all out for this one. My smile gets broad.

There's a small gag-moment when Cal comes up and pinches me on the ass (and there's not much to pinch, thank you very much). "Look at you, tonight! V, V, V. A man just wants to eat you up." There are slurping noises accompanying this tribute to my sexuality, but I've seen Cal eat. Not in a million years, buddy. I crack a smile. "It's so nice of you to be here."

Lucy comes out and is playing hostess as well. I give her a wave and a wink. Amy's getting nervous, running up to me every five minutes to ask if everything is going okay.

"Doll, you need to relax. It's going to be a night that people talk about for a long, long time. She smiles and pinches my arm (OUCH!). "You're the best, V."

Yeah, don't I know it?

Promptly at 7:30, Amy takes the microphone to start the show. The lights go down, and the music starts out low. The ladies from the shelter walk out onstage, dressed in some Salvation Army coats and rags. Then as they go down the walk, into the light, they shed the outer trappings, and voilà, they're nattily dressed in some of New York's hottest designs.

An appreciative "oohhhh" springs up from the audience. Sandra goes from a stained tweed overcoat into white silk from Vera Wang. Svetlana loses the tattered rags and is left in a beautiful green pantsuit from Ralph Lauren. And a short Chinese woman is the star of the evening in a dramatic silver Zac Posen gown.

After the applause dies down, Amy walks back onto the stage. "Ladies and gentleman, tonight we're here to celebrate a special sort of bravery. The ability to recognize the darkness and oppression that physical abuse can cause and the determination of these ladies to walk away. Every day thousands of New Yorkers are abused, and tonight they need your help. We're about to start the auction for the evening. Don't be shy. Don't be cheap. The lives of so many women depend on you to help. Let your conscience be your guide."

And the bidding starts. The dollar amounts quickly go from cheapskate to stratosphere, and I can see Regina bouncing up and down on Paolo's arm. Tamsin looks more refined, although she's blinking a lot behind her glasses as the bidding goes machine-gun fast.

Franz the auctioneer is hammering and pointing, and hammering and pointing, and it's all fabulous. Eventually, we've sold it all, and raised buttloads of cash. And now it's my turn. I see Lucy watching me, and I give her a last wink. This is my turn to shine.

Can I do this? Can I really do it? I walk up on the stage and take my place in front of the podium. Quickly I take a drink of water.

"My name is Vivian Leeza Rosetti, and I sold my soul to the devil."

The room is filled with nervous laughter, and I barrel onward. "It's the stupidest thing I've ever done in my life. Now, I'm not alone in this, and I know it. This is New York, the city of the most beautiful people in the world. The city where riches are beyond compare. Look at who's sitting next to you. You should wonder where all that perfection came from. She's got that great skin—is it Kanebo, or is it a kickback from the bastions of hell? Go ahead. Check everybody out. Go on. Go on."

The heads start to turn. Nobody wants to look like they're doing it, but the eyes are darting, wondering if I'm right. Of course I'm right.

"There's a price for everything. What do you think he paid for that full head of hair and perfect smile and the six-pack abs? Some of you paid with your soul. I don't know who you are—well, I know who some of you are, but most of you are anonymous to me." I pick up a glass of water and drink. My throat is scratchy with fear, but this is too important to me.

"Everyone thinks that a soul is useless, but I'm telling you, it's more valuable than ten years of steely thighs or an adoring fan base. It's worth more than a birkin bag or the Manolos. Fifteen minutes of fame? Bullshit. That's peanuts. Your soul is your humanity, and if you've lost that, you turn yourself into something that's not even human. You think I'm kidding about this? I swear, you're nothing more than the devil's minion, a little humpbacked guy with an Eastern European accent running around, and not to do some evil deed for the Queen of the Damned, oh no. She's trickier than that. All we have to do is *nothing*. So we sit around on our well-toned yet allegorically flabby asses, doing our best faux royalty imitation and laughing at everyone else, like they're not good enough to be in our club. It's a club of morons. Do you really want to be a part of it?"

I look around, and my God, they're listening. I'm talking off the cuff here and just made that last part up, but it sounds really good, don't you think? And the important thing is Lucy. She's getting more and more steamed. I take a good sip of water, and lay it on even thicker.

"Tonight's your chance to regain that humanity. If you're like me, you're not getting your soul again, but you've got a chance to borrow it, just to remember what it feels like. To be whole. To be human. To know that the world is a better place simply because you're in it. Ladies and gentlemen, I know what I'm asking here. She's gonna be pissed, but don't you want to do it? Aren't you tired of being the devil's dancing bear? What's she going to do? Damn us all again?"

The glass of water bursts, and everyone (including me) jumps. But Lucy's not a show person and that's as far as she's going to go. There's a lot of heads turning and people looking around, and some are watching Lucy nervously, which is a dead giveaway of the soulless among us.

I smile into the audience. "There's a hat on every table. The auction's over, but this is your chance to give without anything in return. We're looking for money here for Svetlana, for Sandra, for all these women who need our help. Tonight, help us out."

There's a rustling sound in the audience, and it's growing louder. People reaching into their pockets . . .

And then, I get a surprise. A woman, platinum blond, killer bod, stands up. "I'm Muffy Bandicott, and I sold my soul to the devil."

Dear God, I can't believe someone else is as much of an idiot as me. I start to wave her back down in her seat, but it's too late. There's somebody else. A sportscaster from WNBC stands up. "I'm Charles McAllister, and I sold my soul."

A *New York Times* reporter is next. "I'm Stephen Safire and I sold my soul."

Shelby—my God, Shelby!—is standing. "Hello, I'm Shelby Cohen, and I sold my soul to the devil." At this point I can't restrain myself. I look at her and whisper quite loudly, "Shel, are you fucking nuts? Sit down."

But does she listen to me? Noooo.

Even the auctioneer stands up (actually he's already standing, but he comes forward). "I'm Franz Schubert, and I sold my soul."

And so it goes.

Nicky Muller.

Dr. Andrew Pierce.

The Honorable Phillip Gelman.

Debbie Vanderbilt.

As I look around me and see the numbers, it's scary to realize how much power Lucy has. And just in this one room.

Out on the floor, someone slowly starts to clap. It's Cal. Good ol' Cal. And then everyone starts to clap. And then the applause is thunderous.

Yeah, tomorrow's not gonna be pretty, but I'm okay with that. In fact, I think it was worth it. I think I could handle forty thousand snake tongues burning my feet, because I can look back on this and remember how it feels to be alive again.

Reality comes back fast, and the crowd breaks up quickly to leave as they realize, like I did, there's gonna be hell to pay, and they want to get out of Lucy's firing range. I can't blame them for their fear.

I make my way down from the stage, and Amy launches herself at me. "V, that was brilliant!! I was in tears. Invoking the devil imagery to induce fear, it was inspired! We did that on the show one time. The priest was possessed and making babies, but it didn't do that well in the ratings, but tonight . . . I've never seen anything like it. Obviously the satanic tide has turned since the eighties. Who knew?"

I give her a hug. "Yeah. Who knew?"

A man approaches me and hands me his card. "Robert Gottlieb. I'm a literary agent. Have you ever given thought to writing up your story?"

I blink at him. "You really think it'd sell?" I'm thinking to myself, Who's going to want to read about a stupid person? but I don't say that, of course.

He grins. "Absolutely."

I see Lucy parked in the corner, looking elegant and confident, like I haven't just exposed her whole Life Enrichment bullshit for the Ugg Boot scam that it was. A book would really piss her off even more. There's possibilities there. I turn to Mr. Gottlieb. "Let me think about it. Okay?"

Now I have bigger things to do, like going to rub Lucy's face in it. She's going to kill me, but not before I thumb my nose at her.

Her eyes watch me like a snake, and I know she's plotting her revenge, but now I'm ready for her. I've gotten to my fighting weight. Damn it all, I'm gonna lose the war, but I got in one good battle, and that's enough to put a smile on my face for the rest of my life, piss-poor as it probably will be.

When I get within her mind-radar, I'm careful to keep my thoughts innocent and pure. The game's not up yet.

"I bet you're very proud of yourself," she starts in.

"Yes, yes, I am. Proud is the correct word. Happy, that's another good one to use," I answer back.

"Do you think that little homily just bought you humanity? That now you've made up for a lifetime of self-centeredness and the unmitigated pursuit of pleasure? Do you think it's going to bring back the child you killed? V, you didn't even make a dent."

"You know something? You're absolutely right, Lucy. And when you're right, you're right."

"Then why? What purpose could you possibly have for ruining everything?"

I laugh and put a comforting arm around her. She looks so torn up, so disappointed with me. I must relieve her suffering, and I know just the way.

"You thought that I meant all that crap? You thought I was sincere? Oh, no," I gush, because being good had nothing to do with my reasons. Meegan's not here, but tonight's only for her. I grin at Lucy.

"Sorry, sweetie. You've been punk'd."

Twenty-One

Lucy has been called away for a sudden family emergency. We anticipate her column returning in next week's paper. Liz Smith will be covering in her absence.

There's a familiar face lurking in the back. I'm surprised he's here; I'm even more shocked because he's in a tux (and might I add that he looks very nice).

He also looks a bit nervy, which is good, since I'm trembling and shaking myself (and it has nothing to do with my Lucy fear).

"That was a nice speech you gave."

"We made a lot of money. Mission accomplished. I'm surprised to see you." I lock my hands together, because he's back, and he's not mad. And where Nathaniel goes, hope follows.

"I was thinking—" he starts.

"You know, thinking is a very dangerous preoccupation of yours."

He clears his throat. "As I was saying, I was thinking. I'm leaving tomorrow, and I have to ask you a question."

"G'head."

"That last morning, was that PMS? Hear me out. I've thought about it a lot, and I couldn't come up with any reason for it, and I never pretended to understand females, most times they're really confusing, but I came up with that as a possible explanation. Or maybe I didn't say enough nice things about your hair, or some other unforgivable sin that I didn't know I committed. And if so, I'm sorry. I racked my brains, and I couldn't find one possible reason, except that you were playing me." He stares me down. "I don't buy that, Vivian."

This Nathaniel is one smart cookie, but I don't say anything because his words are like ambrosia from the gods, and I want to hear more.

"I don't like having regrets, and I knew that if I left without asking, it'd bug me for the rest of my life, so I came. To see."

He stops talking, and I realize it's my turn. He needs an explanation, and the truth isn't believable to people who see so much good in the world. "I've changed a lot of things about me since that night."

"I noticed. You look great."

He's working so hard to do the right thing here, and he's doing it just because of me. My eyes start tickling, and I think I'm going to cry. "You're a good man, did you know that?"

He gives me a kiss, and this time it's the kiss of true love (no magic, swear), and then he whispers in my ear: "Can we go home?"

We head out the door, and I turn around to take one last look at the ballroom, holding the memories close. This time I did do right. No, I did more than right. I did good. I did really, *really* good. I shoot him a saucy smile because tonight there's magic in the air, and this time it's not about the illusion. No, Nathaniel is very, very real, and for tonight, he's got my heart, and I've got his soul.

On Sunday morning I wake up very early. The sun is already bright, and I wait for the devil to strike me dead. But no, there's a hard arm around my waist, and wait, the hand begins to move, and there's a devil in my bed, and he's about to strike.

Nathaniel raises himself over me and kisses me good morning. "Good morning."

"When's your plane?"

"Oh-fourteen-hundred."

"So we got a few hours?"

"Yeah."

"I'm going to miss you, Nathaniel."

"I'm going to miss you, Vivian. I can call. And I'll be back. Eventually."

Yeah, but that's not quite the same, and we both know it. I give him a kiss, and he starts to love me, and for a few more hours, I have heaven. Life is good.

*   *   *

That afternoon I meet Blanche in the park. I thought about calling and canceling, but I want to talk to Blanche. I've been thinking.

Blanche is already sitting down, ready to play, when I show up. "You're late, Vivian."

"I bet your watch is fast, Blanche."

"The watch is correct. Do not blame old woman for your own blunder."

I glare at Yuri. "Can you call off the attack dogs, Blanche?"

"Yuri, be nice." She smiles shyly at him. "Besides, we have news."

"Let me hear, let me hear."

"Okay. I hope you're going be happy for us. We're getting married. In Russia. It's so romantic." She pitches her voice low. "I don't want to wait. Who knows how long we really have? Don't you think it's romantic?"

Today, I think everything is romantic. That's what happens when you're blessed with several all-natural mind-blowing orgasms before the crack of dawn. "I think it's very romantic. And I think Yuri is a lucky man."

We move into a heated game of chess, with Yuri advising Blanche, which makes a serious dent in my winnings. "I can't believe you're letting him coach you like this. Where's your independent feminine spirit?"

She looks at me over the frames of her glasses. "My independent feminine spirit would have lost a cool Andrew Jackson to you, missy, so let's not color the issue with that feminine sophistry. How was your auction?"

"It was good, Blanche. You remember me telling you about Lucy? I got her, Blanche. I fixed her good."

She points a finger at me, the bracelets ringing. "Vivian, you're smarter than this. You've got to be careful when you're messing with the devil."

I look at her, amazed that she's held out on me all this time. "You knew? Good God, Blanche, you're not in the Life Enrichment Program, are you?"

"Do I look like an idiot to you?"

No, she doesn't. And there you have it; the prime differential between Blanche and me.

Twenty-Two

Thank you for all the cards and letters in my absence. Everything is much more in control now, and I'm deeply touched by everyone who cared enough to write.

So, why did the chicken cross the road? Because the latest demon-slaying installment was premiering at Radio City Music Hall, and traffic was a bitch as fans lined up for miles. Seriously, the chicken was the only thing moving on the Henry Hudson yesterday.

And I'm happy to say that the fall bag is going to be something new, something innovative, a design by . . . Shel-B. I've heard the buzz, I've seen the heads turn. Yes, It Girl turned fashionista is going to give the Sonata Girl a run for her money.

*   *   *

The next day starts out nice enough. The skies are blue, the sun is shining, and I'm thinking that I might have beaten the devil. Mom calls; she wants me to meet her at Tiffany's. She says she's got something to show me. Yeah. I bet I know what it is. A twenty-carat diamond tiara. But I humor her, and find her on the second floor of Tiffany's with Shelby. There's a bloom in their cheeks, and the sparkle of diamonds in their eyes. Everybody looks to be normal, and I notice no live animals nearby. Okay, beggars can't be choosers. If it keeps my rugs clean, I'll spring for a tiara.

"Vivian, watch this."

And there, before my eyes, my mother poofs up a platinum-initial toe ring.

Good God, NO!!!!

I kick the toe ring under the counter. "WHAT HAVE YOU DONE?"

Mother twirls around like a little girl. "I signed up for the program."

Shelby's wearing the guilty look. "Don't be mad. The devil made me do it."

I stare at her. "Why?"

Shelby squirms uncomfortably. "She threatened my thighs, Vivian. Can you imagine? Fat thighs?"

I can hear your thoughts. You're thinking: "Vivian, why didn't you see this coming? I saw it coming." Well, excuse me, but were you concerned with saving the world from the child of Satan? No? Were you cooking up a whole anti-fraud fraud to keep your ex out of jail? No? Did you have animals slaughtered all over your pristine living room? No? Is your boyfriend, the only cool man you've ever known, being shipped off to some war-torn country that I CAN'T EVEN SPELL? No? No? No?

There's a quiet chuckle from across the room, and Lucy emerges. "Hello, Vivian." I turn my evil eyes on Lucy and run through my repertoire of spells, thinking that having a salesgirl skewer her with a diamond-studded dagger in the back would not be brutal enough. "What the hell have you done to my mother?"

The Tiffany's girl appears, blue box in hand (but no dagger), and looks at me, "Vivian? You're Vivian, aren't you? Can I just say what an honor it is to meet you? I'm on the waiting list for the Sonata bag. Oh"—she coughs—"I'm sorry. Forgive me, I just get so excited. May I help you?"

Can she really help me? Can anybody help me? No. I look over at Mom. My four-foot, ten-inch dwarf of a mom who is now going to hell.

Along with me.

Because of me.

Lucy reads my mind. "Guilt sucks, doesn't it? I would have left her alone, too, but it seems like a big ass just doesn't mean anything to you anymore."

Mother picks this particular moment to speak up. "Don't listen to her, Vivian. I made my own choice."

Like that's supposed to make me feel better? "Mother, stay out of this. Okay?"

The salesgirl looks at us, worried, for good reason. "Can I get you anything?"

I'm wondering if you can buy your mother's soul at Tiffany's. It shouldn't cost a lot, I bet it'd fit in one of those gift boxes, and even if there is a waiting list, I'd stand on line for it.

No, I bet you can't find it at Tiffany's.

I turn to Lucy. "What do you want? You want a million souls? Great. I'll get 'em for you. You want the entire U.S. Senate? I bet I can do that, too. Just give her her soul back."

Mom comes over and looks up at me. "I don't want it back. Why didn't you tell me about all this? It's just like you to keep something like this to yourself. I would've signed on ages ago. If I can just get to Level 2, then I'll be able to get rid of the liver spots on my hand, and Henry would just love it if I had a real rack instead these old sacks of oranges."

She's actually glowing, so happy in her newfound soullessness. Aw, Mom. Why did she have to do this now? Two months ago, I really wouldn't have cared.

"You had a great life before. Why couldn't you have been happy?"

"A great life? You're such a kidder. Besides, it was too much work to be happy. I'm tired of working that hard. For once, I just want to relax and take it easy. Just like you. I'm proud of what you've done, taking your soul and shoving it right up the ass of the world. That's courage."

"No, Mom. That's a moron."

She picks at the alligator belt on her rayon capris, and I realize that even as a Level 1, she cannot dress worth shit. But that's not my concern anymore. That's not my problem anymore. Mother owns that problem. Lucy owns her soul.

Lucy adjusts the scarf around her neck, looking perfect as always. "Well, I'm sorry to have to shop and run, but I've got a column to write. Ta-ta."

I'm ready to run after her, call her out, bitch-slap the devil right in front of Tiffany's, but that's really not going to help my mother at all. No, there's nothing that will help Mom, and she learned it all from me. The greedy, selfish, vainglorious V.

I walk out the door, into the teeming masses of Fifth Avenue, where everyone is working to get someplace else. There's models striding through the streets in their size double-naught dresses and their ten-inch heels. There's Upper East Side princesses chasing after their Upper East Side condos and their Upper East Side husbands. There's a Broadway singer waiting tables at the Stardust diner, chasing auditions.

It's enough to make a smart woman stupid.

It's enough to make you lose you soul.

"Are you people never satisfied?" I mutter under my breath, over and over. I get louder and louder, but New Yorkers know how to tune out the noise of the street.

But I want someone to hear me.

"ARE YOU PEOPLE NEVER SATISFIED?"

No one stops to answer; no one even stops to stare. This is New York. Anything goes.

I go faster down Fifth, passing the windows at Prada, Fendi, Asprey, shoppers stopping to look at the latest dress, the lastest shoes, the latest bag. And through the glass, it all looks so easy to have. You can almost reach out and touch it.

Well, fuck that. They want it all? They can have it.

Wired and wealthy, muddled mass, let their avarice shatter glass.

And all around me, the windows start to break. Chanel, Harry Winston, Henri Bendel, Louis Vuitton, even the gift shop for St. Pat's. At first, everyone is confused. Shocked. Oh, yeah, a crazy woman yelling at the world doesn't do it, but God forbid, break a window on Fifth, and the world must stop.

And then it starts. They're grabbing stuff. At first it's just the riffraff, but then everyone gets in on the act, and I stand back to survey the evil I have wrought.

But it isn't enough. I want more. The story of my life, I always want more. And so I lift my hands to the sky,

Washington, Lincoln, Franklin, more, heavens empty of your store.

And there we have it. It's raining fifties on the streets of Gotham.

You don't have to sell your soul to have it. You want this crap? You take it, but God damn you, do not trade eternity for a goddamned fucking bag. Do you understand?

Can't you people learn anything from me?

My cell phone rings, but I don't need Caller ID to figure this one out. Lucy has decided to reach out and touch.

Like most everyone who actually lives in New York, I've never been to the top of the Empire State Building. First of all, it's fucking expensive, the lines are too long, and eighty-six floors above ground is not a good place to be in the city anymore. But that's where Lucy wants me to meet her. I'll be damned if I'm going to stand in line for three hours to meet the devil, though, you know? I poof myself to the top, where she's waiting for me.

We walk past the school kids and the tourists from Kansas, past the bomb-sniffing dogs and toward the west side of the building, where you have a beautiful, unobstructed view of—

Jersey.

The smokestacks, the factories belching out the jaundiced yellow air. I know how that miserable state feels, sitting alone on the bench, watching the world pass by.

"It's marvelous up here, isn't it?" Lucy asks, her eyes dismissing everything but the statuesque skyline of downtown Manhattan. "This is as close to heaven as I get in New York." Her voice gets soft and wistful. "It's my own creation. God created heaven, but I created the greatest city in the world."

At first I think Lucy is making a joke, but Lucy doesn't have my sense of humor, and it gradually dawns on me that she's serious.

I don't think so.

She looks at me and smiles. "You don't think I did this?"

"No."

"That's neither here nor there. We need to have a little talk. Discretion is a huge part of the program, Vivian. And raining money down on Fifth Avenue is not being discreet. There's questions being asked that I don't want to be asked. I already had to clean up one mess of yours. This is getting ridiculous."

Do I care? Ask me if I care. "Maybe it's time everybody started asking questions."

"Don't be silly."

"I'm not being silly. I'm dead serious. I can blow this pretty city of yours wide open."

Her smile loses a bit of its luster. "Don't threaten me, Vivian. You saw what happened the last time you did this."

"Yes, you took Mom, but I don't have that many friends." And it's the first time in my life that I've been grateful for that. I gamble a bit, because there's something I want to know. "But you could kill me. That would shut me up forever."

The smile turns to a frown. "I told you I couldn't kill anything. I wasn't lying to you."

"Oh."

"Yes, 'oh.' You killed Meegan's baby. I didn't. I told you I didn't."

I fall silent, processing that last bit. I had thought that maybe . . .

But no. But the upside is that Lucy's stuck.

"Okay. Here's the situation. I'm calling CBS, BBC, NBC, Fox, CNN, and the *Daily News*."

"Unless?"

Oh, she knows me so well. "Roll back time, Lucy. Roll back to the merry days before I met you. If I don't know about the program, there's no way I can blow the whistle on it."

"No."

I pick up my cell phone. "I've got Wolf Blitzer on speed-dial. I'm going to call."

She holds up a hand. "Stop. You're not getting your soul back. You can't undo your contract."

"Okay, go back to the day after I signed my contract. You can have my soul, Lucy. Just get rid of all the others."

For a moment I think she's going to refuse, but then she smiles at me.

Lucy looks out over the city and nods. "Alright. They're released."

She checks her watch. "And we'll set the clock back, starting now."

As if in slow motion, the people around us start to change. There are new faces, and the wind is colder.

"October 31, 2003. Right after you signed on, in fact."

Okay, this was too easy. Why do I know there's a catch somewhere that I'm missing?

"Because there is," she says, reading my mind again.

Damn. I hate that. "What is it?"

"I don't trust you. I don't trust you. I don't trust you. "

Yes, there is that, but I had hoped she would overlook that fact. "I give you my word."

She laughs. Okay, so that won't work. "We're going to put you to the test. The ultimate test. You want this so badly? You want to save all these people that you've recruited? Here's your chance. Unfortunately, you're going to have to walk off this building in order to do it."

Slowly the security fence melts in front of my eyes.

And suddenly I see where's she headed. I focus on the sprawling arch of the GW, watching the cars crawl along the Henry Hudson.

"You want to be good and honorable. Here's your chance. I'm letting you trade your soul for the ones you've recruited. It's the ultimate battle of good vs. evil."

"How do I know I can trust you? How do I know you won't go back on your word and move time forward again?"

"I don't lie, Vivian. I spin and manipulate, but I don't lie. The souls are back with their owners, just the way you wanted it."

"And you won't recruit them again?"

She shrugs. "I didn't promise that. But you will be out of the picture."

"And all I have to do is die?" I say, swallowing hard. Death means hell, and I'm not sure I can face that.

"Yes," she says, with such confidence, and I know what she's thinking here. Vivian isn't going to do this, because Vivian doesn't have an unselfish bone in her body.

"And if I don't?"

"We go back to where we were. Back to the present."

"And I go back to the media."

This time she's mad, and I can see it. "Don't kid yourself. You think I can't stop you? Don't forget who I am, and I know all your hot buttons, and don't think I won't use them."

"Then why the deal?"

"Because the idea of you living with your failure is just too much fun. The gamble of a mere ten souls is worth it, because, well, I don't believe you can do it."

Now this is where Lucy is wrong about me. She was always right before, but I've learned, and I've grown.

My hands fasten onto the now-pliant steel bars, finding them hot to the touch. That's okay; it can't be any warmer than where I am headed.

"It's beautiful, isn't it?" I say, pointing to the skyline, stupid chitchat because I'm not going to let her beat me. Not this time.

The trees are no longer green, starting to lose their leaves. I know I don't have much time, and I wish the last pictures I had were of something that was blooming, rather than dying, but there you go—unsatisfiable me

Sometimes you have to have faith. I've damned nearly everyone that I've met. Hopefully without me, they'll do the right thing. I don't know, but all I have now is hope, and I like that.

I push in the bars and take a deep breath. There's so many people up here, but I've never felt so alone. Somebody tell me, where is Charlton Heston when you need him? Not on top of the Empire State Building, that's for sure.

I close my eyes, and I do allow myself seven words. It's not really my style, and my repertoire of four-letter words is much bigger, but sometimes all you have is a wing and a prayer.

"Now I lay me down to sleep . . ."

And I step off into the air, getting the devil out of my hair once and for all.

Epilogue

November 2, 2003

I've been writing this column for what seems like forever, and some things never get easy. It was a somber day in New York yesterday, as most of the city gathered in St. Patrick's Cathedral as we laid to rest one of my dearest friends.

I don't know how to describe the magnificent woman who touched the soul of everyone she met. Every so often, a legend is born in New York—this city has had more than its share—but Vivian Rosetti was a special woman who held a special place in my heart. From modest beginnings, she was on her way to carving out an empire. I wish you all could have met her. Women everywhere would be emulating her irrefutable style. But for her untimely demise, I can't imagine how far she could have gone.

Most people don't realize the road that Vivian traveled to get to her Fifth Avenue store. Born to modest beginnings in New Jersey, she had aspirations, dreams to climb to the top of the designer chain, with only her love of life to guide her.

She embraced life in a way that few truly have the guts to do. Vivian's gone at the age of thirty-eight, a victim of her own genius. Honey, we hardly knew you.

Epilogue Part Deux

April 1, 2004

Did you think that was the end? I told you I was a kidder. I don't remember actually dying, just wishing I'd done myself in some way that was a little more—elegant. When I woke up, I wasn't sure where I was. There weren't any flames or screaming wraiths or shit like that. And I didn't see angels with harps, either. It took me a solid six hours to figure out that yes, I was alive. No, I didn't look like myself, and yes, God is an even bigger kidder than I am.

I'm not in heaven.

I'm not in hell.

I'm in Kansas.

Yes, that's me, amid the tall fruited plains and amber waves of grain. Actually, I'm not *in* the cornfields. I've discovered that I—Suzy Wong, to be precise—live in a one-bedroom apartment in Wichita.

Fucking Wichita. That probably makes me a bad person, doesn't it? I get my soul back, and I sound ungrateful. It's not everybody that gets a second chance, and to be perfectly frank, I'm not sure why God is wasting his time with me. But for the last few months, I've been trying to earn my stripes. I hang out in the park on my lunch hour (I work at a flower shop in town) and try to find a suitable chess partner.

Or maybe just a friend.

I don't begrudge Blanche her happiness, I think it's pretty cool. At age fifty-nine (okay, she's really seventy-three, oh, wait, we're back in 2003, she's only seventy. I hate math), she gets to start over, too. I just wish I could share it with her. Mom is still back in Florida with Dad. Now that I'm out of the picture, there's no reason for her to ever set foot in New York. She always hated the city. I wrote Marv's stock-tipping stripper a letter and told her that Marv was a Middle Eastern terrorist and she needed to stay far away from him. I'm not sure if it will work, but I have high hopes. As for Shelby, well, I've got an idea on how to get to her. I don't know about Meegan, but I think Meegan's got a hell of a lot more backbone than I ever did.

I hope so.

Anywhoo, it's a lot different here. Not everybody is a size two, and there's a lot of polyester. I'm whining again, aren't I?

I'll tell you a secret, though: I wouldn't trade it for anything. Sometimes I wake up smiling, bursting with happiness, for absolutely no apparent reason. Of course, then I remember where I am, but I still have the little moments.

The whole job thing wears on me. I could go back into accounting, or fashion, but I'm not ready yet. Just the other day, I was thinking of being a manager, and then I started plotting to get the regional manager's job, and before two hours had passed, I was ready to take over the whole Roses Are Red franchise. Okay, I'm still a work in progress, but I am getting better.

Today's just another day, but I've learned to take them as they come. When I sit down with my lunch (Hungerbuster with cheese, and an Oreo Blizzard; I've decided that Dairy Queen is very godlike in the breadbelt), the sun feels extra warm, the sky looks extra blue. No skyline here, just an unadulterated view of heaven.

I dive into the burger, just as I hear a dog barking. He comes into my periphery, bounding across the grass, his leash tearing behind him. Now, although I have gone through a life-transforming experience, I do still hate dogs. This one is no exception, especially when he grabs the burger right out of my hands (and please note that florists do NOT make the equivalent wage of a New York bag designer). I chase after my lunch, just as another little voice starts echoing in my head.

"Fluffy! Come back!"

It is no echo. There's a kid trailing behind the dog.

Oh, God. V's life redux. I'm doomed to repeat my life forever.

In Kansas.

The dog jumps in the lake.

The kid jumps in next.

Can she swim?

Let's repeat this all together: "Of course not."

I run to the edge of the lake, and this time I dive right in. It's much easier this time. I'm wearing tennies and jeans. Water won't do shit to denim.

But—holy cow—this water is really COLD! I swim over and grab the girl's ponytail, ignoring her cries of pain. "Get Blebb—," the girl says before her head bobs under the water, which I translate to mean, "Get Fluffy."

I give the ponytail a hard yank, and the Little Mermaid appears and takes a deep breath. Next up, the dog.

Fluffy's leash dangles just out of the edge of my fingers, but I give it an extra kick underwater, and then I've got him.

I think I've ruined my shoes, but I'm sure another 50-percent-off sale will come around soon. I tow the two in (Fluffy's actually a good swimmer) and then hit the ground, the girl in one arm, Fluffy barking and pulling at his leash. The crowd starts to gather.

This doing-good stuff really starts to grow on you.

"Carly!" The mom appears, enfolding the girl in her arms, and she gives me a tearful smile. "Thank you. Thank you, thank you, thank you. I don't know who you are, but thank you." She keeps repeating herself, burying her face in her daughter's hair.

It kinda hurts me, 'cause I miss Mom, not that I had a great relationship for very long, but still . . .

However, I'm through living in the past (technically it's the future, but that just sounds weird), so I start looking around for the newspaper guy to appear (I've seen this movie before), but the coast is clear.

I guess my little redux is done.

I'm almost disappointed, then I look down at my sopping shirt (it was a very nice Ann Taylor), and disappointment turns to relief because I really do look like—

"Are you all right?"

SHIT.

I jerk my head up, and there I am, looking into dark, familiar eyes. Eyes that don't recognize me at all.

Oh, God, don't let this be a dream. If it is, don't wake me up. Ever. "Do you need a jacket?" he's asking. Like a moron, I stand there in dripping clothes. But I will take a moment to say that Suzy has perfect thighs and a very hot little body, and men notice it. Including *Nathaniel*. I would have mentioned this fact earlier, but, I believe it would have detracted from the inherent pathos of my story.

"Here, take it."

As he wraps familiar brown leather around me, my nose starts to sniffle. It could be the start of a cold, or my brain could be leaking water through my nose. Most likely, I'm just now realizing that the world is a fucking cool place.

Nathaniel shakes his head. "Sorry for staring. But I just had the weirdest déjà-vu experience. You ever get that? A memory that you can't quite place?" he asks in a muddled voice. It's the same way he sounds when he wakes up in the morning. I know all that about him, and he doesn't even know who I am.

"No, my memory's pretty good. There's a lot I wish I could forget, but—" I shrug and wrap myself up tighter in his jacket.

"Your name's Suzy?"

"You know me?" I ask carefully.

"It's written on your name tag."

Okay, not an alternative universe. But I'm still a good person. Nobody can take that away from me anymore. "Yeah. Suzy Wong. Who are you?" I ask, because I already know, but he doesn't know I know.

"Nathaniel."

"You from Kansas?" I ask casually.

"I'm on leave here. I want to visit my family."

"Your parents are here?" I say, the light beginning to dawn.

"Yeah, Mom and Dad."

"I lost my mom recently."

"I'm sorry."

I'm sure he's wondering why an absolute stranger would bare their soul to him, but I don't care. If you got it, flaunt it, that's my new motto. "You know, it's hard for me sometimes. We weren't really close. I'm going to share something personal with you, because I think others can learn from my mistakes. When your parents are alive, you need to get things right. You don't know when you're going to see them again. Know what I mean?"

He gets a polite look on his face, like I'm overstepping my bounds. "That's nice, but I can't do that."

I stop and grab his arm. "No, this is important. You don't want to be regretting this for the rest of your life. You can fix it. Trust me."

He shakes his head and smiles. "A family counselor from Roses Are Red, huh?"

"The thorns are a bitch, but I'm getting there."

"Why flowers?"

"To be frank, I have no idea. I just ended up with the job, but I've got some aspirations and some dreams."

"Like what?"

"I've been considering a career in fashion, and I'm currently working on my memoirs."

He laughs at me. That's what I love about Nathaniel, he's the only one who laughs at me. "You look really young to be working on your memoirs."

"What I don't have in years, I make up for in experience."

"Good luck with that. Maybe we could go out for breakfast tomorrow."

Breakfast. Wouldn't you know it? But I smile at him. "I'd love that."

We walk away from the lake, and the people start going about their lives, as if today wasn't a special day at all. Just another day in Kansas. I look up, and on the far corner of the hill, I see a man standing there, just watching us walk. "Can I ask you a strange question?"

"Strange is a relative term. Go ahead."

"That guy at the top of the hill. Isn't that Charlton Heston?"

Nathaniel starts to laugh. "Maybe on a bad day. Your eyes aren't very good, are they?"

"I think my eyes are just perfect, thank you very much," I answer, and Charlton Heston is walking away, but that's okay. I have a good life, and most of all, I have a not-so-good-but-passing-grade soul.

Just remember, you can have it, too.

Up Close and Personal
With the Author

THE RELATIONSHIP BETWEEN V AND NATHANIEL WAS VERY HEARTWARMING AND TOUCHING. DO YOU BELIEVE THAT A WOMAN MUST BE RESCUED BY A MAN?

Actually, if you'll pay attention to the ending, V rescues the entire world, and nobody ever knows about it. That's my definition of being a woman. Women rescue the entire world every day, and you'll never hear them whine or complain about it. Or at least not very much. As for Nathaniel, he's just eye-candy, and V has to fix his life, too.

YOUR GOSSIP COLUMNS WERE SO REAL. WERE THEY MODELED ON ANYONE IN PARTICULAR?

Yes.

WHAT WAS YOUR INSPIRATION FOR *DIVA'S GUIDE TO SELLING YOUR SOUL*?

Actually, when I heard the title *The Devil Wears Prada,* I said to myself, "Wow, what an awesome story! The devil has invaded New York and is running the place." Then I found out the book was about the fashion industry, and I was really disappointed (if you could see my wardrobe, you'd understand), so I realized that there was this great story that needed to be told. And voilà! V, or Everywoman, as I tend to say, emerged.

THE NEW YORK POST FIGURES VERY PROMINENTLY IN YOUR STORY. DO YOU READ THE POST?

Yes, every day, cover to cover. I call it "research." If I had more spare time, I might read the *New York Times* cover to cover as well. However, I suspect that's not really true. I don't think anyone has that much spare time.

IS THIS A CAUTIONARY TALE? DO YOU BELIEVE THAT OUR SOCIETY IS TOO OBSESSED WITH MATERIALISTIC THINGS AND BEAUTY?

I just wrote the book to make money. If you get a message out of it, well, more power to you.

WHEN YOU WERE RESEARCHING THIS BOOK, DID YOU ACTUALLY SELL YOUR SOUL TO THE DEVIL? IF NOT, HOW DO YOU KNOW HOW IT WORKS?

Well, there are those in the literary genre that believe you must become your characters in order to mine the complex psyche of your protagonist and provide an uncorrupted lens to the story. However, I am not a stupid person, and I'm fairly content with my life (although I think I could kill to be a size four), so no, I didn't. However, I did do extensive research and talked to many people who have sold their souls so that the story would ring true. In spite of my soulful status, I think I captured the pain and emotional turmoil that comes about from the loss of a soul. It's hard, it's really, really hard, but it's a problem that so many people face. It's truly alarming how many clients have signed up for the Life Enrichment Program, and the numbers are growing every day.

WHERE DID YOU COME UP WITH THE TITLE *THE DIVA'S GUIDE TO SELLING YOUR SOUL?*

The original title for the book was *The Diva's Guide to Thin Thighs in Thirty Seconds;* however, marketing had issues with that, and believed that the book-buying public might believe it was an exercise book. Now, I know where *The South Beach Diet* sits on the lists, and I was thinking, Is that a bad thing? But my editor said no. She, title-goddess that she is, actually retitled the book. So now I'm considering writing an exercise book. And possibly a personal finance book as well. *The Diva's Guide to Making a Million* has a nice ring to it.

I'VE HEARD THAT ALL WRITERS MUST HAVE HAD BAD CHILDHOODS IN ORDER TO WRITE, OR POSSIBLY DABBLE IN SOME KIND OF ADDICTION. IS THAT TRUE?

I do believe that having a bad childhood helps. As for addictions, they're overrated. Poe, Hemingway, Fitzgerald. Hacks, all of 'em. In today's world, you gotta have a gimmick. If you've killed someone, slept with someone famous, or knew someone that slept with someone famous, that's what you need. If not, you might as well hang up the typewriter, because it's not gonna happen. In my case, I had a friend who had a coworker who had a cousin who went to a wedding with Dennis Quaid. Am I going to use it in a book? Of course!

WHY WRITING? DID YOU ALWAYS HAVE SOME DEEP-SEATED DESIRE TO BE A WRITER?

No. Writers don't make enough money. I never wanted to be a writer, because I wanted to be rich. However, after I kept getting hit over the head with opportunities, I realized that I had to suck it up and be a writer. It was what I was meant to be. I still want to be rich, though.

SO WHAT'S NEXT FOR YOU?

I've got an idea. You see, there's this psychic . . .

Be the Next Downtown Girl
Contest Rules

NO PURCHASE NECESSARY TO ENTER.

1) ENTRY REQUIREMENTS:

Register to enter the contest on www.simonsaysthespot.com. Enter by submitting your story as specified below.

2) CONTEST ELIGIBILITY:

This contest is open to nonprofessional writers who are legal residents of the United States and Canada (excluding Quebec) over the age of 18 as of December 7, 2004. Entrant must not have published any more than two short stories on a professional basis or in paid professional venues. Employees (or relatives of employees living in the same household) of Simon & Schuster, VIACOM, or any of their affiliates are not eligible. This contest is void in Puerto Rico, Quebec, and wherever prohibited or restricted by law.

3) FORMAT:

Entries must not be more than 7,500 words long and must not have been previously published. Entries must be typed or printed by word processor, double spaced, on one side of noncorrasable paper. Do not justify right-side margins. Along with a cover letter, the author's name, address, email address, and phone number must appear on the first page of the entry. The author's name, the story title, and the page number should appear on every page. Electronic submissions will be accepted and must be sent to downtowngirl@simonandschuster.com. All electronic submissions must be sent as an attachment in a Microsoft Word document. All entries must be original and the sole work of the Entrant and the sole property of the Entrant.

All submissions must be in English. Entries are void if they are in whole or in part illegible, incomplete, or damaged or if they do not conform to any of the requirements specified herein. Sponsor reserves the right, in its absolute and sole discretion, to reject any entries for any reason, including but not limited to based on sexual content, vulgarity, and/or promotion of violence.

4) ADDRESS:

Entries submitted by mail must be postmarked by July 31, 2005 and sent to:

Be The Next Downtown Girl
Author Search

Downtown Press Editorial Department
Pocket Books
1230 Sixth Avenue, 13th floor
New York, NY 10020

Or Emailed By July 31, 2005 at 11:59 PM EST as a Microsoft Word document to:

downtowngirl@simonandschuster.com

Each entry may be submitted only once. Please retain a copy of your submission. You may submit more than one story, but each submission must be mailed or emailed, as applicable, separately. Entries must be received by July 31, 2005. Not responsible for lost, late, stolen, illegible, mutilated, postage due, garbled, or misdirected mail/entries.

5) PRIZES:

One Grand Prize winner will receive:

Simon & Schuster's Downtown Press Publishing Contract for Publication of Winning Entry in a future Downtown Press Anthology, Five Hundred U.S. Dollars ($500.00), and

Downtown Press Library
(20 books valued at $260.00)

Grand Prize winner must sign the Publishing contract which contains additional terms and conditions in order to be published in the anthology.

Ten Second Prize winners will receive:

A Downtown Press Collection
(10 books valued at $130.00)

No contestant can win more than one prize.

6) STORY THEME

We are not restricting stories to any specific topic, however they should embody what all of our Downtown Press authors encompass—they should be smart, savvy, sexy stories that any Downtown Girl can relate to. We all know what uptown girls are like, but girls of the new millennium prefer the Downtown Scene. That's where it happens. The music, the shopping, the sex, the dating, the heartbreak, the family squabbles, the marriage, and the divorce. You name it. Downtown Girls have done it. Twice. We encourage you to register for the contest at www.simonsaysthespot.com in order to receive our monthly emails and updates from our authors and read about our titles on www.downtownpress.com to give you a better idea of what types of books we publish.

7) JUDGING:

Submissions will be judged on the equally weighted criteria of (a) basis of writing ability and (b) the originality of the story (which can be set in any time frame or location). Judging will take place on or about October 1, 2005. The judges will include a freelance editor, the editor of the future Anthology, and 5 employees of Sponsor. The decisions of the judges shall be final.

8) NOTIFICATION:

The winners will be notified by mail or phone on or about October 1, 2005. The Grand Prize Winner must sign the publishing contract in order to be awarded the prize. All federal, local, and state taxes are the responsibility of the winner. A list of the winners will be available after October 20, 2005 on:

http://www.downtownpress.com

http://www.simonsaysthespot.com

The winners' list can also be obtained

by sending a stamped self-addressed envelope to:

Be The Next Downtown Girl
Author Search
Downtown Press Editorial Department
Pocket Books
1230 Sixth Avenue, 13th floor
New York, NY 10020

9) PUBLICITY:

Each Winner grants to Sponsor the right to use his or her name, likeness, and entry for any advertising, promotion, and publicity purposes without further compensation to or permission from such winner, except where prohibited by law.

10) INTERNET:

If for any reason this Contest is not capable of running as planned due to an infection by a computer virus, bugs, tampering, unauthorized intervention, fraud, technical failures, or any other causes beyond the control of the Sponsor which corrupt or affect the administration, security, fairness, integrity, or proper conduct of this Contest, the Sponsor reserves the right in its sole discretion, to disqualify any individual who tampers with the entry process, and to cancel, terminate, modify, or suspend the Contest. The Sponsor assumes no responsibility for any error, omission, interruption, deletion, defect, delay in operation or transmission, communications line failure, theft or destruction or unauthorized access to, or alteration of, entries. The Sponsor is not responsible for any problems or technical malfunctions of any telephone network or telephone lines, computer on-line systems, servers, or providers, computer equipment, software, failure of any email or entry to be received by the Sponsor due to technical problems, human error or traffic congestion on the Internet or at any website, or any combination thereof, including any injury or damage to participant's or any other person's computer relating to or resulting from participating in this Contest or downloading any materials in this Contest. CAUTION: ANY ATTEMPT TO DELIBERATELY DAMAGE ANY WEBSITE OR UNDERMINE THE LEGITIMATE OPERATION OF THE CONTEST IS A VIOLATION OF CRIMINAL AND CIVIL LAWS AND SHOULD SUCH AN ATTEMPT BE MADE, THE SPONSOR RESERVES THE RIGHT TO SEEK DAMAGES OR OTHER REMEDIES FROM ANY SUCH PERSON(S) RESPONSIBLE FOR THE ATTEMPT TO THE FULLEST EXTENT PERMITTED BY LAW. In the event of a dispute as to the identity or eligibility of a winner based on an email address, the winning entry will be declared made by the "Authorized Account Holder" of the email address submitted at time of entry. "Authorized Account Holder" is defined as the natural person 18 years of age or older who is assigned to an email address by an Internet access provider, online service provider, or other organization (e.g., business, education institution, etc.) that is responsible for assigning email addresses for

the domain associated with the submitted email address. Use of automated devices are not valid for entry.

11) LEGAL Information:

All submissions become sole property of Sponsor and will not be acknowledged or returned. By submitting an entry, all entrants grant Sponsor the absolute and unconditional right and authority to copy, edit, publish, promote, broadcast, or otherwise use, in whole or in part, their entries, in perpetuity, in any manner without further permission, notice or compensation. Entries that contain copyrighted material must include a release from the copyright holder. Prizes are nontransferable. No substitutions or cash redemptions, except by Sponsor in the event of prize unavailability. Sponsor reserves the right at its sole discretion to not publish the winning entry for any reason whatsoever.

In the event that there is an insufficient number of entries received that meet the minimum standards determined by the judges, all prizes will not be awarded. Void in Quebec, Puerto Rico, and wherever prohibited or restricted by law. Winners will be required to complete and return an affidavit of eligibility and a liability/publicity release, within 15 days of winning notification, or an alternate winner will be selected. In the event any winner is considered a minor in his/her state of residence, such winner's parent/legal guardian will be required to sign and return all necessary paperwork.

By entering, entrants release the judges and Sponsor, and its parent company, subsidiaries, affiliates, divisions, advertising, production, and promotion agencies from any and all liability for any loss, harm, damages, costs, or expenses, including without limitation property damages, personal injury, and/or death arising out of participation in this contest, the acceptance, possession, use or misuse of any prize, claims based on publicity rights, defamation or invasion of privacy, merchandise delivery, or the violation of any intellectual property rights, including but not limited to copyright infringement and/or trademark infringement.

Sponsor:

Pocket Books,
an imprint of Simon & Schuster, Inc.
1230 Avenue of the Americas,
New York, NY 10020

Try these Downtown Press bestsellers on for size!

GOING TOPLESS
Megan McAndrew

DINNER FOR TWO
Mike Gayle

**THE DEAD FATHER'S
GUIDE TO
SEX AND MARRIAGE**
John Scott Shepherd

BABES IN CAPTIVITY
Pamela Redmond Satran

UPGRADING
Simon Brooke

**MY FAVORITE
MISTAKE**
Beth Kendrick

BITE
C.J. Tosh

**THE HAZARDS OF
SLEEPING ALONE**
Elise Juska

**SCOTTISH GIRLS
ABOUT TOWN**
Jenny Colgan, Isla Dewar,
Muriel Gray, and more

CALLING ROMEO
Alexandra Potter

GAME OVER
Adele Parks

PINK SLIP PARTY
Cara Lockwood

**SHOUT DOWN THE
MOON**
Lisa Tucker

MANEATER
Gigi Levangie Grazer

CLEARING THE AISLE
Karen Schwartz

LINER NOTES
Emily Franklin

MY LURID PAST
Lauren Henderson

**DRESS YOU UP
IN MY LOVE**
Diane Stingley

HE'S GOT TO GO
Sheila O'Flanagan

**IRISH GIRLS
ABOUT TOWN**
Maeve Binchy, Marian Keyes,
Cathy Kelly, and more

**THE MAN I SHOULD
HAVE MARRIED**
Pamela Redmond Satran

**GETTING OVER JACK
WAGNER**
Elise Juska

THE SONG READER
Lisa Tucker

THE HEAT SEEKERS
Zane

**I DO
(BUT I DON'T)**
Cara Lockwood

**WHY GIRLS
ARE WEIRD**
Pamela Ribon

LARGER THAN LIFE
Adele Parks

ELIOT'S BANANA
Heather Swain

**HOW TO PEE
STANDING UP**
Anna Skinner

*Look for them wherever books are sold
or visit us online at www.downtownpress.com.*

 Great storytelling just got a new address.

PUBLISHED BY POCKET BOOKS

11226